Barricade Girl
A Novel by Emely Gottwald

ISBN: 978-3-9825903-6-3 (Paperback)
ISBN: 978-3-9825903-7-0 (E-Book)

Any references to historical events, real people, or real places are
used fictitiously. Names, characters, and places are products of the
author's imagination.

Front cover image by Malin Vollbrecht.
Editing by Romy Dolgin.
Editing and formatting by Faith Fawcett.

Printed by Amazon, Inc., in the United States of America

First printing edition 2024.
Emely Gottwald

Leichlinger Straße 20, Düsseldorf, Germany, 40591.

www.emelygottwald.com

To all the fangirls, never stop.

Content Warnings

Sexual assault, drug and alcohol use, explicit sexual content.

Playlist

1. *The Scientist - Coldplay*
2. *Unendlich - Silbermond*
3. *Free Now - Gracie Abrams*
4. *Girls - Girl in Red*
5. *All My Love - Noah Kahan*
6. *Better Anyway - Lauren Sanderson*
7. *Hotel Room - Lauren Sanderson*
8. *Pretty Girls - Reneè Rapp*
9. *First, Best, Hottest... - Beth McCarthy*
10. *Dress - Taylor Swift*
11. *Lunch - Billie Eilish*
12. *Don't Wake Me Up - Mercer Henderson*
13. *Good Luck, Babe - Chappell Roan*
14. *The Smallest Man Who Ever Lived - Taylor Swift*
15. *Begin - Lauren Sanderson*
16. *Be Your Man - G Flip*
17. *Light on - Maggie Rogers*
18. *Still Into You - Paramore*
19. *sun to me - MGK*
20. *Shh... Don't Say It – Fletcher*

Chapter 1
The Scientist - Coldplay

My thumb stopped scrolling at the little image of Marina in her black leather jacket. I pressed play and the comforting tunes of *Fourteen* sounded through my dusty iPhone speakers. The sound was jagged, the loud bass beats turning into crackles, and Marina's voice was barely audible. But I knew exactly what she was singing.

Before Marina could sing the last lines of the song, my phone pinged with a notification. The little alert stopped the video and a widget at the top of the screen indicated that *Paper Rings and Promises* had posted on Instagram.

My heart jumped to my throat. The band had disappeared after their tour two years ago, without any indication as to when they would be back. Fear lingered inside me as I pressed the notification to open the app.

What if they are breaking up? What if it's really over now?

My fears dissipated as soon as the post appeared on my screen.

We're back, stronger than ever. We gave each other a promise and that counts for our fans as well.
Bound by paper rings. And, while they might look temporary, paper rings are forever. So, after a breathing break, here we are!

Our tour starts this summer!

And, we need your help. We are looking for a social media intern to support us for the next tour.
We want it to be one of you because you know what the fans want best. Experience in photography and social media marketing would be preferable but isn't a must.

If this sounds like you, reach out to us under this email: Paperringsandpromises@info.de

We can't wait to meet you.
And, of course, we can't wait to sing with all of you again!
Tour dates will be posted within the next month <3

I was already working in social media, for the Green Party, to be precise. I was used to taking photos of semi-famous politicians but working for my favorite band, working for *Marina*, sent shivers down my spine. I could never function if she was around 24/7.

The next second, my phone rang and Chloe's face appeared on my screen.

I picked up the phone. "No way," I said, before Chloe could say a word.

"*Yes* way," Chloe responded.

"How is this supposed to work? I couldn't even sing into the microphone when Marina held it out to me two years ago. How the hell am I supposed to work for her?" Of course, something inside me wanted to do this, wanted to apply, but every rational aspect of my brain was holding me back.

"I don't know, Kari. But what I *do* know is that you're the only one of us that's qualified to do this. No way in hell am I gonna miss the chance to experience this through you." Chloe's voice was so bright, encouraging, but I felt like crying.

I knew I had to do this. This was a dream; not just mine but *ours*. "Fuck," was all I could say right now.

"Not *fuck*. Hell yes!" I could hear Chloe smiling from ear to ear through the telephone speakers.

I let out an audible breath. "Chloe, we both know this is a bad idea."

"Well, as I've heard, they make the best memories," Chloe said.

11

Seemingly, bad ideas were what brought us together in the first place. Every parent considered talking to a stranger on the internet a 'bad idea' but it was the best one I had ever had.

"I really don't know, Chlo. This is a lot; I don't know if I can do this. Even if we put the thought of working for the hottest woman on earth aside, what if I'm not good enough for the job?" Chloe was the only person I would admit this to; the one person for whom I didn't need to maintain my perfect facade. She knew my insecurities, what held me back.

She'd been by my side when my family fell apart. She held my hand as my father left and my mother couldn't keep herself, or the family, together. My family slipped away. I felt as if I'd lost control of my life. When a mother needs her child to hold *her*, you stop being a child altogether. That's when I started trying to control everything I could. It gave me security. With a mask of perfect make up and painfully slicked back hair, I feel safe, even if I'm crumbling on the inside.

As I got older, I tried to find control in relationships, in my sexuality. I hated it when women touched me because I didn't want my body to loosen in chaos; I decided to be the one to touch them. I loved the way I could make them come. In bed, I was the one in charge.

Chloe had seen me go through all those phases and chose to stick with me. She chose to be around me, to make me laugh, to be there when I cried. She'd seen me hurt girls and be hurt *by* girls, but she never judged. Most importantly, she let me be myself, fully myself, so I could lose some of that control and just breathe.

"Kari! Don't talk about yourself that way. You are amazing. Incredible. Breathtaking. Not just as a person but in your job as well. Your photos and posts have changed lives!" Chloe's voice threw me out of my thoughts.

"Oh, I don't know about changing lives, girl." But something deep inside me wanted to believe what she said.

"And what about the hundreds of young people that started voting Green because of your strategy? The photos you took of refugees that made people feel seen and spurred massive donations?" Chloe spoke about the parts of my work I was most proud of and the reason I was doing it in the first place - to influence people in a way that makes a change in the world.

My heart glowed with pride. "I know. And I'm not trying to talk myself down when I say I might not be good enough for this job. But working for a band is completely different from taking a few photos for a political party."

"It's not as different as you might think," Chloe said encouragingly. "It's all about influence. And the people you have to influence here are just like you, you know them. We both know you can do this."

"I kinda know you're right. I just wish my heart would accept that too," I mumbled into the telephone. "I promise I'll think about it, okay?"

"Okay," Chloe said. "Let me know when you send over your application!"

"*If* I send it in the first place. But yes, I will." Usually, I was the one radiating confidence to the world but, this time, Chloe's voice was the one full of confidence... probably because it was confidence about me, not herself.

"Bye, love you!" Chloe said and hung up the phone.

I dropped the little device into my lap, unable to comprehend what had just happened. I didn't feel ready to face this decision right now so I pushed it aside.

I wandered into the kitchen to make myself an iced matcha latte and was greeted by my hyperactive little dog. I still lived at home, saving up money that could be used for concerts or traveling instead of wasting it on an apartment nearby. I also had a great relationship with my mom so I didn't have to move away to find my peace. I was looking forward to moving out, though. Living in such a small town close to Ulm was not a great place to be, not for work and not for dating.

Loki was jumping up and down my leg, trying to get my attention, when I mixed some green powder with oat milk. This dog had been able to make me smile in my darkest times. He was our family dog, the one thing bonding all of us and one of the reasons I didn't want to move away from home. Loki, and the fact that I didn't want to leave my mom alone, kept me here.

"Good morning!" I laughed and bent down to scratch his head. He leaned into my touch.

Then, he started barking which, for him, sounded more like a squeaking. He was asking for breakfast. I let out a huff and put my morning coffee aside to give him his portion of dog food for the morning.

When my matcha was ready and my dog was happy, I walked back into my room and set up my desk for the day. I didn't really need anything but my MacBook, my camera and my little drink.

Right when I was about to edit the first photo of the day, my phone rang again.

It was my boss.

Holy shit, what the hell does she want now?

My boss was great most days but her schedule was busy; she didn't tend to call her employees. Ever. This couldn't be a good thing.

"Hey, Kari! Do you have a second?" Celeste's voice chirped through the speakers. No matter the time of day, she was always so *positive*.

"Celeste, of course I have time for you!" I said, trying to match her eagerness, even the slightest bit.

Actually, I don't. I hadn't even been able to take the first sip of my matcha; how was I supposed to chirp through the telephone at an unexpected call from my boss?

Celeste chuckled on the other end. "Perfect, perfect." She was still speaking in that same high-pitched voice. "What we have to talk about is a little more serious." It was hard to take her *seriously* when she was speaking like a bird.

No matter how happy her tone was, something told me that this call was not good news. "Now you're worrying me, Celeste. What is it?"

Are they cutting my pay? Firing me?

Worry crawled to the top of my throat.

"We want to promote you!"

Promote me? Why?

"And what exactly would that mean?"

"Becoming the social media manager of the Green Party in *Germany*!" She let out a full on squeal on the other end. "This means no more field trips for you, no more editing videos and taking photos. You'd be the one leading our media team, collecting their posts, assigning and scheduling them. Less work, more pay. Oh, and you'd also finally move away from Ulm and into the big city - Berlin. Doesn't that sound great?"

Her words overwhelmed me. I wanted nothing more than to hide beneath my blanket and forget this morning had even happened. The rational part of me knew that what Celeste was saying was great information. She was telling me I was amazing at my job. This was what I had wanted, climbing the career ladder and making a name for myself in politics. I always planned on moving to Berlin eventually, even worked toward getting a job just like the one I was being offered by Celeste. But, was that really what I wanted for my life? There was the emotional part of me that just wanted to hang up the phone and shut her up. I loved my job, at least the one I was doing right now. But oftentimes, I found myself wishing I could take even more photos, focus less on marketing and strategies. The thought of changing my responsibilities to just the opposite made me sick.

The internship opportunity came back to my mind. It didn't pay remotely as well as my current job and I shouldn't have even been considering it. But I knew that with that internship there would be a lot more artistic freedom and a focus on the photos. It was stupid but knowing what I *didn't* want to do, I knew even better what I *had* to do. I didn't want to manage social media for a political party, where every post was staged and every smile a mask. I wanted to photograph real people, real emotions. And what's more raw and authentic than concerts?

"Kari, are you still there?" Celeste's voice sounded unhappy for the first time that day because I had made her wait.

17

"Oh, I'm sorry. I will need some time to think about this. Moving away is a big step, you know?" I said, hoping she'd take my answer without freaking out. Celeste always thought she knew everything about the people around her and she hated nothing more than guessing wrong.

I could hear a loud intake of breath through the line. "Oh, uhm, if you think so. I thought you'd be a little more excited about this but I guess you're not."

"Oh, Celeste. Don't get me wrong; I am beyond excited about this opportunity. But I don't know if I'm ready yet. Also, how am I supposed to ever accept a boss other than you?" I tried to make her feel good, feeding her ego just a spoonful.

"Well, that is a valid point indeed. I guess I'll leave it up to you." Her voice turned back to serious. "We do need an answer by the end of the month, though. And, be aware that we cannot promise to keep your current job if you decline the offer."

My heart dropped to my stomach.

They are going to fire me if I decline?

All this time I had thought that I was such an important asset to the Green Party, gaining new voters with every post. They probably figured out that any Gen Z-er could grow their following in some way and decided to turn my position into an unpaid internship. My work wasn't cheap, that was for sure. They paid for my experience, after all.

"I'll let you know as soon as possible," I said as brightly as I could manage, hanging up the phone before Celeste could say another word to persuade me.

This turned the internship opportunity into an even bigger thing than it had been before. Even if I applied, I wouldn't know the outcome in time to still get the job on offer from Celeste. If I did it, I would have to be all in. And if I *got* it, it would turn my life around completely. Maybe it would open doors for me, open up more job opportunities to become a full time concert photographer one day? My heart glowed at the thought.

Politics had been my dream since I was little; the thought of changing and influencing the world one day used to fuel me like coffee. Now that I had dived into the industry, it didn't feel quite right anymore. Politicians weren't what I expected them to be; they weren't as strong or as good as they were presented. Most of them didn't even have that much influence. It was all a mask: their real selves and opinions hidden behind marketing, media, and make-up teams.

Pushing this childhood dream aside and going a different route felt wrong. I was disregarding my younger self, turning away opportunities she had dreamed about.

But maybe it had all been about concerts from the start. Maybe this moment was what my inner dreams had been waiting for. As complicated as this decision seemed, it was actually quite easy. I had always been a head-person, disregarding every feeling inside of my stomach. I was realistic while Chloe was emotional and impulsive. But maybe this was the time to finally start following the little spark inside me. And that spark was telling me to do the unexpected.

Being a fan had saved me from losing myself to chaos. I never fit in at school or work. Instead, I gravitated toward the internet, where I could find people like me, people who made me feel seen and understood. Relatives, teachers, and friends had called me crazy. They worried about me when I chose to spend all my money on concert tickets instead of going shopping or buying my first car. After what we'd been through, my mom let me do the things I deemed good for myself. She never judged when I left for a week to go on tour, as long as I was safe. Other people went on their first vacations without their parents when they turned sixteen, but I went to every single concert of my favorite band, touring around Germany with my favorite people. I found my chosen family, the safety I couldn't find at home, with the people in the front row of *Paper Rings and Promises* concerts.

The older I got, the more serious my life became. A new generation of fans appeared that changed the dynamic, and things didn't feel the same. Chloe found a new fandom and a new home in Willow. When I turned

18, people around me talked about careers, and decided tours kept me from growing. I stopped going to concerts, or at least going to *as many*. I distanced myself from the fandom and concentrated on a career that never fully captivated me the way live music could.

Maybe that was never the right thing to do.

Maybe my career was right there in front of me.

Maybe my future was in front of a stage.

I opened my phone back up to the video of Marina I'd been watching before. I followed her movements with my gaze, letting her voice distract me from the present for a moment. Sometimes I missed my old self, the careless fangirl who could get lost in music. Memories of my last *Paper Rings and Promises* concert filled my mind.

Chapter 2

unendlich – Silbermond
2 years ago

I looked at the golden ring on my finger as my hand held onto the metallic pole in the train. A crooked, carved heart decorated the piece of jewelry. My own heart warmed at the memory of Chloe putting the little paper ring on my finger 6 years ago. It was now a golden ring to do what it is meant to - last forever.

When the train came to a halt, I grabbed my suitcase and disembarked. As soon as my Docs met the ground, someone wrapped their arms around me from behind; a strand of red hair tickled my skin. *Chloe!*

"I missed you *so* much," she said and rested her head on my shoulder. Her right hand was wrapped around my belly, her finger shining with a silver ring, decorated with the same crooked heart as mine.

I laughed as she let me go. "You ready?"

"To be honest, not really."

I grabbed the handle of my suitcase and walked toward the exit of the platform.

The next day was my tenth *Paper Rings and Promises* concert. In the same place where everything had started. This was our friendship anniversary and our first concert for this band in a long time. It had been six years since we made our promise. *Forever.* And she was still here. That redhead, who was always there, no matter how much distance was between us, was still here. She was the first person that ever stuck with me. Friends came and left but she was always just one heartbeat away.

Even *Paper Rings and Promises* had made their way into the background of my life, their music still my soundtrack, but the band disappearing into the back of my mind. I was 20 now and my priorities had shifted. Hanging out in fan groups, reading and writing fan fictions and spending days queuing for concerts was my youth. But, after Covid, my career had taken the lead. There were too many voices telling me to stop spending all my money on concert and train tickets, traveling around Germany for a whole tour at least once a year.

Now, looking back, the only good thing I had gotten out of the fandom was Chloe. No one else really stuck. We always used to be the young ones, never really belonging to the "cool fans" because we couldn't attend every concert like they did.

In Germany, it was a regular thing to trade your vacation days for a tour, going to every concert of your favorite band every year. If you didn't or couldn't do that, other fans considered themselves better. At least that's how it was with *Paper Rings and Promises*. The fans that went to every show were able to form some sort of relationship with Marina, while others were just one of many faces.

When I was younger, around 16, I had done a few tours but I never really fully fit in with the high-end fans, the ones that were everywhere and claimed the band as theirs. My own people, the ones I called family, left the fandom before I turned 18.

In most fandoms, different groups of fans form and there will always be some sort of competition between them. Sometimes it seemed just like high school, different cliques fighting each other. They did everything to be more popular with the band than others. I could never identify with that so I didn't really belong.

Chloe was different. She attended a lot more concerts and was part of one of those sub-groups for a while. After she left for her exchange year in the States three years ago, she just never really got back to it. She found something else in Willow, another singer. That fandom was different than anything I'd ever seen. There was so much love between the fans, so much familiarity and seldom any competition.

"I'm especially not ready to see *some* people again. Do you think they're still around?" I said.

Chloe took a second to catch up with me. "I bet they're still there. They did nothing but live for this band. Do you really think they just found something else to live for?" She let her hand wander through her red curls, chuckling. "I hope they moved on, though."

"Isn't Val still involved in the fandom? Did she say anything about the oldies?" Val was one of Chloe's friends that she met through Willow, a singer she'd discovered a few years ago. I was incredibly glad she found her; there was nothing but genuine support coming from both Chloe and Willow. The way Chloe glowed at her concerts made me feel warm and happy. I believed she finally found what she was looking for. A place that felt like home.

"She is but she just started going to their concerts recently and doesn't really know how it used to be. She does get to stand front row every time now so I don't think some of the older fans are still there." My friend was now walking right beside me.

I chuckled. "You just never know with Dresden, right?" The concert in Dresden was supposed to be special every year. It was the band's hometown and they tended to provide some surprises during the shows. At our first concert six years ago, they even had another artist join them on stage. A so-called "home-game" concert meant that every person that has ever considered themselves a *Paper Rings and Promises* Fan would show up for the sake of nostalgia. Obviously, we were doing the exact same thing so we couldn't complain.

Chloe nodded and manoeuvred her own suitcase between a crowd of people.

You never knew what to expect in this city. For our first concert, we showed up at the location at 8am and didn't even get close to making the first row. We walked the rest of the way toward our Airbnb in silence. We didn't need to talk much; each other's presence was more than enough.

As soon as I opened the door, Chloe stormed inside and let herself fall onto the bed. I was always the one carrying the keys, opening the doors, while Chloe was here for funsies.

"When are Liza and Maxine coming?"

She reminded me that we weren't going to be by ourselves this weekend. Two of my friends were joining us for the concert. I had met Liza and Maxine through my work at political events. When I distanced myself from fandoms, I started going into politics and ended up doing some social media for the local representatives of the Green Party in my area. We quickly connected through similar interests for concerts. I enjoyed spending time with them but they'd never be as close to me as Chloe was.

"I actually have no clue." I laughed, took my phone out of my back pocket and let myself fall onto the bed next to Chloe.

A few hours later, I got a text from Liza.

Liza, 3:05pm
will be at the airbnb at 6!

Before I could tell my best friend about the recent news, her eyes were already scanning my phone screen. Most people think Chloe is shy and socially anxious when they first meet her but, with me, she could be the nosiest and most excitable person one has ever met.

"Coolio," Chloe mumbled and put her hands over her head. A crackling sound rang out as she pulled her hands upward in a stretching motion.

"So, how are you doing girl?" I turned around and propped my head on my left hand.

"Do you mean life wise or love wise?" Chloe propped herself up in the same motion.

"Both," I answered.

"Well, life is great. Cologne is starting to feel like home which can be overwhelming at times because I'm not used to feeling that way." There was a content smile on her lips, though.

Chloe had finally taken the step to move away from her small hometown, and from her judgemental mom, last summer. I was proud of her and it seemed like she loved being in Cologne.

"It just feels good to walk into my own 4 walls without having to bend my head down in fear of judgment," Chloe said.

An image of Chloe walking into her apartment flashed through my mind's eye, like I had been there when she had realized that that place was her home. The corners of my lips bent upward at the thought; there was nothing I wanted more than seeing my best friend happy. She had gone through so much in her hometown, had so many years of fighting with the small mindedness of her hometown; it seemed now like she was finally able to move on.

"Why are you smiling?" Chloe asked.

"I'm just happy for you. It sounds like you're finally healing. And it looks like it too with that glimmer in your eyes. You made it."

"I think so too." A tear wandered down her cheek, like it was marking its path for her new future.

"I love that for you," I said.

I was about to change the subject to her dating situation when she took the words right out of my mouth.

"And, as for my love life, it's a mess as always," she chuckled. "Actually, it's been quiet for a while now. But the thing with Mel still hangs over my head. I mean, it hasn't been that long since we went no contact. I don't think our story is over yet."

"To be honest, I'm kinda glad that it's sort of over *now*, even though you're hoping for a revival," I laughed. "That story was emotionally draining, even for me."

I let myself fall back onto the pillow and started untangling the hair tie out of my ponytail. It was a relief to let my hair fall down on the mattress. It probably looked messy around my head but I felt safe to not be the best version of myself around Chloe.

"But, nevertheless, I get it if you're still holding on. I only wish the best for you and maybe it was 'right person, wrong time' but who knows?" I looked over at her while I brushed through my brown waves with my hands. The knots scratched at my fingers, making me irritated.

While my love life was basically non-existent at this point, Chloe was able to keep me on my feet this year. She had fallen head-first into a situationship after meeting the love of her life at pride. I didn't mind her ditching me for women at parties and it always made me happy to see her get her occasional kisses. Before she got involved with Mel, it just all seemed really superficial and I got used to seeing Chloe jump from woman to woman without ever feeling anything deeper. She might have acted as if she liked that lifestyle but whenever someone talked about long term relationships or love, she felt insecure, even though she didn't admit it. There was so much love inside of my best friend and she craved to connect deeply with someone. I just hated that the first time she actually felt this for someone, her love wasn't reciprocated and all she got was disappointment. While she craved connection, I just craved to see her flourishing.

At the time she met Mel, I fell into something between situationship and relationship with Tate. It seemed almost perfect from the start, the way Tate love bombed me and let me meet her parents on the first weekend. She accepted the fact that I didn't want her to touch me or maybe she even *used* that fact. Every night, she let me please her and never once asked if she could touch me. She was never fully into it, I guess. She didn't take the time to learn about me, to gain my trust, so I'd hand her the control.

When times were darker and my need for control grew, she ran away as fast as she could. I tried to keep her, tried to hold onto her while other things slipped out of my grasp but that pushed her away even more. There was a medical emergency; my body turned against me. A cyst grew inside of me, probably for years, and I'd had no clue. When it started pushing my organs to the side and I looked like I was pregnant, I was rushed to the hospital. Neither Tate nor my dad ever visited me. I was too much of a burden if I wasn't the one taking care of them.

Tate's words still rang through my ears: *God, you're such a mess.* She'd said it on one of our last phone calls. I had been crying and I didn't really know if it was because I was scared of dying or because everything was falling apart again.

Get a grip, Kari. You're not gonna die just because your makeup isn't perfect and you can't lift your arms to put your hair in a ponytail.

She scolded the things that kept me alive.

I had thought she liked the way that I was put together.

I couldn't listen to her words anymore, I couldn't keep hearing her voice.

When I didn't answer for a few minutes, Tate spoke for the last time: I *don't think I can do this, Kari.* And then she hung up the phone.

"Yeah, maybe." Chloe sat up on the mattress and bent over the bed frame.

Shuffling sounds appeared from the other side of the bed. I kept laying around for about a minute as keys were clinking and packs of cigarettes and tissues were thrown onto the bed.

"What the hell are you doing down there?" I asked as a hair scrunchie hit my arm.

"You will laugh when I tell you." Chloe's eyes peaked over the side of the bed.

"Your vape?" I crawled over to her.

"What else would it be?" Chloe resumed her search, now emptying the last contents of her tote back onto the floor.

"Girl, have you checked your jacket pocket yet?" I laughed.

She didn't answer and lifted herself into a standing position by holding onto the bed frame. A second later she was out of the room and yelled through the flat, "Why do you always *know*?" She sounded like a child complaining to her mom and that dynamic couldn't have been more accurate in this situation. The next moment, Chloe was back on the bed and inhaled a deep breath of her vape.

"Girl, sometimes I just can't with you." I shook my head with a laugh.

A few hours later, Liza and Maxine entered the apartment with a bang. They were buzzing with excitement. With a forceful hug, Liza even lifted me off the ground for a second.

I'd met both of them through my job; they were the only other young queer people that were part of the social media team of the Green Party in Germany. They'd been my friends for 2 years now and we occasionally saw each other at events or concerts. When the three of us met in person for the first time, we quickly became friends and the meet-ups always cheered me up. They were from a different part and time of my life but I was excited to introduce them to Chloe and my favorite band.

"I'm so happy to see you!" Maxine screamed as she wrapped her arms around me.

"I missed you guys so much!" I laughed.

Chloe stood to the side but there was a smile on her lips. Their loud energy might be a bit overwhelming for her but I knew she'd tell me if she felt anxious.

"This is Chloe; the girl you've heard so much about!" I said and pointed toward my best friend.

"Nice to finally meet you!" Maxine and Liza embraced her in a little group hug.

Chloe laughed and hugged back and I could see her shoulders visibly relax.

As soon as Liza let go of Chloe, she stomped toward the middle of the room and clapped her hands together. "*Okay* but have you guys heard about the new development in Marina's love life?" Liza was in full on speaker mode. She loved having the spotlight, almost as much as she loved gossiping about middle-aged women.

"What are you talking about?" Maxine took a step closer, the nosiness visible in her movements.

I took a step back; I didn't like engaging in theories about real people's love life.

"What is it?" Even Chloe spoke up now.

"Well, you know we, well no, *everyone* has been speculating about Marina's sexuality, right? And we all know that Marina can't be fully straight, *right*?" Liza was now supporting her words with increased hand movements. Both Maxine and Chloe were glued to her words, nodding along. "Well, there have been some rumors-"

"Rumors? Seriously, Liza?" I intervened. Marina was a real person after all and no matter how much I wished my gay awakening was queer, she wasn't. At least, not until she said so herself.

Every fandom I'd been a part of, or heard of, had been full of queer fans. I guessed it was because they started crushing on the lead singer and queer people were usually the ones having to search for a community somewhere that wasn't part of their daily life.

That had been my case in some way and definitely Chloe's case. I didn't know I was queer until I read sapphic fan fictions about Marina and got to know queer couples within the fandom. It was so different to be in a space that was fully queer and there was no need for coming out or any fear of judgment.

Of course, all those stories and narratives that were made up about Marina led to rumors being created about her. As soon as people started writing about a person that existed in the real world, it became hard to differentiate between reality and fiction. It wasn't surprising that all those queer fans saw things in photos that weren't really there, wishing for their little stories to be true.

"Wait, wait. Let me finish." Liza took out her phone, and turned it around. "A fanpage posted this today and it looks like Marina and her co-host on *Sing Along* are kissing!" She pointed at the picture and motioned for us to move closer.

The image was blurry in purple lights, posted by an account named *Papergirl4life*. There were two women in the image, one with dark hair criminally close to another one with light blonde hair. The woman in the front was wearing platform Docs and black tight jeans, unmistakably Marina. The image was so indistinct that there was no way to tell if they were actually kissing but I couldn't deny that my heart fluttered at the sight of the image.

Chloe was the first to react. "How the hell did I not know about this?!" Her cheeks were red with excitement.

"Oh, new tea! They literally just posted." Liza said in a rather stable voice, seemingly feeling superior for knowing this first.

"Wow! Marina and Lara? I can't believe all my fanfiction dreams are coming true here!" Maxine snatched the phone back out of Liza's hand to stare at the post again. "This was posted just a few hours ago; I can't believe we're witnessing this."

"Yeah, right?" Liza exclaimed and hugged our blonde friend from the side. "This is insane."

Chloe took the phone next. "People are starting to comment! They are all saying this has to be legit."

"They just *wish* this was legit," I mumbled, not really meaning for the rest of the group to hear.

"Come on, Kari. You're wishing the same thing here. Accept that we're clinging on to our last hope," Liza said, putting her hands on my shoulders. "Marina is finally realizing that she's one of us."

"Liza, she has a *husband,* and a child," I said. Something inside me wanted to protect Marina, keep her safe from rumors that could hurt her family, even when warmth swelled between my legs at the thought of her being with a woman.

"You don't have to agree. But just let us be delulu for a second!" Maxine laughed and leaned against Liza.

I let it go, took out my phone and stepped aside, leaving them to speculate.

The sound of loud, out-of-tune singing shook me awake the next morning. A grumpy "hmmph" emanated from Chloe's side of the bed as the voices of my friends echoed through the apartment. A *Paper Rings and Promises* song played in the background, Marina's voice barely audible beneath the loud singing which could almost be called screaming. I pulled the blanket over my head, refusing to open my eyelids which felt glued together from lack of sleep. *What time is it?!*

I almost dozed back to sleep, the noises fading into the background, when the door to our room burst open and Marina's angelic voice forced itself into my right ear. Now, I was the one to groan before I pulled the blanket off my head and forced my sticky eyes open. My friends had thrown the bluetooth box onto the bed and the music was now blasting between my head and Chloe's. Maxine and Liza were standing in front of the bed, the only sounds left from their singing were the tapping of their feet on the wooden flooring.

"Have you checked the clock? Jeez, the sun's not even fully up!" Chloe was pointing toward the window. It was indeed still gray outside.

"Doesn't matter, we gotta hurry! The first people are lining up already!" Liza knocked on the wooden frame of the bed. "This is your tenth concert Kari; you gotta make the first row."

I propped myself up on my elbows to look at my friends; my eyesight was still blurry from sleep and a slight headache had developed behind my eyes.

"Do you really think we even have a chance?" I rubbed my right eye with the back of my hand. "What if we sit there for 10 hours just to end up in a space we could've made at any time?"

"It's about the *experience*, Kari!" Maxine's hand grabbed my right ankle and shook it for a second.

Chloe let herself fall back onto the bed with a groan.

"Do I really want to experience 10 hours with the people I decided to distance myself from? With that fandom? I'm not 15 anymore." I shook my head which was followed by another flow of pain.

"Valerie said it's not as bad anymore," Chloe mumbled. "But anyways, I'd prefer some more sleep." She pulled the blanket over her head.

"This is about nostalgia, Kari. Do everything the way you would have done it 8 years ago. One more time." Liza grabbed my other ankle and both my friends pulled me off the bed.

I laughed at their effort. "Okay, okay. Let's get this party started, I guess." There was truth to their words, after all. And some eye contact with Marina during the concert wouldn't hurt either.

"Cool, we're leaving in twenty minutes," Maxine said and left the room, followed by Liza.

"Your friends are something else," Chloe murmured and rolled to the side.

"I know but I love them. They mean well." My hand wandered toward the nightstand and searched for my phone. "I mean, they are new to the fandom as well. We've had all this for years; we're done with the early queuing and first rows. They aren't. And this is Dresden after all, the big thing." The bright light of the phone screen stung my eyes. *6:45am. Jesus.*

"What time is it?" Chloe crawled over and appeared behind my back to look at my phone screen. "Jesus Christ, I haven't been up this early since high school. I'm gonna need multiple energy drinks. And maybe a bit of alcohol." She let her face rest on my side.

"Alcohol at a *Paper Rings and Promises* concert? I wouldn't say no to that!" I laughed and pushed Chloe off my body to move to a sitting position. Guess I just gotta force myself through getting up now. "Come on, let's do this." I gave Chloe another push and got out of the bed.

I collected my black suit pants and a tight azul top out of my suitcase and wandered into the bathroom with an audible yawn.

That morning, my hair did not want to be slicked back; with every bit of gel I put on, a new strand of hair spiked up. I grunted but kept trying. When I applied my foundation and concealer, my skin didn't want to take it in.

Breathe. This is a good day.

I checked the clock on my phone. *7:00.* They wanted to leave soon but Chloe hadn't even made an appearance in the bathroom yet. But there is still time.

My hand was shaking when I blended the makeup on my face but I forced my movements to be calm and careful.

Today is the big day.

Everything's going to be perfect.

I let out an audible breath and applied another bit of gel; this time, all of it stuck.

This is going to be great.

I finished my makeup and applied some mascara.

You look great, I thought to myself.

When I walked back into the room, Chloe had just made it out of bed and passed me on her way to the bathroom. I chuckled at her predictability and let myself fall onto the bed to scroll through TikTok for a moment.

An hour later, all of us were seated on a tram, each clutching two cans of Red Bull and baked goods. Chloe's bag clinked with two bottles of secco when she stood up to let an older person take her seat. My eyes were still stinging and sticky but the anticipation for the night pushed energy through me.

"I still can't believe that it's been 8 years." Chloe took a sip from her energy drink. "We've been friends for eight full years. Can you believe that?" Her smile was so bright that it lit up her eyes.

"I can't. And I can't believe that today is my 10th concert in the same location we met. Seven years after we hugged for the first time. The exact same date. How full circle is that?"

"Insane." Chloe bent forward and squeezed my hand from her standing position.

Liza leaned in from my right. "What kind of sentimental thing are you two talking about at this early hour?"

"Just about the fact that tonight will be such a full circle moment," I said.

"And we're so grateful that you let us experience this with you."

My heart warmed. Of course, this night was about Chloe and I but bringing more people couldn't hurt. Their energy was unmatched and this concert could only be better with them around.

"Of course, the more the merrier." I told them.

I looked around the group. All of us were wearing Doc Martens in different styles. Mine were black with a slightly higher platform to make up for my height. Chloe's were similar but with sprinkles of pride colors on the sides. Maxine's were normal height but had 3D flowers in pastel pink colors on their ankles, while Liza's were the typical black ones.

Hers reminded me of the first pair I bought right after discovering *Paper Rings and Promises*. I had scraped bits of pocket money together and found them on some second-hand platform. Chloe had found the same in a different size at a flea market and we put them on for the first time together on Skype. That day, we jumped up and down in front of the camera. It felt like we were finally real *Paper Rings and Promises* fans and we were connected by wearing the same shoes. That was long before we beat the distance and were able to wear our new shoes to our first concert.

Maxine had her blonde hair tied up into two space buns, glitter sparkling on her head. She also had glitter on her face and sparkling winged eyeliner. Two strands of hair were braided along the sides of her face, butterfly clips at the ends. The small pink butterflies matched her flowing purple dress. She looked like a little fairy and I loved everything about it.

Sometimes I wanted to go all out like her, dressing up as something magical, but I so often found myself resorting back to the basics. Since I was behaving like the adult in the group, I thought I needed to dress like an adult as well, compensating for missing authority. Even if I didn't have everything together inside, I always looked like I did on the outside.

Liza was going full-on Marina-style today. She wore tight black jeans just like Marina did every day and a basic white top. Her shoulder-length brown hair was down and one of those lesbian black beanies that didn't slip down over your eyes decorated her head. It might have been fall but the temperatures outside felt like late summer; I was sweating even with my hair in a ponytail. I had no clue how Liza was surviving in that beanie.

"Okay girls, enough sentimentalities. We gotta get off now." I got up from my seat and motioned for the others to leave their spots.

The breeze of fresh air reminded me that I had forgotten to breathe inside the humid tram carriage. I took out my phone, typed in the address for the concert and took the lead. Sometimes, I wondered if I was the only one with any sense of direction because I always took charge. On the other hand, I never gave anyone else the chance to navigate because I couldn't stand it when they guided us wrong. We were the fastest when the control was with me anyway.

When we arrived at the corner just before the entrance, I took a deep breath and braced myself for a line full of people I hadn't seen in years.

Chloe took an audible breath right next to me. "I'm not ready to see some faces again."

"Do you think there are many people already?" Maxine asked from behind before I could respond to Chloe.

I lifted my shoulders to signal that I had no clue. There was no way to guess what was waiting for us. Then I turned toward Chloe: "Me neither," and I kept walking.

The line was surprisingly short and, except for Valerie, I didn't see a single person I knew. There were only about 15 people around, all of them wearing Doc Martens in the heat. Sometimes the uniform made me feel like I belonged but *sometimes* it felt a bit cringe for all of us to be copying Marina's style.

The faces around were all new, some older and some not even 18. Ever since Marina had been a judge on the talent show *Sing Along*, there had been a new wave of young fans.

Chloe stepped forward to greet Valerie and I followed. After leaving Chloe with Mel and going to a party with Valerie alone during Cologne pride 2 years ago, we could be called friends as well.

I greeted Val and left them to catch up and walked back to my friends at the end of the line. They were setting up our camp for the day and pulled out a picnic blanket. As soon as it was set in place, I let myself fall onto it.

The air might have been warm but the hard ground felt cold through the blanket.

Why did I ever agree to spend ten hours sitting on the ground?

There was a reason I stopped doing concerts the way I used to. Arriving late, standing somewhere in the back, even buying seat tickets to avoid lining up completely, was just so much more comfortable.

As soon as Chloe got back to the blanket, we resorted to all sorts of queuing activities, from playing cards to making friendship bracelets and eating every kind of snack we could find. Social interactions tended to wear me out, so I started reading a sapphic book on my phone.

I was engulfed in a sex scene when Chloe clinked the secco bottles together to signal the start of day drinking. I checked the clock on my phone.

2pm.

It felt like I'd spent a lifetime sitting on that road but it has only been a few hours. We had 5 more to go.

"Already?" I asked with a laugh when Chloe uncapped the first bottle.

"I swear I cannot survive a second longer without alcohol. Have you seen the people that showed up? Or listened to even one conversation around us?" Chloe shook her red curls and took a swig from the bottle.

My eyes scanned our surroundings. I had been so zoned into the words of my book that I hadn't even realized that the line was now going all the way to the corner. There were even more people wearing Docs all around us. Some of them didn't just wear Marina's *clothes*; they had the same wavy dark brown shoulder-length hair as well. There were a few faces I had seen before, people I hadn't interacted with except for a few evil glares.

When I focused on the conversations around us, I cringed. A group of blonde girls right behind us was aggressively chatting about Marina's love life. Some talking about Marina and Lara, others arguing about the love between Marina and her husband. One of the girls even went as far as saying Marina was secretly dating the drummer of *Paper Rings and Promises,* Dari. The girls were actively waving their hands and each of them talked like they were superior and had some information the others didn't.

Is this how we were when we joined the fandom?

"These girls make me understand why no one wanted to hang out with us 8 years ago!" Chloe laughed and pointed the bottle toward the group of girls. She had been watching me watch them.

I slowly started to understand why the older generation of fans used to avoid us.

"Were we really as bad?" I hid my face behind my hands in embarrassment.

"Oh, probably worse," Chloe said as took another swig from the bottle.

"Probably." I held out my hand.

"Certainly," Liza said from my side and grabbed the bottle from Chloe's hand before she could hand it to me.

I nodded with a laugh. "Says you! You're probably the worst of us." I snatched it from my friend quickly.

"The loudest fan and proud of it." Liza made a saluting motion and took the bottle back after I had taken a chug.

"Okay girls, let's play a drinking game." Maxine let the half-done friendship bracelet she had been working on fall onto the blanket and took the bottle next.

"Like truth or dare?" I asked. "You know that none of us ever have any ideas for questions *or* dares!"

"Oh, I have an idea." Liza exclaimed and moved closer to the middle of the blanket. "What about turning all these annoying people around us into a drinking game?"

"Sounds intriguing." Chloe muttered.

"How exactly would that work?" I asked.

"We gotta drink whenever they do or say specific things. Like, whenever we hear a *Paper Rings and*

48

Promises song, we gotta drink. Or whenever they mention Marina or Lara."

"I got another idea! Whenever someone talks about all the concerts they have already been to!" Chloe exclaimed.

"Good one." Liza's eyes scanned the group. "Any other ideas?"

"Whenever another person wearing Docs shows up," Maxine said with a laugh.

"Gosh, Maxine. We'd all be drunk within a minute," Liza replied.

"Isn't that the point?" Maxine chuckled.

"I'll give you that," Liza exclaimed.

"Okay, let's start. But maybe without the Docs to begin with." I pointed toward the end of the line. "The girls in the back just sang the verse of *Fourteen*."

The two drinks were empty faster than we could blink and I soon found myself on a hike with Chloe to the next grocery store.

"How are we feeling?" Chloe asked, as we turned around the corner.

The alcohol made me feel comfortably bubbly and warm. "Ready to stare at Marina on stage, for sure." I theatrically closed my eyes and let the image of Marina on stage flow through my mind. Even just the thought of her made my body tingle.

"Agreed." Chloe took a hit from her vape, the first one in a few hours. "What about all the memories this brings up? Good or bad?"

"Good," I answered. "It feels good to be here with you."

We didn't speak anymore until we returned to the group.

The rest of the wait flew by incredibly fast and we soon found ourselves in front of the door, ready to run in. We had downed two more bottles between us and I had never been this calm before the entry time.

Everyone around us was looking around in a panic when the security guards found their spots around the door. Some sounded like they were about to collapse. I knew exactly how they felt, it was refreshing to approach a concert with enough distance this time. We just laughed at them, giving each other funny looks.

"Ready for this?" Liza asked into the group.

Chloe hugged her from the side. "So ready!"

We grabbed each other's hands to make a chain. When the doors opened and people aggressively pushed me to the side, bumped their elbows into my body and stomped on my feet, I kept smiling. Liza led us through the tumult and, when our hands bumped onto the metal barricade, I couldn't quite believe my eyes.

While everyone else was busy arguing with each other, focused on preventing other fans from getting their desired spots, we had sneaked our way through and ended up right in the middle of the first row. When I looked straight ahead, my nose was level with the microphone stand. We had fought for a spot like this for so many years but were never quite able to make it. We had experienced other concerts at the barricade but always had to bend over and turn our heads to the side to even see a glimpse of the stage. When we missed the barricade, the second or third row were the best spots we got.

Maxine wrapped her arms around us. "We made it. Thank you so much, Liza."

"I didn't think I'd ever thank you for forcing me out of bed this morning. But, *thank you.* I'm beyond grateful for your excessively loud screaming at 7am," Chloe looked at Liza and laughed.

This was worth every second we had spent on that cobblestone ground. My heart felt warm, my head comfortably fuzzy.

For a second, I felt like I was 15 again, holding Chloe's hand for the first time, ready to experience the best night of our lives. It was just that, this time, we were older, bruised but stronger. Everything my 15 year old self had feared on that day came true. But everything she had dreamed of had come true as well. The fact that this was the first time we would see Marina from a spot like this felt meant to be. We had been swimming, fighting, running, for the past few years. Now, we had reached the shore, the spot where we were supposed to be all along.

"I can't believe we made it," I said. Those words meant so much more than the fact that we had got the spots we wanted. Chloe and I had made it through.

Together.

"I don't know how I'll survive seeing Marina from this close." Liza was stepping from one foot to the other in excitement.

"Oh, me neither," I answered, followed by Maxine and Chloe echoing their agreement.

Even just imagining Marina's body on that stage, the thought of seeing her this close in real life, sent electric shivers through me. I would be able to see her rings, her hands, the way she pulled her hair back, the sweat dripping down her throat. *I will see the sweat dripping down her body. I am going to die.*

"I think I might die right here." Maxine put my thoughts into words.

Chloe nodded and let her upper body fall over the barricade. "If she wears that same black top she wore back then, I will faint."

"Guys, please don't die; I still need you, even though I might have a heart attack when she steps on stage," I giggled. Then I took a deep breath. "But I also kinda need to pee and would love to get an Aperol." I pointed toward Chloe. "Wanna tag along and help me carry?"

Chloe nodded and put her jacket over the barricade. "Are you two going to be fine with keeping our spots?"

"Sure thing; I'll just do the butterfly and it'll be fine." Liza stepped half a meter away from Maxine and spread out both her legs and arms, taking in the space of three people as one.

Getting out of the crowd was a fight as no one made the effort to step away. I am not looking forward to pushing through to the front on our way back.

Before we reached the bathroom, Chloe grabbed my upper arm and stopped me in my tracks. "I feel like I should text Mel."

Her words came fully out of nowhere, catching me off guard. Chloe hadn't talked about her ex summer situationship for a while now which should have been a good thing.

"Don't," I said and stepped in front of my best friend. "Why the hell would you think something like that?"

"I mean, she said I could text her when I was ready." Chloe looked to her feet, her arms crossed in front of her chest. "I wonder what's going on in her life."

"Or maybe the alcohol is just making you horny."
My words were harsh but meant well; she knew that. "Do
you really feel like you're ready to talk to her again?" We
both knew she wasn't and never would be; they should
stay no contact for the rest of their lives.

Still, the fact that she'd said Mel's name summoned
Tate in my thoughts. It would be a lie to say that I didn't
feel like texting my ex whenever I drank. I knew that it
was wrong, though, so I didn't.

"I don't know, maybe I am." Chloe started fiddling
with the scrunchie around her wrist. "I feel like it wasn't
fully over; I'm missing some form of closure."

"Well, closure doesn't mean you have to let her back
into your life, Chlo." My voice softened and I grabbed
her hands. "What if you finally let her out of your life
instead of holding on?"

"I don't think I can do that." Chloe hid her
insecurities under a sarcastic laugh; she always did. "I
guess I miss the sex as well."

"Jeez, Chloe. You can find sex everywhere," I
laughed and pushed her into the bathroom.

I wanted nothing more than to see my best friend
happy and I knew Mel had hurt her deeper than anyone.
She had to let her go, leave her behind and move on, even
if it had only been a few months since their 'break up'.

When Chloe came back out of the bathroom and met
me outside the door, I stopped her from walking out.

"What if you say goodbye to her tonight? What better place is there to let go of someone than the concert of your favorite band that is gonna make you cry all night anyways?"

Chloe laughed, even though I knew she didn't want to hear my words.

"Give me your phone." I held out my hand.

She gave it to me without resistance.

Chloe 8:15pm

Hey. Thank you for everything but I don't think I'll ever be ready to reach out to you. Maybe we're going to meet again, maybe we won't. But I don't think we can ever be friends. Goodbye.

The words flew from my fingers fast. I was the rational friend here, solving the issues that Chloe was unable to solve. Ready to help and fix wherever I could.

I wrote the words I wished that I could've written to Tate. I wished I could've found closure the way Chloe was hopefully finding now. It's not like I ever wanted her back, I definitely didn't. She'd hurt me too much, had made me feel like a burden and never reached out to me again. Somehow, I wished that she would apologize.

I handed the phone back to Chloe. She didn't even read the text I had typed, didn't even scan it. She hit send, then blocked her.

"Thank you. I trust that you said the right thing." She hugged me and pulled me toward the bar.

I was happy with my work; even if she reversed the block the next morning, this stopped her from desperately texting Mel tonight. Tonight was for us and Mel had to move to the background. Unconsciously, I pushed Tate there as well.

We clawed our way back through the crowd, balancing two cups of Aperol Spritz each. The others took their cups and gulped down a few sips. We resumed our drinking game to pass the time until the support act came on stage.

And then, the first beats of the intro drummed through the hall. With every beat, my heart beat faster, aligning with the drums. This concert, this band, became my heartbeat, taking in my entire being. When I looked over at my friends, tears sprang to my eyes. They were glowing, jumping up and down in excitement.

"*In the dimly lit room, where whispers turned into sighs.*" As Marina's voice appeared in the room, something caught fire inside me. "*Fingers intertwined, tracing secrets in your eyes.*"

"*Lost in your touch, we dance a delicate line.*" I started singing the lyrics with the crowd, a choir of people connected through the same band.

"*Bodies in motion, syncing in perfect time.*"

I was 15 and 22 at the same time. I felt lost and hopeful as well as content and free.

"It's like a melody, soft and sweet."

Chloe's hand found mine in an anxious and clingy way when Marina stepped on stage.

"Our bodies moving to the beat."

My heart dropped to the bottom of my stomach when the woman of my dreams appeared in front of us.

"Exploring depths in ecstasy."

Her Docs hit the floor in the beat of the drums, a smile brighter than ever was on her face.

"Lost in the rhythm of you and me."

It felt like she was glowing more the older she got. Even 6 years later, she was still wearing her signature black jeans and they still shaped her legs in a heavenly way.

"Breathless gasps and tangled sheets."

Marina took the mic and let her body glide down the stand and back up.

"Skin on skin, our hearts meet."

My mouth was agape. When I looked straight ahead, I was looking right at the space between her legs. I forced my eyes to wander upward and scanned the rest of her body on the way. She was wearing the black top we had been talking about, the deep cutout revealing her gorgeous decollete. The older she got, the better her boobs looked, the little wrinkles marking the years she had spent touring with my favorite band. Her arms were hidden under a cropped leather jacket, the reflection of the spotlights making her face glow. Her hair was gelled back, giving it the wet look before she even started sweating. Sizzles of electricity burned through my body. I had to suppress a moan when Marina let her head fall back and a high note vibrated through the crowd.

"In the silence, our desires speak."

Marina lifted her left arm to the sky and the audience reacted with loud cheering.

"A symphony of passion, reaching its peak."

"Fuck. Fuck. Fuck." Chloe shook my hand and forced me to look to her side.

I giggled and made a fainting motion.

Liza bent over the barricade to look at me, ignoring that Marina was currently dancing above us. "MILF!" she screamed.

How is she not scared that Marina might hear us?

Sometimes, I wished I would give less fucks about what the people around me thought, allowing myself to be as loud as Liza. Both Chloe and I nodded enthusiastically.

When I focused back on Marina, she was looking right at me. She was smirking while she sang.

"It's like a melody, soft and sweet."

If my heart hadn't reached the floor yet, it had now. Everything inside me vibrated under her watch.

"Our bodies moving to the beat."

Every word of the song shot through me like a shock wave. This song had always been the hottest *Paper Rings and Promises* song and now Marina was singing about sex, staring right at me.

"Exploring depths in ecstasy."

Her eyes were pinning mine. Then, she took a step forward, less than a meter from our bodies.

"Lost in the rhythm of you and me."

In the next second, Marina had shoved her microphone in front of my face. My heart jumped back up to my throat, closing every inch of breathing space. Marina stopped singing, waiting for me to scream the bridge into the microphone. I was frozen in place; the lyrics were ashes on my tongue.

Silence.

There were only the sounds of the band playing in the background.

For a second, it felt like only Marina and I existed on this planet, her brown eyes staring right into my soul. *You're supposed to sing*, the conscious part of my mind screamed, desperately trying to keep it together. Marina nodded at me with encouragement which made a cough slide up, itching at the top of my throat.

When it was about to burst out, Chloe pushed me aside and bent over the barricade toward the microphone.

"In every touch, a story unfolds."

Marina moved the microphone in Chloe's direction, shifting her attention toward my best friend. Chloe's voice grew louder.

"*A masterpiece of love untold… With every kiss, we rewrite the script.*"

The room was screaming with my best friend now.

"*In its intimate dance, our souls eclipse.*"

Marina thanked Chloe with a high-five and got back into a standing position. When she found her space in the center of the stage to finish the song, she winked at me.

After embarrassing myself in front of her, she just *winked* at me?!

I wanted nothing more than a hole in the ground to swallow me.

When Marina finished the song, and greeted the audience, I took Chloe's hand. Pride filled me at the touch. This must have taken so much courage. My best friend's anxiety held her back so often and years ago, she never would have sung into a microphone. She beat her fears to save me and I could never thank her enough. I looked at our hands; my gold ring was glowing in the spotlights. A reminder why I was at this concert right now. This night was about Chloe and me, our journey and our shared love for this band.

For the rest of the night, I turned back into a 15-year-old, focusing on my friends and screaming the lyrics that had shaped me over the past six years.

When *Fourteen* came on, I cried happy tears, hugged my best friend tighter than ever and it felt like I was coming home. With every word and every beat, everything was coming together. We had made it. We were right where we were supposed to be. My heart felt warm and safe.

We had made it.

The weight I had carried over the years fell off my shoulders. The worries of my fifteen-year-old self floated away with every word I sang. I was 20 again. *We* were 20 again. This was our shore. It was time for us to stop swimming and to start walking, soaring, flying.

Together.

Forever.

Chapter 3
Free Now - Gracie Abrams

Instead of posting my three TikToks of the day, I started working on an application. Probably the most important application of my life so far. It felt almost impossible to put every thought into words and to convey what this opportunity meant for me.

5 hours and a work day later, I pressed send on an email I had poured my heart into. I was careful not to focus on the fact that I had been a fan for so long - that was what everyone was writing. I leaned into my own development and experience with photography.

When I opened my phone to text Chloe the news, another message appeared on my screen:

Tate 12:31pm
I miss you.

Pain erupted from the space where my heart sat in my chest.

What the fuck?

The pain turned into anger and back into pain within seconds. Tate was the last person I thought I'd hear from. Though I couldn't quite formulate the thought yet, she was also the last person I *wanted* to hear from. I used to love her; now there was almost nothing but hate.

Two years ago, I met her parents and she met mine. We dated, she took me to her graduation, we spent most days together. And then, when things got darker, she decided I was "too much", saw her ex-girlfriend and couldn't distinguish who she loved anymore. She probably had never loved me fully and instead made use of me pleasing her. Once she had to take care of me, when I ended up in the hospital, she distanced herself from me. She'd left me in one of my darkest times and, now that things were better, she *missed* me?

While Chloe's situation was ended by Mel, I had to end mine myself. It seemed like Tate couldn't quite let me in but couldn't quite let me go either. It had been more than 2 years and there had never been any closure. And, now, she was reaching out to me. What was I supposed to do with that?

I didn't respond to the message and called Chloe instead.

"Tate just texted me," I said, before Chloe could greet me.

She made a growling sound. "What the actual fuck?!" I had never heard Chloe's voice this angry. Then, she let out an audible breath, seemingly calming herself. "How do you feel? What did she say?"

"She said she misses me." My voice was surprisingly calm. "I don't know how to feel. It's been so long, Chlo." I put the phone on speaker and pulled on my ponytail, tightening my hairstyle. A slight pain shot through my head; but the pain in my heartfelt less threatening.

"Do you *want* her to miss you?"

Chloe's question went right to the core, sending a shiver down my spine. Tears welled up in my eyes but I gulped them down. Chloe knew me in all stages of my life but I scarcely cried in front of her. The only tears she'd seen were happy tears. I was the put-together one here, the realistic one, the strong one; not the one to ugly cry.

I took a deep breath. "Not in the way that I see hope. More in the way that it makes me feel good for *her* to miss *me*, I think." There was no hope in this situation; I knew she would hurt me again. "Like, I feel accomplished by knowing that she's suffering too."

"I get that," Chloe said.

"But do I need to feel bad about that? I don't want to wish harm on anyone or sit here and hold a grudge forever," I mumbled, my breathing calming to a regular level. "I don't miss her. I feel angry. The fact that she even has the audacity to reach out makes me so furious."

"Oh, girl, you have every reason to be angry. And better to be angry than sad, right? Definitely better to be angry than taking her back." Chloe let out a chuckle, trying to shift this conversation to a more ironic tone.

I wished I could join in with her laughter but the pain in my chest didn't let me. I put on a sarcastic voice anyway. "Why can't I just date Marina, for God's sake? She would treat me right." There was no way it'd ever happen, as Marina was sitting at home with her husband, but talking about impossible fantasies distracted me from reality for a moment.

Chloe laughed. "Oh yes, definitely. But you'd have to share her because I couldn't let you date the woman of my dreams without including me."

"A throuple it is then." I did have to smile at the thought and the pain in my chest eased a little. "I sent out an application, by the way."

"No way!" Chloe's glow was back; I could hear it in her voice. "I'm so proud of you. And I'm 100% sure you're going to get it. There is no way they'd take anyone else; you're perfect for this job."

"Thanks, girl," I said. "I do have to go now, though. I spent all morning writing this email and haven't actually done any work yet. Not looking to get fired before I even have a reply to this application." I forced out a laugh.

"Text me later," Chloe replied. "And block Tate; she doesn't deserve an answer."

Before I could reply to her, the beeping sound of a disconnected phone line rang in my ears.

I looked at myself in the mirror next to my bed. My eyes were red. My ponytail wasn't as sleek as I wanted it to be, a little bump developing on the top of my head, even after I had religiously tightened it. I divided my ponytail into two sections, pulling even harder and forcing the bump to go down. The tears were back now, caused by the pain shooting through my scalp. I shook my head and buried my face in my hands for a second. Then, I pressed my palms against my eyes.

This day was just too much.

I took 5 deep breaths, counted 5 things I could see, 5 things I could smell and 5 things I could hear. Then, I opened up the TikTok of my local party to post the video for the day. I did the same for Instagram and shot out a quote to Twitter. After that, I linked my camera to my MacBook and transferred around a hundred photos from a climate protest we did last week. I scrolled through, found the best ones and edited them. When I finished the tenth photo, I had forgotten about the message from Tate and was fully concentrated on my work.

When there was no more work to do, I closed my MacBook and removed my hair tie. With my brown hair falling down my cheeks in a mess, I started crying. I wandered from my desk to my bed with wonky steps, the tears blurring my vision. My breathing came out in huffed motions. I felt like I couldn't breathe. I crawled onto my bed and let my head fall onto my pillow face first. While the pain on my scalp slowly eased, the pain in my heart grew stronger. I couldn't breathe with my mouth and nose pressed into the pillow. I screamed. I screamed into the fabric, leaving snot on my pink pillow. My right hand started beating the mattress until I was forced to lift my head so I didn't suffocate.

Once my breathing returned to normal, I dragged myself back out of bed to get my phone. I texted Tate:

Kari 5:15pm
I miss you too.

Then, I threw my phone to the other side of the room and hid my face back in the pillow.

Why did I do this?

I knew that this was a horrible idea. I knew that I was throwing away 2 years of progress by responding to her. I couldn't be strong and realistic in *every* aspect of my life. I deserved to lash out sometimes, right?

Right?

Tate didn't respond to my message and a week later I got an email from the manager of *Paper Rings and Promises*.

I got the position.

Chapter 4
Girls – Girl in Red

This is all going to be fine. She won't think you're weird.
Just be normal.

My thoughts were roaming as my platform Doc
Martens found the pavement of Stuttgart Central Station.
I let out a grunt and I lifted my black suitcase which was
covered with rubbed-off stickers from all the concerts,
events and places I had traveled to.

When I stumbled a few steps away from the door,
my right hand felt the rough surface of my Paper Rings
and Promises sticker. I stopped in my tracks, bending
down to take another look at the sticker which had
accompanied me for the past 10 years. The familiar lines
of two hand-drawn rings entangled into what looked like
an infinity sign let a warm, homey feeling develop in my
heart. This band was my home after all.

And I have to go meet them now.

I straightened my legs and intensified the grip on the
handle of my suitcase. A breath of anxiety later, I

shuffled through the masses of people at the station, bumping into unamused travelers with my suitcase. Every bump made me breathe heavier and I felt sweat developing under my armpits; there was no way I could impress Marina now.

At the end of the platform, I took my iPhone out of the back pocket of my mom jeans, and pulled up my mail app.

Dear Kari,
We'd love to invite you to an internship with Paper Rings and Promises!

My heart still leaped at every word of this email, that weightless feeling lurking in my stomach. I scrolled down to the Google Maps link before I re-read the whole email for the 100th time.

My phone pinged with a notification.

Tate, 5:25pm
Do you have time to talk soon?

I scoffed and archived her chat. I had almost forgotten about the little message exchange between Tate and I. How could she have the audacity to reach out and then ghost me for months? Her behavior was so weird but still typical for her; she had loved to keep me waiting, reaching out only when it was convenient. Old me would've immediately organized a date to meet up with her. New me was on her way to an internship that would take up all of her time for the next 2 weeks and a future that was unknown. There was definitely no space for a person like Tate. My whole brain was consumed by the thought of Marina and the dream that was awaiting me. I kept going.

There was no reason to question reality again; my feet were already taking me through the hall of Stuttgart Central Station on the way to the 1st tour stop. I was supposed to meet the crew and band at the event location, getting used to the job and environment before the first show tomorrow.

Getting used to... Such a weird phrase for something that seemed so delusional. I would never get used to it.

I caught the time on the big clock in the main hall: 5:30pm.

Shit. I'm supposed to be there in 30 minutes.

I quickened my step, my breathing getting heavier and the fabric under my armpits wetter. The tunnel from the hall to the tram station was never-ending. I felt thrown back to the day I ran down that hall to find my place in the line of a concert venue. Concerts had brought me to 100s of different train stations and Stuttgart had always been the biggest pain in the ass. The construction on site was supposed to be temporary but it had been making me sweat for the past 8 years.

12 minutes later, I jumped onto a tram, huffing and puffing from the endless walk through the station. The little train car was packed and my body squeezed against the dirty window.

I should have never agreed to this.

A strand of brown hair came out of my claw-clip, sticking to my forehead.

They will fire me on sight if I show up on my first day like this.

All I wanted was to make a good first impression and, of course, the summer heat and public transport had to ruin my plans.

I redid my claw clip tighter as the tram stops were passing. I felt like I was 14 again, on my way to my first Paper Rings and Promises concert. Or 16, on the way to my 1st date with a girl. And still, this moment had felt so much bigger than all of the ones before. People kept telling me "never meet your heroes" and there was so much fear in the anticipation of finally doing exactly that. I was scared that the moment wouldn't live up to my dream. At the same time, I was scared it would be so much more, overwhelming me to the point that my heart stops beating.

What if she's even more gorgeous in person?

And she's actually nice to me?

How will I stand, walk or even talk?

My hands trembled at the thought of meeting her; how would they be able to hold a phone while filming her at the concert tomorrow night?

The voice on the speakers announced my stop. Warm, sweaty bodies pressed against me as I made my way toward the door. Even if I tried to ask them to step aside, I knew no words would come out of my mouth right now.

A warm summer breeze stroked my face as I stumbled outside. Before I could take a calming breath, people pushed into me and forced me into the corner. Once I could grab the barrier of the platform, I breathed in. My suitcase hit the barrier with a metallic clack. I took my tote bag off the handle and let myself fall onto the heated plastic of my suitcase. My hands were shaky as I rummaged through the contents of the bag, looking for something to ease my sweaty smell. I didn't dare to check the time on my phone.

Why do I even use tote bags if I can never find anything in these things?

A light squeak escaped my lips as my right hand closed around the small deodorant I had thrown into the bag just 5 hours earlier.

I knew I wouldn't have left the house without deodorant!

I sprayed every corner of my body. I was shocked that I didn't empty the can in one go. At least I smelled more like a field of tulips mixed with chemical odors than the sweat that was still dripping down my forehead.

My hair resisted my attempts to get it back into the claw clip 3 times. Only on the 4th attempt did I manage to get every bit of hair out of my face and semi-safely clipped back. The motion of putting myself together calmed my nerves with its familiarity.

As soon as my appearance was in order, my insides started feeling less messy. Another deep breath entered my lungs and came back out as a huff. I nodded toward an invisible person before I pulled my tote bag over my shoulder, grabbing the handle of my suitcase and taking on the last 300 meters toward the location. My hand anxiously felt for my phone but I refrained from checking the time.

I can't help it if I'm late now.

"Hi! Kari? Is that you?" A warm voice sounded from a few meters away on my right, just as I stepped onto the driveway of the location.

It's her.

I silently counted to 3 before I stopped. The first thing that caught my eye were the same Doc Martens I was wearing, stepping toward my direction. My breath caught in my throat, making me cough.

I got it now. I was a hypocrite, laughing about other fans when they hyperventilated because of her; I was just the same.

Marina was approaching me. She was wearing black skinny jeans, the same she always did. I had spent countless hours zooming in on pictures of her from every show she had ever done. Now, she was right in front of me, forcing me to blink a million times to prove I wasn't hallucinating. Marina was even more gorgeous in person.

"Hello? Are you Kari?"

Her words made my eyes dart up to her face. She wasn't wearing any makeup, the wrinkles around her eyes making her seem even prettier, warmer. The top part of her dark hair was up in a bun, only a few loose strands framed her face. I wouldn't have dared to leave them loose but for her they just added to her beauty, framing her angelic features.

I couldn't breathe.

She stretched out her hand. A different silver ring decorated each of her fingers, the dark nail-polish making them seem even more graceful than I ever thought possible.

"Hello?" She was about to remove her hand.

Before she could call me a 4th time, I grabbed her hand and shook it without a word. An electric wave sizzled from the space where our hands connected, up my arm and down my back.

"So, you're Kari?" she asked again.

I tried to speak; nothing but a cough came out. My free hand shielded my face as I nodded to answer her question.

My suitcase fell to the ground with a loud thump; I wanted to sink into the ground with embarrassment right then and there. Marina moved and grabbed it herself before I could lift it back up. I tried taking it from her but she pulled it away.

"Oh, dear, let me carry that; you don't sound good." Her thumb gently caressed my hand and I thought my legs wouldn't be able to stand all that electricity coursing through my body. "Well, I won't force you to talk. But, let me show you around so you can rest as soon as possible." Instead of letting go of my hand, she turned around and pulled me after her. I thought I might faint right there.

How am I supposed to survive the next week?

She pulled me as much as she pulled my suitcase. My feet stumbled over the cobblestones like 4 little plastic wheels did.

About 50 meters into the stony road, the tour bus came into view. It was black, except for Paper Rings and Promises in hand-written letters on its side. I knew this bus from photos but had never dared to approach it. I could have, of course. Sometimes, it was even parked in front of the location, reachable for anyone that wanted to look at it or even knock at the window. It wasn't uncommon for a few fans to wait in front of the bus for hours, hoping to catch band members on their way to bed or their morning cigarette. Whenever that happened, selfies appeared: Marina in pyjamas, sometimes even with a toothbrush in her mouth.

I mean, who likes to be disturbed by strangers on their way to bed?

I was proud of being part of this fandom but people doing things like that sometimes made me scared to admit it.

"This is the bus code." Marina let go of my hand and I almost tried to grab it back. "I believe Milo also put it in the email. But in case he hasn't, this is it." She started typing numbers into the keypad next to the bus door.

1-2-2-3-3.

I had no clue if that code had actually been in the email I got and I had no clue if I was able to memorize a code in a situation like this.

The door opened with a whoosh, the smell of a new bus coming my way. It smelled so modern; I was scared to ruin it with my dusty boots.

Marina stepped inside without hesitation, her dirty boots climbing the steps of the bus, lit up by colored LEDs. My suitcase bumped against the steps right behind her. Her butt appeared behind the black plastic of the suitcase here and there, sending a shiver down my back.

It was almost scary how much impact her presence had on my body.

Kari! Stop thinking about your boss this way!

I didn't like that I reverted to a fifteen year-old hormonal teenager in her presence. It didn't seem so bad when she existed on my screen or on stage, but now, seeing her right in front of me, she was more than just a hot celebrity.

I was frozen in place. There were fan fictions describing the interior of this bus, their details collected from various backstage photos. Stepping onto the bus now was like trespassing.

It's their home, their most private space. They sleep here, change and live.

I had an image in my head but there was no way for me to know what exactly was waiting for me around that corner.

"Do I have to drag you with me again or can you take the steps of the stairs by yourself?" The warm tone of Marina's voice rose, accompanied by the sound of water splashing into a glass cup. There was not a hint of annoyance; it had more of a joking air to it.

Come on, Kari. Get yourself in there. It's just a bus.

I fixed my posture.

It's just a bus.

I inhaled deeply.

The soles of my Doc Martens touched the first step of the stairs. Red lights made its steel cap glow.

It is just a bus.

I breathed out.

It. Is. Just. A. Bus.

I stepped inside.

Marina stood in the narrow hallway, next to a small kitchen counter. She was holding out a glass of water to me. "After coughing your guts out, I thought you might want a sip." She took a step in my direction and the scent of lavender immediately hit my nostrils. I stepped back, feeling the tip of the last step beneath my soles.

"You know you live on this bus now, right?" Marina let out a soft laugh; one of the most beautiful sounds I had ever heard. "No need to be scared. This is your home now." She motioned for me to come closer.

Stop embarrassing yourself.

I stepped toward her and took the water with a grateful nod. Our hands brushed for a mere second when I took it, sending my heart into an unsteady rhythm.

"Thanks." The word was barely audible but I was still proud of getting it past my lips.

"Okay, let's get to it." Marina winked and suddenly there were countless 'getting to it' versions in my mind. I used to think these things in private, quietly in my own room. I didn't like how my mind jumped to sexual images in her presence. I was no different than the screaming and hyperventilating fans. My knees felt weak under the pumping sensation developing from the space between my legs.

As soon as Marina turned around to step back toward the kitchen, I gulped down the water. It evaporated on the hot surface of my throat; I was burning from the inside out.

For God's sake; get your shit together.

"So, as you can see, this is the kitchen. There are no appliances to cook but a sink for fresh water and washing your hands, as well as a water cooker for tea." She bent down to open the little fridge beneath the sink. "This is mainly for drinks or anything you need to cool. If something isn't labeled, anyone can have it."

The fridge was almost empty at this point, a single coke can was sitting in its back corner. Marina pulled back the strands of hair that had fallen into her face and pushed herself back up on the counter.

"This is the bathroom." She touched a door opposite the kitchen.

Note to self: Never go to the bathroom if there is ANYONE on this bus.

She let out an audible huff as she turned around to the back of the bus. A gray curtain was shielding the rest from view. She pulled it aside and stepped behind without another word.

Before I followed, I placed the glass cup on the sink and rubbed my sweaty hands on my pants. I carefully stepped forward; my nose almost touched the curtain in front of me.

So, this is it. This is the sleeping area. Her bedroom. The place countless fans have envisioned in their writing.

It felt wrong but I still forced my hand to push away the curtain.

"So, this is where we sleep."

The walls were lined with bunk beds that looked more like sleeping capsules. 6 on each side, 3 on top of each other. Each bed was made out of wood and had a smaller version of the big gray curtain for privacy.

Gosh, I hope I won't have to sleep in one of the top bunks. The third row seems a bit too high.

At the end of the hallway, which was also the end of the bus, was one double bed.

Oh, so there actually is a double-bed on these things.

I felt the immediate urge to text Chloe about this. We had spent countless hours theorizing about the 'bed' situation on tour buses.

"And this," Marina raised her voice again, my eyes darted back toward her, "is where you'll sleep." She pointed at a bottom bed in the second row on the right.

She pulled my suitcase up to her side and heaved it onto the bed.

It was right in front of her double bed.

Fuck, a bit too close to her.

"I know it's no 5 star hotel but it does the job. Most days, we only sleep on this bus anyway. Not much time spent here besides that." She leaned against the frame of the bunk beds and crossed her arms, pushing her boobs together. "My husband used to visit on tour years ago, but they never stopped booking a bus with a double bed."

My eyes darted down to her neckline for a millisecond.

Stop.

"Ready to go on?" Marina pushed herself away from the beds and walked toward me.

I nodded.

"Cool." She squeezed past, her body almost pressed against mine. It felt like that moment was the only moment to ever exist in the space-time continuum. "You can leave anything that you don't need right now on your bed." She disappeared behind the curtain and left me choking on air.

I threw my tote bag right after my suitcase and breathed in what felt like the millionth calming breath that day. It was just that the air entering my lungs felt anything but calm. My hands shook as I felt for the claw clip on the back of my head. I opened it, pulled and twisted my hair even tighter and closed it again.

Get a grip, Kari.

A pulsating pain was developing in the back of my head.

"You coming?" Marina asked from somewhere behind the curtain.

"Yes, just a second!" I shot out a short text to Chloe before I followed Marina:

Kari 6:27 pm
I have no idea how I'm going to survive this.
She is even hotter up close.

Marina was already leaning against the wall across from the bus door. She was typing something on her phone but smiled up at me when she heard the stomping sound of my boots on the stairs.

"Are you ready to meet the rest of the crew?" She pushed herself off the wall with her right foot and I think it might have been the most graceful motion I had ever witnessed.

I decided that it was better to go with cute insecurities than saying nothing at all. She knew I wasn't ready for it anyway. I let out a soft laugh.

"I hope so."

No, not at all.

I looked down at my shoes and a strand of hair fell out of the clip. I instantly wanted to fix it.

Marina laughed; it seemed genuine. "They don't bite." She waved her hand at me as if to say there is no need to worry. "I get if this is a lot, though. I can't imagine how I'd feel seeing all this for the first time."

"Yeah, it is a lot," I agreed.

She placed a warm hand on my shoulder. "Just give me like 30 more minutes to get through everything and then I'll leave you to settle and process. Okay?"

"Okay," I answered with a slight nod of my head.

But please stop touching me or I won't ever be okay again.

A warm, sizzling feeling developed in the space her hand had touched.

Or never ever stop touching me because this actually feels amazing.

She motioned for me to walk into a white tent that was set up right next to the wall she was leaning on. The last corner of the tent's wall was hanging loose which functioned as some sort of door. There were just about 3 meters of space between the bus door and the loose part of the tent, minimizing the area where the band could walk freely without being seen.

A wall of hot, humid air brushed my face as I entered the tent. The space was surprisingly big. There were 3 long tables set up to my right and some plates with a bit of fruit were still scattered on them. It looked like they'd had a pretty big lunch buffet.

A man with long brown hair picked up a piece of watermelon and took a bite.

Dari.

The drummer.

In the back of the tent was a big leather couch and two leather chairs. It looked like they'd been standing there since the first concert this town had ever seen.

A middle-aged man with short blonde hair was hunched on the couch and was aggressively typing away on his phone.

That must be the manager.

Next to him on the chair, a man with short black hair and a leather jacket covered in patches was snoring away.

Brad.

The guitar player was known for never taking off his leather jacket, even in 30 degree heat.

There were a few other people roaming around the space, chatting or still carrying around bits of equipment. All of them were male.

Marina grabbed my hand again as she walked past me and pulled me toward the tables on the right. "Hey, Dari!"

He looked up, half of his face was still covered in brown hair.

"This is Kari. She'll be taking photos for socials."

He held out a big, lanky hand to me. "Hey Kari. I'm Dari." He pulled a strand of hair behind his ear with his other hand; it immediately fell back into his face. His hair was greasy, like he hadn't showered in weeks. "I'm the drummer."

I took his hand. The handshake felt sweaty but I couldn't distinguish if it was his sweat or mine. His eyes wandered down my upper body in a way that made me feel uncomfortable.

"Coolio. Have fun meeting the rest of the gang. I'm gonna go smoke a J." He turned around as soon as he let go of my hand.

I tried not to dwell on the way his eyes had scanned my upper body.

"Don't take him too seriously; that's just the way he is," Marina laughed. "These tables are where we get our catered food. It might look different in other locations but the rule is: if there's food in the backstage area, anyone can eat it."

I nodded and Marina took hold of my hand again. She pulled me toward the seating area and motioned for me to sit in the free chair while she wrapped her arm around the man's shoulders, forcing him to look up from his phone.

"Hey, Milo. Your intern is here," Marina said.

So, that's the person I've been talking to for the past week.

He moved his head as if he wanted to look back down.

Oh, it's gonna be a blast working for this guy.

I stepped forward. Straight cis men didn't feel half as intimidating to me as Marina's smile. My hand shot out before he could even look back up. He looked at my fingers directly.

"Hi, I'm Kari. We talked over email."

Milo stared at my hand for a second, before his eyes scanned the rest of my arm and shoulder up to my eyes. "Ah, yes. Kari. Nice to meet you." His big hand shook mine. It was dry, as if he applied hand sanitizer a bit too often. "Glad you could make it." A second after he let go of my hand, his eyes were glued back to his screen.

"Okay, guess we're not getting any more out of you today." Marina gave her manager a slap on the back and jumped back up. "Now, let me show you the best part: the stage." Marina's strong arm pulled me up from the chair before I could even comprehend what was happening. The warmth of her hand in mine almost felt familiar at this point.

"Don't expect too much of Milo," Marina said as she pulled me through the tent's second entry. "His job is literally planning things and that is impossible without his phone. And, for some reason, he's never really off the clock." She stopped me in front of a set of black steps. "Okay, here we go. These are the stairs to the back of the stage." Marina was holding out her arm toward the stairs.

I stood in shock for a second. A sliver of fear ran through my body.

What awaits me on the other side of these steps?

Are these concerts ever gonna be the same for me once I cross this line?

I wanted to know how it feels to walk up this stage not like you adore it but like it belongs to you. I had made the decision to cross this line long before this moment, staring at the steps in front of me. I had made the decision by sending out that application. And still, walking up to the stage now felt like standing on the edge of a precipice.

I'm on the wrong side of this stage.

For the first time that day, my heavy breathing wasn't a reaction to the warmth of Marina's hand in mine; I was afraid of change.

"Ladies first." Marina let go of my hand and gave me a little push toward the steps. "Don't hesitate. You belong on that stage as much as I do now," she winked. "And, believe me, you'll regret not model-walking onto that stage at least once while we have it to ourselves. I promise it feels amazing!"

I chuckled, even though I felt like crying.

"Okay," I huffed and placed my right foot on the first step. It made a creaking sound under the weight of my Docs.

It's just a stage.

This doesn't mean you're changing your whole life.

You're still a fan girl, even if you've seen the other side.

I wasn't quite sure if I could believe the thoughts I was telling myself. Who knew what was going to happen in the future? Who knew if I would ever find myself in front of that stage again?

"What are you waiting for? The stage is yours!" Marina laughed and gave me another nudge.

My feet carried me up the stairs one by one. I counted 8 steps before the soles of my shoes touched the smooth surface of the vinyl ground. The stage floor was made of square plates, each lined with a metal frame. I bent down to touch the ground, before I could give it a second thought. The surface was smooth, almost slippery, not soft but also not completely hard. It felt warm beneath my fingers, charged with energy.

Why have I never wondered about the way the ground feels?

It's amazing.

I didn't dare to look up as my knees fell onto the stage, followed by the rest of my body sliding down. My eyes were shut as my back laid flat down on the ground.

There was a cracking sound as the claw clip on the back of my head hit the vinyl. The palms of my hands were soaking in the energy of the ground.

I belong right here, right now.

I had forgotten about the person that had pushed me up here. I had forgotten that this was the space I had spent so many hours admiring from the other side. I had forgotten about the fear I had felt just moments before.

There was no way to know what this tour would do to me, how many things would change, if I would still be the same person when this tour ended. What I did know was that I had to be here. If this experience changed me, it had to be for the better. This was my childhood dream, after all.

Chapter 5

All My Love - Noah Kahn
8 years ago

The day that I had heard *Paper Rings and Promises* on the radio for the first time, I had no idea how much impact that band would have on my life. When Marina's warm voice rang through my ears, singing about a lost love, something inside me felt seen, even though I had never been in love. Her voice felt soothing, like summer rain after a long drought. My mother had been speaking to my dad on the phone, one piece of her wired headphones in her ear, while the other hung down her front. She hadn't wanted me to hear my father's side. Her fingers were aggressively tapping the steering wheel. I could still hear the faint noise of his screams through the headphones. The song had pushed her conversation into the background for a moment, giving me a sense of quiet that I hadn't felt in weeks.

I was just 14 at that time. My parents were constantly fighting, turning my home into purgatory. I hated to see my mother hurting; she cried often since their relationship had become complicated and I was often the one picking her up from the ground. What used to be my safe space, my stability, fell apart. My mother had lost control over our family and herself. I was only a child but I was the one keeping me, and her, together. They had needed to separate but something told me that they stuck together because of me. Every time that they had fought, a dark sense of guilt developed like an ice block slowly forming inside my stomach.

Now, hearing Marina's voice, a humming feeling of comfort developed instead.

A few months later, I knew everything about *Paper Rings and Promises* and had joined multiple fan groups for the band. Most people in them had been going through something. And most importantly, they had always listened.

When a girl named Chloe had texted me for the first time, asking me if I was okay, I poured it all out. I even told her about the way I pulled my hair together to ground myself and confessed that I liked the pain sometimes. Instead of judging me, saying that other people had bigger problems or that I should be happy that my parents were still together, she had listened. I had felt seen for the first time in a long time. She might have lived on the other side of Germany but I felt closer to her than anyone. I think that she felt the same way. We then started our own little fan group, gathering people that were just like us.

We called their song *fourteen* ours because we were that age too and the song was about friendship. It originally told the story of the band, the way they met at 14 and became inseparable since. It made me hopeful for the future, hopeful that Chloe and I would stick together through it all and hopeful that we'd get somewhere in life, just like they had.

About a year later, we'd met for the first time at a concert. It was our first *Paper Rings and Promises* concert and it was pure magic. Our first hug had felt like two lonely puzzle pieces falling into place.

"Kari! I'm so happy to finally hug you," she'd said. I would have pushed other people away, keeping them at a distance, never letting anyone in, but this felt like summer after years of winter.

"Just happy?" I'd laughed. We knew it was so much more than happiness.

"You know exactly what I mean," the sight of her smile had summoned a mirrored reaction of my own.

I nodded and she took my hand, pulling me towards the entrance.

When Marina had come on stage and I saw her real, physical body for the first time, it had felt like everything was falling into place. The shape of it had looked angelic and, when she danced, something tingled inside me. The way she had let her hand wander through her sweaty hair had made my legs shiver.

When people had asked me why I was so obsessed with her, I referred to her talent or described her as a role model and mother figure which was honestly what I believed at that time. When I had seen her in person that day, I had known that it was something entirely different. I wasn't able to name it. I hadn't yet fully grasped the concept of sexuality. But I had known that I didn't want to *be* like her anymore. I wanted to be *with* her. And I liked that feeling.

There, between sweaty bodies and the smell of beer, I had felt at home. We'd danced and hugged and cried and I had never felt more alive.

When our favorite song *fourteen* had come on, Chloe had let herself fall on one knee with a laugh and pulled out a paper ring. It had a little hand-drawn heart on it, just like the band's logo.

"Will you be my best friend forever?" she had mouthed, inaudible. She was never the person to scream over songs but I knew exactly what she was saying.

I had jumped up and down, giggling, something I would've never done in another situation. When I'd held out my hand, she had pushed the little paper ring onto my finger.

It didn't matter what happened in my life.

If my family was falling to pieces.

If I felt alone.

If I was freezing.

I had her.

I *have* her.

A *promise*.

Chapter 6
Better Anyway - Lauren Sanderson

"Kari?" Marina's Docs made the same stomping sound on the steps that mine did.

I was startled, my upper body darting into a sitting position. Her trained legs appeared in my vision before I could stand up. The shock, or call it embarrassment, must've been visible on my face when I looked up at her.

"No need to rush. Believe me, all of us have been lying here at some point." She put her hand on my shoulder and an electric shockwave erupted from the space that she touched. A second later, Marina laid down on the stage, right next to me. She patted the space next to her without saying a word.

I lay back down, the soft surface meeting my back. Marina didn't say another word. The only songs filling the stage were our slow, calm breaths. The floor felt charged with energy, not just the one I had felt before but another kind that flowed between our bodies. It almost felt like the floor was connecting us; energy ran through the ground.

"You know, it still feels breathtaking to walk onto this stage, even for me." There was a shuffling sound from Marina's side as she turned her head in my direction. "The air just feels different up here, like the floor is charged with magic."

A bright, beaming smile greeted me as I turned my head, and tiny little dimples appeared next to Marina's perfect round lips. Her eyes were glowing and I could almost make out little stars in their brown depths. My calm breaths quickly advanced into huffing. Her dark hair traced the ground beneath her as she lifted up her head.

She was the prettiest woman I'd ever seen.

"How do you feel?" Marina's head turned to me in concern. "Not in general but like… How does being on this stage make you feel?"

"Amazing." My words were barely a whisper. A cough was sitting at the top of my throat and speaking an octave too loud would have sent me into another coughing attack.

"Have you ever been on a stage before?" Marina's breath stroked my cheeks as she talked.

I shook my head and another strand of hair fell out of my claw clip. I didn't even consider redoing my hair.

"The first time I got on stage, I cried like a baby!" Marina bent her arm so that she could rest her head on her hand. "And I wasn't even performing. I wasn't even an intern like you." She looked up at the roof of the stage, either dreaming or thinking.

"What were you doing?" my voice came back with curiosity. "I mean, if you feel comfortable sharing."

"Don't ever hesitate asking me things." She lifted her head. "I'm an open book for my crew. And, to be honest, I don't think the way that I started out in the industry is much of a secret." Her hand wandered back under her chin. "I was working actually, scrubbing the stage ground to be precise. Working as a cleaner at an event location was the closest I could get to performing so that's what I did. And still, entering the stage and looking over the barricade from this side got me. The moment I set foot on a stage, it just felt right; I knew that it was where I was meant to be."

Every word that Marina said felt like it was coming from her soul. My heart went through a loop at the thought that she was opening up to me, sharing vulnerable thoughts, even though she barely knew me.

Does she feel comfortable around me?

Does this mean she likes me?

That I made the right decision?

"I knew it back then. The guys and I had already started the band a few years prior but didn't get anywhere. I still refused to give up. *We* refused to give up and now I'm right here, with you. I was scrubbing stages

101

like this back then and now I'm owning them." The corners of her lips lifted slightly more, her dimples deepening. "Do you ever want to perform on stage?"

Her question startled me for a second.

Do I ever want to be on stage?

I had spent countless hours in front of stages but I had never envisioned being up there myself. Lying on the soft vinyl of a stage felt right but that didn't necessarily mean I was supposed to *perform*.

Do I want to be like Marina?

I admired her, yes. But I knew I didn't want to *be* like her. *With* her was more accurate.

"To be honest, I don't know what I want." Better to be honest than making something up, right?

"Well, that's fair. You have more than enough time to figure out what you want in life. And, even if you never find out, life's about constant self-exploration, isn't it? That's also what an internship is for, right?" Now, she stood up. "Let me show you the rest of the stage."

I followed her and we spent the next 15 minutes looking at every corner of the stage. She also showed me the way she entered it which was familiar to me from the front but it felt entirely different from the back.

"When I walk onto the stage like this, you gotta follow me with the camera." Marina walked up the steps for the third time that day. "I'll walk all the way over here until I'm standing on that little X which marks my

102

position." She walked toward the middle of the stage and pointed at a yellow cross made from tape. "You'll follow me, maintaining a meter of distance. As soon as I reach the cross, you can walk backwards and toward the back of the stage." She pointed toward the shadows at the back where the crowd probably couldn't see me anymore. "Got that?"

"Sure." I nodded. The thought of following her all the way to the front sent a shiver down my back. I didn't even know how to walk straight in her presence; how could I make sure not to embarrass myself in front of a concert crowd? The comfortable space in the shadows of the curtains seemed a lot safer.

"Great, do you have any questions?" The tone in Marina's voice seemed more distant now, professional. Almost as if the moment on the ground hadn't happened. A painful sting inside my chest reminded me that she was my boss and that we weren't friends or anything else; we never would be.

I shook my head. I just wanted to be alone.

"Cool. That means we're done here." Her boots stomped over the ground and back toward the stairs. "We're just gonna do a final rehearsal and then hang out. You're free to watch and join or do whatever you want. I get it if you just want to rest right now." She stepped down and disappeared around the corner without another word.

I contemplated lying back down on the ground but couldn't imagine myself there without Marina. There was no way that I could survive watching their rehearsal; my whole body felt exhausted just from being around Marina. There wasn't really anywhere for me to go except the tour bus. When I got there, I freed the little personal space I had from my scattered belongings and hid behind the curtain.

I woke from a weird state between sleep and daydreaming to the creaking sound of Doc Martens' soles on the wooden floor of the bus. I didn't dare move. I wasn't ready for another conversation with her, yet. The sounds traveled to her corner of the bus, followed by the whir of a zipper, then hands shuffling through a bag. I turned my head as slowly and quietly as possible. There was a tiny gap between the curtain and the wooden wall of the bed, allowing me a glimpse of Marina's body.

Maybe it wasn't right to turn my head and watch her. Maybe I should have closed my eyes the moment that her hands wandered up to the buttons of her pants. Maybe I should have turned my head to the wall when she pushed her pants down her ass. But even if I wanted to, I couldn't. My eyes were glued to her body, drawn to her every movement. A burning sensation rushed through me with every bit of skin that Marina revealed. My fingers tingled; it almost felt like I was touching her.

Marina's black jeans went down her legs, revealing her round butt and curvy upper thighs. She was wearing lacy black underwear, her round butt cheeks were revealed. There were stretch marks on the sides of her upper legs, the white lines shaped like ocean waves. I imagined my index finger tracing them and I felt the space between my legs heat up.

Stop.

I felt disgusting. Marina was so much more. And my boss. Still, my eyes were glued.

She rummaged through her things until she retrieved a pair of black boxers and pulled them up her legs. They were short, leaving most of her legs bare. I wanted to let my fingers tickle up her legs, to place my hand between the fabric and her skin.

What if I touched her skin just for a second?

My cheeks heated up.

What if my hand wandered upward and beneath those boxers?

I felt heat rushing through my body.

What if I traced the seam of her underwear?

I had to ball my hand into a fist and press it against my lips to keep a moan from escaping my lips. My breath caught in my throat.

I coughed.

Marina stopped in her motions and looked around. If I hadn't been frozen in place before, I definitely was now. I didn't dare move, didn't dare make a single noise. Marina shook her head for a second and resumed her changing. I pulled the blanket over my head and let out a shaky breath.

What the fuck?

I closed my eyes, and pulled the blanket as close to me as possible.

That was stupid.

The sounds of Marina's dressing continued for a few more minutes and the heat and moisture between my legs for even longer. I didn't dare look again. It took me *hours* to finally cool down and fall asleep.

Chapter 7
Hotel Room – Lauren Sanderson

My arm fell out of the tiny bunk bed as my body turned around, startling me. A beam of light fell through the space between the wooden bed and the dark brown curtain that separated me from the rest of the bus. I pushed it aside and sat up. I grunted as my head hit the wooden bunk above, followed by a stinging pain behind my eyebrows.

A sweet female voice spoke. "Okay, it's time to get up."

Marina. It was Marina's voice that shook me out of my sleepiness. I was on a bus, my favorite band's tour bus. This was my first official day working as a social media intern for them.

A shuffling sounded on my right side, a yawn behind me. People started saying their good morning's, naked feet tapping on the dirty floor of the bus.

I waited until I heard Marina's voice outside my window; I felt uncomfortable. Even though I probably would never have a chance to impress her, she still shouldn't see me like this. My hair was up in a messy bun, the structure falling to pieces from sleep, and I was dressed in sweatpants and an oversized t-shirt without a bra. One thing that I prided myself on was looking put together at all times; I practically lived in my uniform of business-casual chic.

I climbed out of bed as quietly as possible, bumping into the drummer with a muffled "sorry". He looked at me in confusion, his forehead crinkled. The smell of alcohol surrounded him. Up until now, I would've thought bumping into him would be soft, the big teddy bear I'd perceived him as. The way he stared at me was almost harsh. His eyes darted up and down my body before he stepped away with a grunting sound.

The rest of the day happened in a daze. My camera captured whatever seemed interesting, from band members carrying around instruments to the manager giving orders to people from the venue. Everything seemed so familiar but still so new. The stage set-up was seared into my memory from the countless hours I had stared at it but until today, I never knew what actually happened before the show.

Marina barely showed her face until shortly before the show. She was hiding somewhere between the bus and the backstage area. Was it to calm her nerves? Avoid interactions? No matter why she was hiding, I wasn't mad about it; it gave me the chance to take a breath and exist without the exploding doom of my heart.

About 30 minutes before the show, I took a stroll through the pit. Chloe was waving at me hysterically from behind the barricade.

"Kari! How are you feeling?" Chloe embraced me in the tightest hug, the barricade pressed into my lower belly. The heated metal almost burned my skin.

"Excited? Stressed? Scared? Gay panic?" This was the first time I had heard my voice within the last few hours; it was hushed and high-pitched.

"I can imagine." Chloe looked down at the ground. "I hope you know that I am beyond proud of you for living our dreams… Even though I am so jealous that you can sleep so close to the hottest milf on earth!" She poked my side with a laugh.

I nodded enthusiastically. Sometimes I wondered why I got to do this and not Chloe.

Because she's a writer, not a photographer.

She still deserves to be this close to Marina too.

More than I do.

Was it really my talent or just the fact that the job required me and not her?

The barricade put distance between us. "I gotta go. The show is about to start." There was enough time to spare but I wasn't in the headspace to fangirl right now. If I talked about the fact that I had seen Marina getting undressed down to her underwear, my body might have collapsed. Chloe would've freaked out, though. I just didn't know if she'd feel sad for missing it or jump up and down with excitement for me. I felt bad that I couldn't share all this with her.

I took off for the backstage area. Familiar faces squeezed in the front row behind the barricade, looking up at me, and there was a jealousy flickering in a few eyes.

They don't believe I belong here either.

It felt unreal to walk past security, even though my AAA pass was dangling in front of my black dress-pants. Did they use one of those tall, hulky security guards to measure the size of this? It most certainly wasn't meant to be worn by people as small as me; another indicator that I wasn't actually meant to be there.

I felt like an intruder when I entered and held up the rectangular piece of plastic in front of security. Isn't it weird that such a small card can grant access to that ominous, magical place you spent so much time thinking about?

I entered the same white tent I did the day before. It felt weird to interact with the band so I tried to hide somewhere until it was time for work.

It was almost embarrassing to be a fan; I was scared the band or crew would judge me for it. Around the people I was close to in my life, I wore being a fan on my sleeve, sharing the pride that came with it. Here, I thought I had to hide it, make sure that they wouldn't know so that they'd respect me as their equal.

I had spent so much time reading, talking and thinking about the band members. So many details about their lives were engraved into my brain, many more than I was supposed to know, and they didn't know a single thing about *me*.

While the band made me feel like an impostor, the crew made me want to turn around and hide in the safety of the first row. It consisted of men that liked to scan my body for a bit too long. We were certainly not going to get along.

There was a camping table filled with what looked like a fancy breakfast buffet set up. I thought about taking a donut to seem busy but the thought of gooey dough on my tongue made me gag.

Before I could take out my phone to dissolve into the depths of *fanfiction.com*, soft fingers lightly traced down my arm.

"Hey Kari, do you feel ready for your first show?" Marina's soft voice ignited a warm sensation in me, followed by hot sweat running down my back. Her voice created both a feeling of comfort and unease. The fact that she thought about me and felt concerned with my well-being made me feel safe in the midst of all this new chaos.

I turned around, hyper-aware of the little bits of skin she was still touching. Her skin was barely on mine; maybe there were even a few millimeters between us but I felt the presence of her touch as strongly as if her hand was grabbing my whole arm. She seemed concerned as I didn't answer her question immediately.

"Sure am," I blurted out with an enthusiastic nod before Marina could second guess my ability to do a good job.

"Cool. I know that all this can feel overwhelming at times. When you're feeling ready, could you take a few pictures of me and the boys on that couch over there? We gotta get some backstage content in as well." She was already headed to the back before I could answer her question.

I stumbled after her, suddenly aware of the fact that Marina wasn't a mother or a friend but actually my boss. My hand was shaking as I knelt on the ground to snap a few photos. I was here to work, and this job was something I could very well lose. As my eyes focused on the image on the screen, I caught what felt like the first real breath that day. Taking photos was something I was good at, something I could center my energy on.

Making all 4 band members happy with the arrangements of the photo wasn't particularly easy. By the time I got the shot, we had to gather by the stage-entry to get ready for the show. My phone caught each member running onto the stage, until I followed Marina like a shadow as she made her way to the microphone. My knuckles turned white with the intense hold I had on the device in my hands. I tingled inside as the roaring sounds of the crowd rushed at me from the front, not the back. I barely looked at the audience; I didn't feel like I was allowed to. But the sheer volume indicated that a few thousand eyes were shimmering with excitement right now. The intense illumination of the stage lights was burning my skin and the camera felt as if I was holding my sanity in my hands, breathing in and out with every photo I took. As soon as Marina sang the first words of the intro into the microphone, I escaped backwards into the cold breeze of the shadows.

I took a few action shots from the back. I had to bite my knuckles to suppress a scream as Marina dipped down to her knees to the beat.

The crowd cheered at her movements and I felt like I was floating. Thousands were screaming the words I held in my heart. My feet jumped up and down with the masses in front of me, but I quickly forced myself to stand still. I was an intern first and a fan second.

My eyes caught on Chloe's hand waving with too much enthusiasm in the front row. I answered with a slight nod of my head and hoped that she would be happy with that. I was on a pedestal here; I couldn't just wave my whole arm at a crowd of 5,000 people. A shiver of shame went through me, fear of Marina finding out about the little fan girl I really was. Something that used to be my proudest asset suddenly felt embarrassing. I felt guilty.

The concert was over in a heartbeat. When the band exited the stage, I held my phone up, recording them as they passed me. I let the camera zoom in on their faces as the cheering crowd marked the end of a magical concert. Marina was the last one to leave the stage, kept there longer by the magnetic force of fan-love.

I stopped breathing. While the other band members were smiling into the phone camera, it seemed like Marina was only smiling for me. Her eyes found mine the second that she turned and they kept shimmering at me as she made her way towards me. There was a lightness in the way she moved, like she wasn't walking but floating. Sweat shimmered on her forehead. Even in this bodily state, she looked like a goddess.

I could still smell a faint hint of lavender as she approached me; it made my cheeks burn. When Marina grabbed my left hand with hers, a flame was lit inside of me. She held onto it for a few seconds. I knew she always did this with the crew after a show but I couldn't quite believe that her hand was holding onto mine. When she let it go, it felt like hours had passed. As soon as I was dismissed for a break, I found myself in the bathroom, splashing cold water onto my face.

Despite my efforts, the moment I came back to the backstage area, I felt my face heating up to strawberry red. Marina was sitting on the couch in the back, her hair now dripping wet from showering, and her fresh white shirt full of watery spots, revealing the black of her lace bra.

Brad, the guitar player, let himself fall onto the couch right next to her. The rest of the band and crew were scattered around the room, hunched on little chairs and cushions. My knees felt shaky; I needed to leave. But my break was over so I had to at least linger around if they needed me.

I was about to sit down on a chair in the back of the room when Marina called out to me: "Kari, whatcha doing over there by yourself?"

My wobbly legs moved me towards the woman that was pushing me to the brink of unconsciousness.

"Is there anything I can do for you?" I asked.

"Oh, you're done with work now. Come join us for a beer!" She patted the space between her and Brad on the dusty leather couch. She still had the same glow in her eyes from performing.

I squeezed into the space between Brad and Marina. As I sat next to Marina, I was hyper aware of the way our knees were touching. For the moment, I couldn't feel anything else. The only part of my body with nerve endings was the little space where her knee touched mine.

Dari soon let himself fall onto a cushion across from the couch. The 3 band members started out with simple small-talk, analyzing the concert. The conversation became increasingly private. I felt myself loosen a bit but the heat between my legs never left. Especially because Marina started leaning more and more into my body.

"You know, guys, I feel like this band and crew is my family?" Marina mumbled at some point, drawing in a sharp breath. "Sometimes even more so than my actual family at home."

Her family?

Her husband, Greg, and her always seem so happy in photos… And her daughter, Joni? She seems like such a sweet girl. Her family was public and the fandom never really stopped speculating about their dynamics. I shouldn't be listening in but I couldn't exactly leave either.

"Oh babe, you are family to us, too. But you don't mean that, do you?" Brad put an arm around Marina's shoulder from her other side, his fingers grazing my shoulder.

"Would it be so wrong if I did?" Marina shuffled in her space. "You know I love them but it just seems like they have ganged up against me."

Wow.

"I know it hasn't been going great with Greg lately. But Joni? You always had such a great connection." The drummer, Dari, slurred. He was sitting on a cushion across from the couch and had his long brown hair pulled up in a bun.

"Well, Joni has been on Greg's side for a while now. She hates that I'm touring all the time and Greg has planted the seeds for her to think being a singer makes me a bad mother."

Now Dari got up from his seat or, rather, let himself fall onto the ground in front of it. He shuffled over to Marina's feet, grabbing her hands out of her lap. "You are not a bad mother." His voice was bleeding with honesty. I would've thought he was drunk and said this because he didn't know what else to say but something in his undertone made me catch my breath. I wished that I could be the one holding her hands right now.

"Come on, Dari. I know that I am a great mother. It's just that sometimes I think I might be a better mother AND wife if I wasn't a musician. You guys are my second family; I just hate that Greg makes me feel like I have to decide between you both." Marina's eyes were tearing up now. "And with these rumors going around right now... I love the fans so much but Greg is acting even worse because of it. I think it hurts his pride."

What is she talking about?

There were always so many going around. I quickly blocked off the thoughts about her private life. I might have acted like an investigator when I thought I could never meet her, staring at pictures for a bit too long and engaging in theories about her life but now the only things that concerned me were the ones she told without asking. It was wrong to even be around for this conversation but I doubted I could have made a good exit from this couch after the beers I had knocked back far too quickly.

"Okay guys, I think we should call it a night. This was just the first show." Milo, the tour manager, appeared from behind us. He stomped to the couch and gave Marina a pat on the back; it made a clapping sound. "Marina, Dari, Stallon and Brad; you guys are sleeping in separate hotel rooms tonight. The rest of us," Milo made a waving motion around the room where all kinds of crewmen were hunched together in different groups and sitting positions before continuing, "are going to sleep on the bus."

I looked around at the people I was supposed to share the bus with. There were 5 people on the crew except for the band. 4 older men and me. The 2 private security guards, who were 50 plus, already had an uncomfortable redness in their cheeks that came out when men at a certain age drank a few beers too many. Their eyes were lingering on my body as I looked over. The others were Milo, who did not exactly inspire trust either, and the soundman, who didn't really say a word to anyone. It's safe to say I didn't feel comfortable sleeping on the bus with them without the band. There just wasn't much I could do about it.

I caught Marina looking around between the men and me. There was concern in her expression. And, as she realized how they were regarding my body, disgust. Then, her eyes met mine. They were warm, protective, almost motherly. Suddenly, I became aware of the way we were sitting on the sofa, of the few inches that were between us. Our lips were only inches apart and she was staring into my eyes. A vibrating sensation erupted from her hand and went up to my middle. The space between my legs suddenly announced itself; it was now the most alive part of my body.

"Can we book another room for Kari?" Marina asked into the room.

Milo shook his head, "I tried. These were the last rooms I could get."

"You can have my room. I'll be fine on the bus," Marina leaned in closer and I was able to smell the faint scent of beer on her breath.

"I wouldn't want that. I don't want you to give up your comfort for me."

Marina nodded, "In that case I can offer to share my room with you. It's probably big enough for the both of us." Her voice was more of a whisper, her words only meant for me. I couldn't quite tell if she was trying to keep a sexy secret between us or if she just didn't want to upset her crew. Probably the latter.

"Oh, it's fine." I shuffled my legs and put a few more inches between us. My body was so close to acting without my permission. Her eyes were still pinning mine, her eyebrows scrunched in concern. "Don't worry. I don't want to bother you on your night of rest."

"You're part of this band now, which means I consider you family." She pulled a strand of dark hair behind her ear; it was dry by now. "And family shares," she added.

"I just don't want to bother you." *I also don't know if I'd survive sleeping in a bed with you.*

"Don't worry, it's completely fine." Her lips were almost grazing my ear. "As long as you feel comfortable with that."

Her words were fully platonic, she'd called me *family*, and still, a shudder ran through my body. Of course, I'd be comfortable sleeping in a bed with her. There was no reason to freak out about this, she was just being nice.

"Okay." The word was more of a whimper.

Marina got up from the couch, leaving my body to sink to the middle. "I'm gonna head to the bus and grab my things. Milo will let you know where to go. Meet me there, okay?"

I just nodded. If she realized my loss for words, she didn't acknowledge it. As soon as her back disappeared out of the room, I took in a visibly deep breath. I took out my phone to text Chloe.

Kari 11:15pm
I think Marina just invited me to share a hotel room with her tonight.

Chloe 11:15pm
You've got to be kidding me.

Kari 11:16pm
I am dead serious when I say I can't breathe.

Chloe 11:16pm
Holyfuckingfuckshit.

Kari 11:16pm
yup.

A little '1' hovering over my archive folder caught my eye. My finger clicked on it before I could stop myself.

Tate 3:11pm
Of course you're ignoring me.
You don't even have control over your text messages, Jesus.
I really thought we could try again.

I couldn't quite believe my eyes when I read her message. I hadn't even thought about her in the past 24 hours. This was so much bigger than the heartbreak I had gone through before. Of course, her words created a stinging sensation in my stomach but the little sizzle of excitement for Marina was more prominent. I had to focus on my dreams now.

I blocked Tate and deleted her chat before I let my phone fall into the back pocket of my pants and moved off the couch. A second of dizziness made me stumble, the beers floating in my stomach. My phone vibrated with another message but I didn't dare look at it. I had to calm down and fueling my delusions with Chloe's theories wouldn't help. The backstage area was empty now; everyone had left with Marina or even before her. Marina's presence had made it impossible for me to register anything else that happened around me.

My next steps were robotic. I grabbed my coat and tote-bag from the hanger in the back and stepped into the night. The cold air lifted the fog from my brain a little but I didn't let my mind wander. I counted my steps until I arrived at the bus.

Marina was leaning at the door, a black sports bag dangling from her shoulder. I gave her a quick nod and stepped past her into the bus. I filled my tote bag with my pajamas, a button down for the next day and underwear, prohibiting myself from lingering inside too long. This night was happening now and I knew deep down that I would regret backing out until the day I died.

Marina pointed across the street "The hotel is that building over there. Milo showed me over already and handed me the key." She started walking and I followed. "You know, I think it's quite unnecessary that he booked this for us? I mean, we would have all been fine with sleeping on the bus. Sometimes he thinks he helps but it's just more stress to leave early tomorrow."

I didn't say a thing, I was concentrating on finding the right spots to place my feet.

"Well, I am glad that you are coming with me now. I don't like being alone. Especially after what has been going on with Greg. And, when I drink alcohol, I don't like the feeling of dizziness I have when I am lying in bed by myself." She took a deep breath. "I am over sharing, aren't I?"

I lifted my shoulders, even though she couldn't see me in the dark. "I like listening to you."

She didn't react to that. We walked in silence until we entered the building and Marina let herself fall onto the hotel bed. My concerns *(or hopes?)* were confirmed as I looked around the room. There was only one bed, no other place to sleep, and it was barely queen-sized. I sat down on the corner of it, trying to take up as little space as possible.

"I hope you're fine with sharing a bed." Marina rolled herself around on the mattress, "I do have to warn you, I get cuddly sometimes."

I pressed out an awkward laugh and waved my hand as if to say I didn't mind. I mean, I didn't mind. But I did.

"Okay, you seem a bit tired. I'll go into the bathroom and get ready for bed. You, get settled." Marina disappeared into the bathroom, the door making a cracking sound as she closed it.

Kari 11:31pm
I confirm, I am sharing a bed with the hottest woman on earth.

Chloe didn't answer immediately the way she usually did so I found myself sitting in awkward silence, waiting for Marina to exit the bathroom. I shuffled around in my bag and laid out my pyjamas and toiletry bag. My bag was red with big white dots; it was probably more than 10 years old now; I wished I had a cooler one.

My eyes went back to scanning my surroundings, trying to make the time pass without seeming desperate. The walls were painted a dark red and there was a floor-to-ceiling window facing the street. It was a modern hotel, probably expensive, and the bed felt soft under the palms of my hands.

My attention darted back to Marina. "I hope none of us have to use the bathroom in the middle of the night 'cause this thing is looooud."

Marina practically jumped back into the room, her t-shirt bouncing up and down with every step she took. My mouth darted open at the view. With every jumping motion, I could see bits of her panties; she wasn't wearing shorts. The burning sensation within my body came back to life with every inch of skin my eyes were able to trace. I could see her thighs, her birth and beauty marks. The more I got to see of her, the more gorgeous she became.

"I hope you don't mind me sleeping without shorts; I forgot mine on the bus."

My eyes must have lingered on her legs a little too long. She was looking at me looking at her legs.

"No, not at all." I shook my head.

Was that too enthusiastic? Too flirty?

My eyes wandered up to her face, stopping at the outline of her braless boobs for a second.

Kari, get a grip!

I forced myself to look away and grab my things. "I'm gonna head to the bathroom now."

There, I found myself fighting the hot flashes inside my body with splashes of cold water on my face, again. What was she doing to me? When I had signed up for this job, I definitely didn't expect to see my gay awakening half naked, let alone be sleeping in a bed with her.

As I started brushing my teeth, my phone buzzed inside my back pocket.

Chlo 11:45pm
Had a sexy dream, just to wake up to THAT message. How is it going? Any spicy details yet?

Kari 11:45pm
She is NOT wearing pants, Chlo.

Chlo 11:46pm
Wait, I need details. Does no pants mean panties yes, or no?

Kari 11:46pm
Gosh, Chlo! What do you expect? Ofc she's still wearing panties.

126

Chlo 11:46pm

Sorryyyy, I guess I am still a bit in a sexy dreamland…
Well, what kind of panties is she wearing?

Kari 11:47pm

Do you really think I am going to tell you?

Chlo 11:48pm

fair game, that's your accomplishment.
Imma head back to sexy dreamland then.
Please just don't die, okay?
You're the only one able to give me details about
Marina's sexy body!

I shook my head and put my phone on night mode. Chloe was my best friend and I loved her. She just was the queen of inappropriate messages, especially when it came to middle-aged women. I spit out my toothpaste, put on my pyjama shorts and an oversized t-shirt, splashing my face one last time. Light brown eyes were staring back at me as I looked at myself in the mirror. They seemed tired, barely visible without mascara on my lashes. My hair was in a messy bun above my head.

Marina was scrolling on her phone when I entered the room. I lifted the blanket to climb in next to her. The cotton on my legs felt soothing while my insides were burning. I could feel the proximity of her bare skin under the blanket, almost like I was touching it. The mattress moved as Marina shifted her body to put her phone onto the nightstand. Then her body shifted my way, rolling over so she could look at me. My eyes were fixated on the ceiling while I felt hers scanning my face. Every millimeter of my flesh sizzled under her gaze.

Is she trying to get my attention?

Does she want to talk to me?

I didn't dare look over. I didn't even know if I would be able to formulate a single word while she was looking at me like that. The fact that we were sharing a blanket, and knowing that she was almost naked beneath its thin cover, made me want to scream.

"Can I ask you something?" Marina whispered. She seemed nervous, her voice shaky.

"Sure," I almost coughed on the word. My eyes were still focused on the ceiling.

"I know I probably shouldn't be talking to you about this. I barely know you." She huffed out a breath. "It's just that you make me feel comfortable. Something about you feels familiar, like I've known you for a long time, even when we had just met." She shuffled under the blanket, scratching her leg. "Do you think it's wrong that I sometimes wish I didn't have my husband holding me back?"

"Hmm." Why was she asking *me* that? I was just a fan.

I tried to find a superficial thing to say. It felt wrong to intrude on her private life.

"I know you don't want to overstep but I really want to know what you think. Don't hold back," she said.

"Well," I said and forced myself to turn around and look at her. "I don't really know. I don't know a lot about your situation but, if he holds you back, it is not a bad thing to think, I guess."

Marina suddenly didn't look like an adult anymore, a puppy-like naiveness coloring her face. "Remember that break we took? It was the hardest time of my life because I didn't feel alive without being on stage. I hated it. And you know why we did it?" Now, she huffed angrily. "My husband forced me to take a break, to focus on family and let the rumors die down."

I nodded but didn't say a thing. It seemed like there was more to come, like there was more she needed to get off her chest.

"Of course, I love him. I love what we have and I love the amazing daughter he gifted me. I would do anything for her. And he keeps saying I have to stay home to be a good mother and that the rumors are hurting her." She propped her upper body up on her elbow. "But I don't think so. She loves my music and she loves to see me happy. Sometimes I wonder if it's just his ego being

129

hurt by people speculating about my queerness. He thinks it makes him less of a man or something. And that makes me love him less."

I nodded again.

"Gosh, I'm sorry. You don't have to answer." She let her head fall back. "I can't believe I just said all that! I shouldn't just trauma-dump on you. I don't even know if I mean that. Oh God."

I looked at her. "It's okay. I get it. I can imagine how this tears you apart. I hate how he's putting you in a position like this. He shouldn't make you choose between your family and the thing you love. That's wrong. You even got together when *Paper Rings and Promises* was already a thing, right?" It felt impossible to find the right words in this situation. But still, I wanted to help. Her puppy eyes made my heart ache. For a second, I felt like a friend, not a fan.

Marina bent her chin down. "Oh, so you have been doing your research on my private life?"

Fear shot through me. Had I overstepped? What was she thinking about me now? Did it bother her?

"I, uhm…"

Marina just laughed. "Don't worry. I know the fans do that and it's not secret information. Of course, I didn't meet my husband at 14." She winked at me and all thoughts of friendship disappeared. "I actually kinda like it when fans speculate about me, when they're interested in me as a person. It makes me feel appreciated. He's the one that wants me to keep everything private." She pulled a strand of hair behind her ear.

"To be honest, I always felt like an intruder when I looked up things about you. You're a real person, after all. I always tried to stay away from speculation." I mumbled, still trying to explain myself.

Marina was staring at the ceiling again. "Actually, if I'm completely real with you, sometimes I wish the rumors were true. It would be so much easier to have a secret romance with a co-host than trying to juggle my family and the band at the same time." Marina let out an audible breath. "I love my queer fans and the community. And, it would make the fans happy; that's all that I want."

I stared at her, speechless. She knew about the rumors? She even gave thought to them. I had always thought that she'd just ignore them, put them away as some delusional fantasies from the queers. She also thinks about ending the relationship with her husband... about what it'd be like to be with a woman.... about letting the rumors come true. The information felt overwhelming. My inner queer child was screaming, longing to hold onto every word she'd just said. I grabbed the blanket, turning my knuckles white, to keep myself from squealing.

She's still with her husband.

She is with her husband.

She loves a man.

I forced myself into reality but all I wanted was to drown in delusions.

"Kari?" Marina asked beside me, reminding me that those exact delusions were lying right beside me.

"Yeah, sorry; I've been thinking for a second." I forced myself to look at her. "You know you don't need to stay with him for your daughter, right?"

She nodded. "I know." Then, she rubbed her eyes with her knuckles. "I'm sorry. This was too much; I shouldn't have said anything." She turned around to turn off the light. "We should sleep. I'm way too tipsy and we have to get up way too early tomorrow."

The room went dark. My mind was roaming, overwhelming me to the level of feeling sick. I wanted to text Chloe but I knew I couldn't. This was too private to talk to anyone about.

Whenever I tried to close my eyes, Marina's presence in the bed felt more real. I could feel Marin beneath the blanket; it was turning my body into flames. The butterflies inside me were nagging at my insides. I let my hands wander to my hips, the fabric of the sheets soft and cold under my palms. I forced my eyes to close.

When my body was finally about to cool down, a warm hand grabbed my hand and electricity shot through my whole body. My eyes shot wide open within seconds. Everything tingled.

Marina was holding my hand.

In a bed.

In a bed that we were *sharing*.

How was this real life?

I focused on her breathing, trying to tell if she was still sleeping. It was steady, the blanket lifting in regular motions... she had taken my hand in her sleep.

I told myself that she was mistaking me for her husband and lay awake for what felt like the rest of the night.

Chapter 8
Pretty Girls - Reneè Rapp

I woke to the tickling of hair on my nose. I grunted. When I tried to swipe it away, thinking it was my own, my hand touched the soft skin of someone's forehead. I opened my eyes. Dark brown strands were lingering on my neck.

Huh?

I rubbed my eyes in confusion.

The wetness of lips nuzzled their way deeper into my skin. A yawning sound emanated and reality rushed back to me in a wave.

Marina.

I thought that I was drowning. Her presence forced me to hold my breath.

How the fuck did we end up in this position?

Her breathing was steady; she was still asleep. Something about the way that her breath tickled my shoulder brought calm over me again. I focused on it, the fact that she felt comfortable sleeping this close to me, that she had sought my proximity. I leaned into her presence, moving so my head could rest on hers. It made me feel calm. Safe.

My breathing slowly started to match hers and my eyes fell closed again.

The next time that I woke, my head was resting on the pillow by itself. A cold wind brushed my ear and sent a shiver up my neck. Marina was gone, the window opened wide. I sat up in bed to look around the room. She was nowhere to be seen, even her clothes were gone.

Where did she go?

Why did she leave?

Did she wake up the same way I did just a few hours ago?

Did she feel embarrassed for the way she slept so close to me?

I grabbed my phone to check the time. 10:15 am.

Fuck.

The bus was leaving for the next tour stop in 15 minutes.

Fucking fuck shit.

I jumped out of bed and changed my clothes. There was no time to think about my outfit for the day so I ended up in the same black dress pants from the day before, matched with a light pink button down.

Why didn't Marina wake me?

136

I wanted to be mad at her for leaving me in this situation but I couldn't quite generate anger toward that gorgeous woman.

I ran into the bathroom. The image in the mirror almost scared me. My hair was a rat's nest and dark circles adorned my eyes.

I checked the time on my phone again. 10:18.

I needed 3 minutes to walk over to the bus so there were only 9 minutes left to get my appearance in order. I grabbed a pink claw clip from my bag and juggled my hair up into it. A few strands escaped, dangling around the sides of my face and making my hands clench in frustration.

I applied some concealer around my eyes as fast as possible. There was no time for foundation or moisturizer. When I applied powder, crumbs refused to dissolve, speckling my face with white dots. I stared at myself in the mirror for a second. I needed another hour to fix the mess that looked back at me. More and more hair slipped out of my claw clip and the concealer was barely hiding my eye bags. I breathed in, turned around and forced myself to leave the bathroom.

I ran out of the hotel and arrived at the bus with 5 minutes to spare. When I opened Snapchat to send Chloe a quick vlog of my misery, I realized that I hadn't applied mascara and wanted to punch myself for it. I looked 12 years old. I recorded a short video anyway, careful not to mention the information Marina had given me the night before or the hand-holding or the cuddling in the morning. That was between Marina and me. And telling my best friend would somehow make it real which I wasn't quite able to let it be. Not yet. I knew that she'd be happy for me, incredibly jealous but also incredibly happy. But she'd also freak out and pump me up about it… she'd scream and spam me with messages… and I really was not in the mood for all that.

Shortly before I reached the bus, Marina appeared behind me. "Hey, sleepy-head!"

I stopped in my tracks and turned around. Marina was running toward me, a glowing smile on her face. Her hair was bound in a ponytail and sweat glistened on her cheeks. She was dressed in short leggings. With every step, the muscles above her knees became visible.

Seriously?

This is why she left?

Her upper body was dressed in a white tank top, cut out on the sides to reveal a black sports bra. She was simply beautiful.

She stopped in front of me. "I'm sorry I disappeared this morning but I kinda overslept and wanted to get my run in. And, you were sleeping so peacefully. I didn't wanna wake you."

A pearl of sweat dripped down to her lips and she licked it off. I was reminded of the way that those lips had touched my skin this morning. Everything felt tingly inside of me.

Kari! What the fuck are you thinking?!

Marina put a hand on my shoulder. "I was worried you didn't set an alarm but it seems like you made it on time. You look good today, though." She gave me a nod and then walked past.

Her words sat with me for a second.

I look good?

I looked the worst that I had looked in months. But I felt 10 times better about myself after she'd said I looked good. Did she like me messy? Did she like the 'natural' look?

I lifted my tote bag back over my shoulder and stepped onto the bus. The rest of the band was already sitting in their beds, ready for take-off. I crawled into my bunk and spent the 4-hour ride hidden under my blanket.

We arrived in Leipzig before I could really catch a breath. I had never been to this city before.

I left the bus and was faced with a giant brick building. It looked like an old factory, something most concert locations in Germany had in common. There was graffiti on the wall that read "FCK AFD." I quickly glanced around; every building around looked just the same.

Then, we had to carry the band equipment into the big building. The rumbling sounds of the cases on the cobblestones reminded me of Ulm. That was the thing with the old towns in Germany that survived the war: they looked and sounded mostly the same.

There was no time for me to explore because we left Stuttgart in the morning instead of the night before, and therefore arrived pretty late. I helped where I could, switching between photographer and roadie. I found myself carrying heavy boxes and suitcases, as well as taking videos during the soundcheck. It was only the second day, and I was already becoming a part of the crew. No one looked twice before handing me a box or giving me something to do, and I'd never felt so grateful to be working. I had been looking up to this small group of people my whole life, and now I was becoming part of it. *What does a fan want more than carrying boxes for their favorite band?*

It was hours before I finally found a moment to myself. As soon as everyone began their last preparatory steps before the show, I excused myself, grabbed my makeup bag and went in search of the bathroom.

The backstage area was a labyrinth of halls and unlabelled dressing rooms, most of which were locked. I accidentally opened the door to a kitchen and turned right back around. I was about to give up and get ready in the bus when I heard the sound of Docs on parquet behind me.

Marina.

I had been able to avoid her for most of the day, focusing on the tasks at hand instead of hyper fixating on her every movement. On the first day, I was aware of her location at all times; I felt her presence in every room. Today, I focused on not noting her location every few seconds. The dark hallways in the depths of this building were the last place I thought that I'd meet her.

"Hey, Kari! It's easy to get lost here, isn't it?" Marina quickened her step and approached me. She was still dressed in her workout clothes, looking effortlessly gorgeous. A big bag was hanging from her shoulder, a men's shampoo bottle sticking out. A wave of lavender made me feel dizzy with excitement when she stopped beside me. "Were you looking for the bathroom as well?" Marina pointed at the makeup bag clenched between my hands.

If I hadn't been pressing it against my breast, it would've fallen out of my shaky hands. I nodded. The thought of Marina showering simmered through my brain and my heart stopped beating for a second.

"Cool, I was just about to shower. I can show you the way." She put her left hand behind my back to guide me in the right direction. "I'm sorry again for disappearing this morning, I just didn't want to wake you at 6 in the morning."

"Oh, it's totally fine." I laughed, far too aware of Marina's touch.

Why is she touching me again?

Does she have any clue how we slept last night?

I wanted to believe that Marina was looking for my company. That she wanted to be around me.

"Okay, cool." She stopped in front of a door on the right. "Luckily, we've played this venue before so I know that this is the backstage bathroom."

When I saw the bathroom, my insides did a somersault. This was a shower room. There were 3 sinks on the wall to the left with big mirrors and good lighting. The wall to the right was lined with 3 shower heads with no stalls or doors.

Is Marina about to shower in front of me?

Marina locked the bathroom door behind her and walked over to a little bench in the corner. "I know this isn't ideal but it's still a lot better than getting ready on the bus." She untied her Docs. "And a lot more private." She took off her socks. "Here, it's just us." She unbuttoned her jeans. "And we've slept together so showering in the same room shouldn't be a big deal." She pulled down her jeans. The waves of stretch marks on her upper legs appeared, drowning me. "As long as you don't mind." She stopped what she was doing.

I was still standing right in front of the door, hoping that I could float through it like a ghost while also in no way wanting to miss this. I swallowed, then forced out a shaky "don't mind", strolling over to the sink.

Was it normal for your boss to just undress in front of you?

Let alone a celebrity?

My hands were clutching my bag so hard that my fingers cramped when I put it down. I had to bite my lip to not make a sound.

I managed not to turn around and look at Marina until she turned the shower on. When I lifted my head to redo my mascara, Marina's body appeared behind my head in the mirror. Her back was turned to me, her face tilted up to welcome the shower rain. Water dripped from her hair, making its way down her tanned skin.

Don't look down.

I couldn't keep myself from following her body with my eyes. I admired her. Marina lifted her hands to apply shampoo to her hair and the muscles in her shoulders flexed. There was a little tattoo on her left one: a group of black swallows flying away to the side. I wanted to kiss each of them and suck on the last one, right at the tip of her shoulder, leaving a little mark like it was flying in front of a red moon. I fixated on a drop of water which slowly made its way down her spine. Her body was curved perfectly, her back widening into round hips. The liquid went onto one of her butt cheeks and I felt the urge to lick it off. Then, it dripped to the floor.

I was about to scan her legs with my gaze when her feet moved so that she could turn around. My eyes flicked

143

back to my own face and the mascara brush had never made it up to my eyes this fast. I almost stabbed my eyeball when Marina's eyes caught mine in the mirror. She walked over to the bench to grab a bottle of shower gel. I forced myself to focus on my makeup until the water was turned off.

I did my best to turn the brown mess of my hair into one french braid, when Marina appeared at the sink next to me. She applied black eyeliner. There was something fascinating about her concentrated face while she created the perfect wing next to her deep brown eyes. I wished that those eyes would sparkle for me the way that they sparkled when she stepped on stage.

My hands subconsciously applied gel to the top of my hair, smoothing down the last few strands sticking up from my head. Marina finished her look with mascara and didn't bother to apply foundation or concealer; she didn't even need to style her hair in any way.

Still, she looked perfect when she turned around to face me.

"You ready? I wanna grab something from the buffet before I have to get on stage." Without concealer, I could make out a few freckles on her nose and cheeks. They looked like little stars decorating her face.

I turned around and checked my hair one last time. It was far from how I wanted it but it would have to do. I flattened it with my hands once more, then turned around to face Marina.

"Sure, let me just grab my stuff and we can head back upstairs."

Marina swung her bag over her shoulder and unlocked the door while I frantically collected the makeup tubes that I had spilled across the sink.

We walked out of the bathroom and back up the stairs without saying another word. I was happy about that; I wasn't sure if I would be able to formulate a single sentence after seeing her naked. The image of the little drops of water making their way down her butt cheek would be engraved in my brain forever.

I caught myself wishing that I could scream about it with Chloe but I remembered that she couldn't make it to the concert that night. She had a university exam the next day and Leipzig was basically on the other side of the world from Cologne. It was practically impossible to reach with public transport. I wished that she was here though; I needed to debrief with my best friend, for her to tell me that I wasn't being delusional about the way Marina flirted with me. The tension and excitement was nagging at me from inside, finding no outlet besides tearing at my organs.

I forced down a veggie sandwich and prepped my equipment before the show started. I was supposed to spend this concert in the pit, getting shots from down there and filming a few fans and self-made signs. Another reason I wished Chloe, or any of my friends, were there; I could have spent the concert with them, like in the old days.

Before the concert started, I interviewed a few fans. Conscious not to choose anyone that I knew, I ended up with screaming 16 year olds that had just recently joined the fandom. It wasn't the most pleasant experience but I did my best anyway; they made for some good content. Some even sang a few lines of *fourteen* for me because they had just turned 14 and their parents were hiding somewhere in the back.

The new fans made me feel nostalgic; my start to the fandom hadn't been any different. But, at the same time, I resented them for showing up and changing everything. I felt guilty for thinking it but it felt like they were taking something away from me, even though *Paper Rings and Promises* was far too popular to gate-keep.

When Marina appeared on stage, singing the first words of *rhythm of you and me,* I was reminded of the time she held out the microphone to me and I lost my voice. I was still embarrassed about the way Chloe had to finish the lyrics two years ago.

This time, I sang along, just like I had back then. Staring up at her from the pit didn't feel that different to staring up at her from the barricade. It was just that, this time, Marina was staring right back at me.

Does she remember the day that she held out the microphone to me?

I was convinced that she wouldn't, that I was just one of many. Maybe I wanted to believe that she didn't know me before my first interview. That she didn't know that I was just one of many fans, that I seemed different, like I did it for the job and not to be close to the band. Yet, here she was, staring right at me, singing a song about sex.

Does she want me to film?

I lifted up my camera to capture her singing but a little wave of her hand indicated for me to put it back down. She was still looking at me when she sang the pre-chorus, approaching me from her space in the middle of the stage. The crowd was cheering her on.

"In the silence, our desires speak."

She bent down at the edge of the stage, a warm, reassuring smile on her face.

"A symphony of passion, reaching its peak."

She motioned for me to come closer, then held out her right hand.

Does she want me to take it?

I took a deep breath.

You can't embarrass yourself another time, Kari.

I took her hand. It fit right into mine. Then, she held out the microphone to me and I sang the chorus with her. I didn't let myself think. I didn't let myself hesitate.

And it felt amazing.

The world went silent and, suddenly, it was just Marina and I. I was so close to her that I could see the stage glow in her eyes; they were almost golden. Marina didn't let go of my hand until the chorus finished and deep waves of electricity shot through my arm with every heartbeat. For a second, it felt like she didn't want to let go. But she returned to the stage and my hand felt cold where she had left it.

"Applause for Kari, our amazing social media intern!" Marina screamed into the microphone before she resumed the lyrics. She didn't take her eyes off me for the rest of the song.

What the hell was that?

I forced my eyes back to the phone in my hand.

Why did she grab my hand?

Did she want to tell me something?

Did she think about me during the song?

I mindlessly tapped on the camera feature to record a short clip for the Instagram story.

She remembered that moment two years ago and wanted to give me another chance; that's all that this was, I told myself; my delusions said something else.

When I lifted my camera up to take some shots of the crowd, my mind was free from Marina for the first time that day. I focused on zoom and lighting and happy tears. No matter how much Marina confused me, I could always get lost in photography. I loved capturing the crowd, catching their emotions on film, seeing myself in them. I took a picture of 2 young girls hugging and crying during *fourteen*. I was reminded of Chloe and me... this was what I was there for. To pursue my passion, to pursue what I had been dreaming of for the past 8 years. Yes, I had a crush on Marina but I also had dreams to chase.

When Marina high-fived me that night, it didn't startle me like it had the day before. I only felt excited about showing her my work, talking about the things that I had seen, the diverse faces and emotions that I had captured.

"Wow; these are amazing, Kari!" Marina put her arm around my shoulder. "I hate that I can't see people this close when I'm on stage. It's almost impossible to make out what they're feeling. This is insane; I feel so much closer to the crowd. I didn't even know people go through this many different emotions during our shows." She looked at me. "This is a gift, Kari."

That night, I went to bed feeling accomplished. Marina wasn't on my mind, even though she was sleeping just a few meters away.

Chapter 9
First, Best, Hottest... – Beth McCarthy

The third day turned out to be an off-day. It was weird to have free time after just two shows but for some reason the planning hadn't worked out in a better way. We had already made our way to the next tour stop during the night which left me with a whole day to waste in Erfurt. I had never seen the city, except from the window of trains I had taken home from Berlin. It reminded me of Leipzig.

Everyone slowly made their way off the bus. I stayed in bed as long as possible, hoping to join someone else's plans once they were already set. Of course, I could have ventured out alone and explored but I didn't quite feel like being alone with my thoughts that day. Truthfully, deep down, I was hoping that I'd get the chance to explore the place with Marina. Even though I should have stayed away from her, kept my professional distance, I was drawn to her presence like a magnet. I wanted to spend every second of every day in her presence.

Marina, Dari, Brad and Milo were gathered outside the bus when I made my way out. A cigarette dangled from Dari's lips while Brad leaned against the bus, looking like he was about to fall back asleep right there. Marina was standing at the wall opposite the bus, looking like a mom waiting for her children as she watched her band mates. She was wearing black round sunglasses, her staple black pants and a cropped leather jacket. It was red today, breaking from her usual black dress code. Sparks kindled inside me, burning like the color of her jacket.

Where she had looked bored and annoyed beforehand, her face now brightened when she spotted me on the steps of the bus.

"Hey, Kari! Wanna explore the city with us?"

"Sure!" I tried my best to sound normal but my words came out raspy.

I already had my hair tied back in a sleek ponytail and my tote bag was dangling off my shoulder with everything that I needed. The most important part of my time here was still to make a good impression, even when I wasn't working. This group of people had shaped me, and they had become my entryway into a new future.

Now that I had joined the group, it seemed like Marina was ready to leave. Dari put out his cigarette, and we soon found ourselves walking through yet another city with cobblestones. Milo was talking on his phone most of the time and eventually left us because he had to take some sort of meeting.

Marina let herself fall back to stick with me.

"I love these guys," she laughed and put her arm around my shoulders, squeezing me closer to her body. "But something about you makes me feel good in a way they can't." Her words were genuine, no trace of flirtiness left. "What is it about you, Kari?"

"Maybe I knew you in another life." I was growing more confident around her.

"No," she stopped to look at me and put her hands on my shoulders, keeping me at arm's length. "It's almost like you know me in this life. You know me in a way the others don't, almost in a way I don't know myself."

"What do you mean?" My heart felt warm because I could finally ask her real questions.

"When you look at me, I feel like you're looking right into me," she was still smiling in an innocent way, like her facade was falling. "When I asked you about my husband, you were more understanding than anyone has ever been before. The guys know him; they know my daughter, and they wouldn't recommend for me to leave him." Her hands wandered down my shoulders and to my arms. "You have a really calming energy, Kari. I feel comfortable around you. You also make me curious. I'd love to know more about you, the way you see the world, what you think about me." She let go and we continued walking.

"I like talking to you, too." Now, I was the one to interlock our arms. "And I guess you feel like I know you because I've been a fan for such a long time." *Did I really just admit that?*

Marina pulled me around a corner. We were now approaching a cathedral. Its tall dark medieval walls were beautiful, and its top looked like it touched the clouds from below. The guys found a bench on the other side of the plaza, and Dari lit a joint. His dark eyes scanned me for a moment when I looked over. His presence made me feel uncomfortable, and I couldn't really grasp why.

"This is pretty," Marina stopped and looked up at the big building. "I didn't know Thuriniga had such beautiful churches."

"It definitely is," I said and walked over to the entrance. The wooden doors were huge with artistic patterns carved into them. "Do you like architecture?"

Marina looked at the sky. "Nope, not really. I've seen a lot on tour but I don't really care about the design or history or anything like that," she looked at me, her brown eyes sparkling in the sun.

"Me neither, I guess," I kicked a stone on the ground. For some reason, I needed to share more with her. "My dad is an architect. He used to tell me about his work, show me buildings. It bored me most of the time. Now, I almost hate it."

Marina let herself fall on another bench, motioning for me to sit down next to her.

"Why do you hate it?"

I stared at a tree across from us. I didn't feel the need to hide my weaknesses from her; I wanted to tell her everything about me. "I don't talk to my dad anymore or, rather, he doesn't talk to *me*. My parents got divorced. I was 14 at the time, and I had to be the one to save my own mother. I hate my dad for abandoning me like that. And I hate him for never apologizing for leaving."

Marina looked at me with compassion in her eyes. "My parents got divorced when I was 14, as well. I didn't really get along with either of them. So, I found the band and made it my family. I really know what it feels like when your own home doesn't feel safe anymore, when it turns into chaos."

"You lose control, right?" I asked, my eyes meeting hers.

"Exactly." She looked over to the guys who were handing the joint around. "These guys saved me. They took me in. That's why we wrote the song *fourteen*. Being on stage and starting this career gave me back a sense of control. I like to give my fans the love I couldn't get from my parents. I know lots of people look for found family in fandoms."

"The band definitely gave me some love I was missing at home. And I did find a family in fans. My best friend Chloe has been with me through my highs and lows. I discovered your music right when my home fell apart, and it has been with me ever since."

"That's why we're doing this, you know? It's sad that I often don't get to hear fan's stories because there are just so many. There is nothing more fulfilling to me than helping other people that have gone through similar experiences."

I nodded.

Marina clapped her thigh. "Now, to more cheerful things. What should I know about you, Kari? What are your dreams and ambitions? What makes you happy? What makes you glow?"

Marina wasn't just my crush or my idol anymore; she was becoming my friend.

"Well, until a few weeks ago, I thought I wanted to be a politician. At least, that's what people told me. Now, I'm pretty sure I belong on stage. Taking photos of you excites me. I love spotting the best angle and thinking about the way fans would react to the pic. I love experimenting with lights, looking for art in the real world. I think I want to be a photographer."

Marina's eyes beamed. "Kari! That's amazing. I have to admit, I haven't seen much of your work yet, but the way you talk about it, the way your voice rises and your eyes beam, tells me that it's the right thing for you."

"Really? This is actually my first time doing it professionally," I mumbled, a nervous hitch in my voice.

"Well, the photos I've seen so far were more than amazing." She stood. "If you believe in it, it's the right thing. I had no clue what being a singer meant when I started but see where my mindset got me?" She laughed and walked over to her band mates.

I jumped up and followed.

Did I really just talk to Marina about my private life?

And did she really listen?

She even told me details about herself that were nowhere to be found in the media. I couldn't believe that she'd trust me this much.

Marina put her hands on Dari's and Brad's shoulders. "So, guys, is there anything else to see in this city? You've been here before, right Brad?"

Brad laughed, smoke coming out his mouth. "Yup but nothing to see really."

"I'm not sad about that. I could do with a beer to be honest," Dari chimed in. He sounded drunk and high. The slur in his voice sent a shiver down my back..

"Well, that's great because I could do with a coffee," Marina said and started walking away from the cathedral.

157

A few moments later, I found myself sitting across from her in a little alternative cafe.

Marina and I were sipping on some chai lattes while Dari and Brad were hunched in another corner of the restaurants with beers in hand. The boys separated themselves whenever they got the chance. Before I got to know them, I'd always thought that they were inseparable from Marina.

Marina took a sip from her cup. "I'm sorry they don't quite engage with you. They can be pretty reserved sometimes," she nodded toward her band mates who looked like they were contemplating philosophical issues, both staring into the abyss.

"Oh, it's totally fine." By talking to Marina about my life, I had become more comfortable in her presence. I was more myself around her, losing some of my fears. Her presence had become regular, almost normal; as long as she didn't touch me. "To be honest, I didn't really expect anyone to engage with me; I'm just an intern." I looked down at my cup. The foam was shaped into a little heart.

"Oh, sweetheart," Marina bent forward and put her hand on mine. "You're a lot more than an intern. When someone joins the team, they become part of our little family." She smiled, revealing a dimple on her left cheek. "And, to be honest, I'm so happy to finally have another woman on board. It can get lonely sometimes, being surrounded by this many guys."

The touch of her hand threw all my progress away. A tingling sensation went up my arm and down my spine. Suddenly, I had lost my voice again and a huffed "thank you" was all I could manage.

"Sometimes you seem so scared, like a puppy," Marina laughed but didn't move her hand from mine. "Do I intimidate you?"

My mouth went agape at her words.

Holy shit.

Something about the way that she studied my face from the other side of the table and held my hand felt like she was flirting. This was what fan fictions were written about.

Is she flirting?

"It's okay; you can admit it." She shook my hand a little, the sweet ring of her laughter surrounding me. It had been my favorite sound since I was 14.

"I, uhm." *Of course, you intimidate me.* "Maybe, sometimes. I just want to make a good impression, you know."

Marina took her hand away; I wanted to grab it and maintain the physical contact.

"Oh, babe. You don't have to be worried. You made a great first impression." She lifted her cup with both hands and took another sip. "An *amazing* one, even."

I chuckled. "Oh, you call coughing my heart out on the first encounter a great impression?" I drank a sip of coffee; my hands were shaky. "That was definitely not the introduction I was aiming for. I had been going over the moment I would meet you for *years*. And then, there you were, standing right in front of me... and every word I had so carefully prepared got stuck in my throat." I probably shouldn't have said those things but something about this setting made me feel comfortable sharing.

"Oh, so you had been fantasizing about meeting me for a while?" Her brown eyes fixated on mine. "That's kinda cute."

And there she was again, making my heart beat like I was right on top of a rollercoaster, just with her words.

"Yeah, I mean, I've been a fan for 8 years now; of course I've thought about what it'd be like to meet you." I lifted my shoulders, like my devotion to the band was nothing.

"I can't believe you've been around for this long," she said. "I mean, I've seen your face in the first row a few times. Who could forget that one time you forgot the words to *rhythm of you and me*?" She winked at me, sending heat into my cheeks. "But, I can never quite grasp *how long* fans have been around."

She recognized me?

I screamed internally but stayed calm on the outside.

"Oh yeah, it's been a long time." I folded my hands around my coffee cup. "I did disappear for a while and I'm definitely not as engaged in the fandom as I used to be."

Marina was still staring at me, her lips slightly parted. "How did you find us? And, why did you disappear?" Marina averted her gaze. "You don't have to answer; I'm sorry if these questions overstep. I kinda feel like a mom asking about what my teenagers were doing with their friends. I just don't really know what the fandom is like. All we see are the things online and the faces in the front row and I just really want to know what your experience was like."

A glimmer of genuine interest and curiosity made her eyes shine as intensely as they did on stage. That intensity was directed at me. Not just at my face or presence but at *me*. My personhood, my experiences, my interests and my history were compelling enough to make her eyes bear into mine. It felt good.

"Uhm, I discovered you on the radio when I was 14. I already told you about my parents splitting up; that happened at the same time. Your fans online listened when no one else did and your music made me feel calm and safe." *Actually, your voice did.* "I met my best friend Chloe, who sang into the mic when I couldn't, through a WhatsApp group that year. We met for the first time a year later at our first concert. Seeing you live felt like coming home."

I stopped for a second, waiting for Marina to react. While I was telling my story, my vision had been focused on the cup of coffee in my hands, avoiding eye contact with Marina. When I looked up at her, her eyes were still fixated on my face. She was waiting for me to continue.

I took a sip and a deep breath. "Chloe and I are still friends, but I distanced myself from the fandom for a while. Don't get me wrong; you, the boys and the music are still amazing but some people in the fandom acted a bit toxic. Because we were the youngest and couldn't go to as many concerts, we weren't fully involved and I think older fans looked down at us for it. Now that I've seen the new fans, I get that we could've been a bit annoying back then but they still could've included us more. Over time school, and then work, became more and more demanding. I just didn't have the time for fan girling anymore. I didn't realize how much I'd missed it before we went to the concert in Dresden 2 years ago. I never really got back into it, not fully, but *Paper Rings and Promises* will always have a special place in my heart. You shaped me and maybe even saved me. I wouldn't be the person I am today without you. Somehow, I'm here now, sitting at a coffee table with you and telling you this story which is the most insane thing I could have ever imagined."

"Thank you for telling me. This means a lot, Kari. I'm sorry you didn't feel welcome. I wish I could know every fan and give them the love they deserve or at least I wish I'd known you earlier. But really, thank you for telling me." She brushed through her hair with her fingers and it fell back naturally. "I gotta admit that this brought up a million more questions but I'll stop bombarding. At least for now." The dimple in her cheek grew even deeper, if that was possible. "But, anyways, what would you think about going to a lake next? We could have a swim. Being in the water really calms me, especially during a tour. I think we can probably leave the boys here; they're happy as long as there's beer."

"Uhm, I don't have a swimsuit with me. Like not here and not on the bus either," I mumbled and scratched my scalp.

Marina laughed. "I don't either. I can lend you a t-shirt. If you feel okay with skinny dipping, that's another option."

An image of Marina undressing and jumping into the lake flew through my mind. I bit my lip.

"I've never been skinny dipping but there's a first for everything, right?" I said, acting like my body wasn't aflame at the thought.

This wasn't something you'd expect from your boss but the way that Marina talked to me, I was more of a friend than an employee.

"Perfect, I've seen images of this lake on Google Maps and I'm excited to check it out. Reviews said it was pretty private during the week and it's one of the best spots to watch the sunset." She was glowing. I wanted to kiss that dimple now.

"I'm gonna tell the boys and pay. Take as much time as you need to finish your drink." She got up and I couldn't resist watching her body.

I gulped down the rest of my chai while Marina walked over to the counter. The fact that she was paying for my drink made her even more attractive. Of course, she was the older person with more money to spare and I was only working for her but, still, she didn't *have* to pay. Did that make this a date? I so wished that it did.

We approached a body of water that was surrounded by tall blooming trees. I was speechless with anticipation at being moments away from seeing Marina naked again, not to mention showing her my own bare skin for the first time.

"Okay, this is it: one of the best swimming spots in all of Erfurt," Marina said, stepping forward. Opening her arms like she was a tour guide, she showed me the most beautiful lake I'd ever seen.

"Really, really pretty," I muttered before walking past Marina and taking a look around.

She had been right; it was really private here. There were no sounds except for a few birds chirping. The lake was spanning my whole field of vision and reaching far into the distance. We were looking at the lake from some form of hideout, the shore lined with trees that hid us from anyone on the other side of the lake. The tree branches also provided nice shade on this warm, late summer day. The other side of the lake was the complete opposite and far from private. There were fields as far as the eye could see and no trees at all. The probability that anyone could be watching us from that area was as good as zero.

"I know. This lake has been around for hundreds of years. Before Erfurt was a big city, the townspeople were already washing their clothes here," Marina spoke in a high-pitched voice that sounded way too happy. She was impersonating the role of a tour guide.

I acted astonished. "Oh, really? That is *so* interesting," I looked around as if I was picking up details in a museum. "Do you know who discovered this lake?"

"Sadly, my knowledge doesn't span that far but I will check in my books and find out." Marina shook her head, as if not knowing this ridiculous fact embarrassed her.

I had to bite back a laugh. "Well, can you show me how good this lake is for swimming?" I asked and winked at her. I couldn't believe I managed to build up enough confidence to wink but her joking tone made me feel bold.

"Sure thing," she laughed and started taking off her clothes right then and there.

I couldn't help but look at her. Her leather jacket fell to the ground first. It was this specific item all of us fans always wanted to own; some using it as a status symbol, letting us know they're better than the rest. The fact that Marina let it get dirty, regardless of its high price tag, made her more attractive. For a moment, she seemed like she didn't care, like she didn't mind what people said. She was effortlessly hot, even without the jacket. She had a wild side, an inner rock star buried somewhere beneath the image of a proper wife and mother.

She took off her black shirt next. Her hair got tangled up in it before falling in waves once she freed her arms. Something about the way her hair fell down her cheeks made me want to comb through it with my hand. Her upper body was now dressed in nothing but a black lace bra. There was a pattern of lace on the cups and I wanted nothing more than to trace those little flowers and pinch them.

What the fuck?

How was I staring at a woman that was 12 years older than me and thinking about pinching her nipples? Let alone thinking about touching my boss' boobs.

Who am I?

Marina stopped and looked at me. "You okay? I won't look if you feel uncomfortable." She nodded toward my still fully dressed body, blissfully unaware of the fact that I had been staring at her boobs for the past 10 seconds.

I shook my head, more to push myself out of my trance as opposed to answering Marina. "It's all good. I don't mind."

I don't mind you staring at me.

I took off my own shirt and then my pants. When I was down to my underwear and about to take it off, I took a quick glance in Marina's direction. Her eyes were lingering on my body. She was full on staring at the little pink rose on the seam of my black panties. Marina was fully undressed now but I forced my eyes to linger at her neck and shoulders. She was my boss and I had no business lusting after her naked body, even when she was staring at my pussy right now.

She didn't even register me looking at her, her eyes were so fixated on my lower belly. Her gaze made me feel good. Before I could think twice, my nails caught on the seam of my panties and I pulled them down, my eyes fixated on hers. When my panties made their way down my thighs, Marina bit her lower lip.

Am I hallucinating?

When I took off my bra, Marina's eyes shot up and found mine. She realized I had caught her staring. For a long moment, we stared at each other. The tension of what had just happened blurring the air between us. I didn't know what to do, didn't know how to behave.

Marina, my gay awakening, a supposedly straight woman, had been biting her lip at the sight of my pussy. How was I supposed to handle that? I wished that I could debrief the moment with Chloe, like we were staring at a photo of Marina making eyes at someone that wasn't me at all. I felt like I wasn't myself, like I was just some part of the queer speculations about Marina.

Before the moment could get any more awkward, Marina turned around and wandered toward the water. I followed without hesitation. I needed to cool myself down. Or heat myself up by getting even closer to her.

Marina jumped into the water before I could even reach the shore. It almost seemed like she was trying to get away from me. She swam further in and didn't turn around until she heard the splash of me jumping in after her.

I dipped my head into the water, the silence of it blocking out Marina's presence for a moment. That was, until I opened my eyes and saw her naked body under the surface. Blurry lines of tanned skin were shuffling to keep her afloat. The outline of her body looked like a modern interpretation of Aphrodite's silhouette. I wanted to place my hands on her hips.

When I came back up, face lifted to the sky and hands on my head to let my wet hair fall back neatly, Marina was looking at me again. Her brow was furrowed, like she was thinking about something.

"Did you know I read fan fics?" Her question came completely out of nowhere.

I swam toward her until only half a meter separated us. "About yourself?"

Marina nodded with a smirk. She swam around me and back toward the area where she could stand.

I followed. "No, I thought you'd avoid things like that."

"Actually, I don't." She scratched her left shoulder, the space where I knew the swallows were. "I kinda like reading them."

Flirting?

My eyes shot wide open. She liked reading fan fictions about herself? Most of them were queer and super smutty. She had to be joking, right? If she really read them and enjoyed them, there was no way she could be 100% straight.

Before I could react, she spoke again. "And I read yours." Marina wandered through the water, closer toward me.

My breath got stuck in my throat again and I had to cough. I used to write fan fictions when I was about 17 years old and my crush on Marina was at its climax. I never shipped her with anyone. Instead, I created characters resembling myself that dated her. Those stories were cheesy and not my best work. And, they had sex scenes in them.

How the hell had she found them?

I hadn't used my Instagram fan account in years and that was the only link between me and those stories.

I thought about the moment Marina stared at my underwear and took a chance. "Did you stalk me?" I took another stride toward her and casually brushed her upper arm with my fingertips. A shock wave ran through my body from the space where we touched.

"Yeah, maybe." She lifted her shoulders and looked to the side like she was insecure. For a second, I was looking at an 18 year old on their first date instead of a woman in her thirties. "Your social handles were linked with your profile. And, um, I wanted to know who you were." Our faces were now only centimeters apart. Her cheeks were tinted pink. "And, maybe, I got lost in your stories. They're kinda good."

Was I making her nervous?

The blush on her cheeks was making me feel more confident. "You know that they're basically smutty stories my teenage self wrote about you and me, right?" I leaned my head to the side, assessing Marina's expression. I could see her brown eyes turn golden; she was glowing. My whole body was hot, even in the cold water.

Briefly, her eyes darted down to my lips. It was less than a millisecond so I told myself that I had imagined it.

"I know." She bit her own lip, sending my stomach through the loop of a rollercoaster. Her hand brushed mine again, just slightly, like she wanted to grab it but didn't quite dare to. She was going to make me go insane. "It was kinda hot."

Everything inside me was on fire at this point. The proximity of her naked body made my skin sizzle with electricity, and her words fuelled every delusion I had ever had about her. The tension between us was unbearable. The magnetic force of her body toward mine drew me in like nothing before.

She grabbed my hand.

Enough.

I leaned forward and kissed her. She didn't kiss back at first and froze at my attempt. Before my head could pull away, so I could disappear from the face of the earth completely, she opened her lips to mine.

Everything inside me burst into flames. Marina, the woman of my dreams, was kissing me back. All the scenarios I had invented in my head disappeared the moment our lips united. Reality became so much more than any delusion I had ever had as I let my tongue wander over her bottom lip just a little bit... and she let it in without hesitation.

Marina's arms wrapped around my neck, drawing me in. She pulled me closer, our bodies connecting under the surface. Her skin on mine made me moan into her mouth. I squeezed her butt for a second, right where that drop of water had driven me insane. Marina's hands were lost somewhere in my hair; I didn't mind them turning it into knots. Her teeth tugged at my bottom lip, biting slightly, before she kissed my chin and then my throat. She was leaving little marks on her way. I was hers long before I even had my first kiss. My head went quiet for the first time in a long time. There was no past or future to think about because the present was better than anything I could've imagined.

Marina pushed me away before my right knee could slide between her legs.

"I uhm..." She put distance between us, then washed her face with the lake water.

I stared at her, didn't dare to say a thing. Her mouth was slightly open, her eyes wide in shock. The golden glow from before was gone.

Did I overstep?

"I'm sorry, Kari. I shouldn't have... This was wrong." She turned around and climbed out of the lake, drops of water falling from her perfect body

My heart wasn't crushed at her reaction. What else would I have expected? She had a husband and she had just cheated on him. However, I still felt warm at the thought of the kiss. I wanted more now and Marina clearly didn't. And she was still my boss. I didn't want to think about the way our dynamic would change, the way this would complicate things.

Marina was already putting her clothes back on when I reached the pile of mine. "It's okay. I get it. This never has to happen again if you don't want it to." I was surprised at the calmness in my voice but there was also no other outcome I could have expected from this scene.

"Thank you," Marina mumbled, barely audible.

I pulled my tight shirt over my head and closed the zipper of my pants without another word. Marina didn't even dare to look at me once on the journey back to the tour bus. She immediately disappeared inside when we arrived. I sat down on a wall across from the bus and took out my phone for the first time that day. Chloe had spammed me with text messages:

Chloe, yesterday 11:21am
How was sleeping in one bed with the most gorgeous MILF on the planet?

Chloe, yesterday 3:42pm
Girl, are you okay? Did she eat you alive?

Chloe, yesterday 8:11pm
Also, have fun at the concert in Leipzig. I wish I could be there.

Chloe 11:57am
Uhm, girl. I'm kinda getting worried here.

Chloe 5:46pm
Okay, now I really think Marina just ate you up.

I chuckled at her messages for a second. I thought about Marina eating me out. Then the closeness of her naked body came back to my mind. Her full, soft lips against my clit.

I shook my head. She had clearly indicated that that it was never going to happen.

Kari 7:51pm
You will never believe me if I told you what I just experienced.

A second later, my phone rang. I picked up and Chloe appeared on my screen. I must have looked rough because her eyes turned wide at the sight of me.

"Do I look that bad?" I asked.

"Well, if I'm completely honest with you, you look like a wet poodle whose owners forgot her in the rain," she laughed.

"Well, that's kinda how I feel."

Chloe moved the phone so close to her face that I could only see her eyes. "So, what the hell happened. Don't spare any details."

I looked down at my left hand sitting in my lap. "I don't know if I can talk about it."

"Well, now that you say that, I'm even more curious." She didn't move her eyes away from the camera. "There's no way you cannot tell me about everything. I will force it out of you if I have to."

I loved Chloe for her persistence. I knew I had to talk about all this eventually.

"Well, I went swimming with Marina in a lake today. Alone."

She moved the phone back to a reasonable distance. "Do you even have a swimsuit with you on tour?"

"No."

Chloe's eyes shot open wide, the reality dawning on her. "No fucking way; you went skinny dipping with

175

Marina?!" Chloe was squealing. Her eyes were so wide that I thought they'd pop out.

Would she faint if I told her everything?

"Yes way," I laughed. It felt freeing to tell Chloe about something. Talking about it made it real.

"So, how does her body look beneath those tight black jeans?" Chloe winked at me. Her eagerness to live vicariously through me made me feel less alone in this mess.

"Breathtaking." I let my mind wander to the back of her body for a second, the water running down her spine. "She has a tattoo on her shoulder blade. It's swallows flying away."

"Damn. I wish I could see the images in your mind." She sat up against her white wall. "What about her booty? Or her boobs?"

I laughed. "Chloe! Of course I tried not to look!"

"Yeah, sure. As if you could withstand that temptation. I'll let you keep those details to yourself." She brushed through her red curls with her right hand. "Tell me more about swimming and sleeping in one bed, though."

I told her about everything that had happened the day before, up to the moment Marina told me about reading my fan fics. I left out our conversation in the hotel room as well as the kiss. That was private, at least for now.

Chapter 10
Dress - Taylor Swift

Do you know the feeling when a dream becomes reality and suddenly everything else seems dull and meaningless? One single moment can cause you to lose any and all ties to the life you were used to. Usually, it's something like publishing your first book or reaching that one position in your career that you've worked for, traveling to that one place you've always wanted to see. And, when it's done, when you've reached it, what else is there to strive for?

For a fan girl, it starts with seeing your favorite singer live and evolves into eventually meeting them in person. When it's a concert, it becomes an addiction and you want to experience that feeling of screaming your favorite songs with a crowd over and over again. That's something you can strive for, going back to the dull normal life just to save up for more concert tickets. If you manage to meet them, it gets trickier. Concerts will not feel the same because you always want more. But what if that one meet and greet was a once in a lifetime chance? What is there to strive for then? In my position, all those things I used to strive for seemed small. Even the little girl that spent hours staring at the giant posters of Marina in her room could never have come up with a thing like my current situation.

And yet here I was, lying in an uncomfortable little bunk bed, touching my lip and still feeling the little tug of Marina's teeth.

That morning, Marina left the bus before anyone else woke up. I told myself that she was fine and had just gone on her usual run. I stretched out in bed. I had barely slept; the electric sensation of kissing Marina flowing through me whenever I closed my eyes. In some way, I still wanted to believe this had been a dream. How was I supposed to keep going now? How was I supposed to function? I knew that it couldn't happen again and still, I wanted to be close to her. I wanted to get to know every part of her, get to know sides of her she didn't show. My heart had been beating in her rhythm for years, and she was about to steal it.

The rest of the crew was still snoring away in their bunk beds so I shuffled through my bags as quietly as possible, grabbed my clothes and makeup bag and crawled out of bed. The sun was already blinding my eyes as I stepped out of the bus. Because it was black inside and outside, and the windows were tinted, it was always night in there.

I stepped over the cobblestones in my Doc Martens and entered the back door of the venue. Luckily, I didn't have to search for any bathrooms this time because we had been shown around the day before. There was no way I would've gone to bed without a shower after swimming in the lake.

When I looked at myself in the mirror for the first time that day, I saw dark bags under my eyes. It seemed like I hadn't slept for days. If Marina had seen me that morning, she would've asked me if I was okay. The dullness in my eyes even scared *me* a bit.

Marina was becoming a friend; have I messed that up already?

I put my hair in a sleek ponytail, pulling the strands as tightly as possible. I winced slightly but pulled tighter. The pain in my forehead was something I could feel.

I hid the dark circles beneath my eyes with multiple layers of concealer and put on black leather pants and a black button down. I left the top buttons open to reveal some cleavage and then, as I scanned myself in the mirror, I told myself that I looked hot.

I knew that I had a reason to be here. I was supposed to work for my career, reach a goal I had set for myself. I just couldn't stop thinking about Marina. Suddenly, the only thing I wanted to work towards was being in her presence, maybe kissing her again.

When I left the bathroom, Marina walked down the hallway. She didn't look at me as she stomped past me, her chest heaving from her run. My own chest stung at the thought that she hadn't even acknowledged my presence. No matter how much I had dressed up, nothing was ever going to happen between us again. Guilt made me feel sick at the thought that I had kissed her, even though I shouldn't have.

Later that day, the backstage area swarmed with reporters wielding huge cameras and microphones. Marina was supposed to do an interview for a big magazine. After the band had announced that they would have a comeback, Marina had also said that she was going to be a part of the new season *Sing Along*. That had led to media exposure and a lot of nosy people.

I was hunched in a corner with Dari, who was taking tiny bites from a pink donut. The way he munched away on the dough was weird. It almost made me sick seeing the wet dough stuck in his beard. He smirked at me, and I saw streaks of pink stuck between his teeth. A wave of an alcoholic smell came out of his mouth. He wasn't the person I'd seen on stage all those years. He was so far away from the comforting teddy bear I'd thought he was.

Marina had disappeared in the bus until shortly before the news crew arrived. She didn't even come out for lunch. At this point, the guilt was eating me from the inside.

As soon as everything was set up for the interview, I pushed myself from the couch, hoping that I could find comfort in doing my job. I started snapping a few pictures of the media situation, a close up of Marina talking into the mic or laughing about a joke here and there. My head felt less cloudy, as long as there was a screen between Marina and me.

There is a reason I am here.

The interviewers asked about the tour and how it was going, how Marina felt about being on stage after such a long time and if the fandom had changed since they'd toured 2 years ago. Marina smiled through it, even though I could see through my lens how she cracked her knuckles and clenched her legs. Her eyes weren't glowing anymore; they were tired. She wanted to leave.

"So, what are you excited for when coming back to *Sing Along*?" the man with the microphone asked. He had white hair and his nose and forehead were wrinkled. He leaned in closely. I wanted to push him away.

Marina chuckled, charming. "The new talents. It always amazes me how many undiscovered talents we have in this country." She pulled her hand through her hair. I zoomed in on the motion and I could see the veins of her hand on my screen. "And, seeing my colleagues, of course!" Marina's laugh was bright but false.

The reporter scratched his head and it made an uncomfortable sound. "Apropos to your colleagues, you'll be working with Lara." He bent forward even farther. "How do you feel about working with *her* again?"

I moved the phone down.

Is he going to talk about the rumors?

It had been a fan theory and nothing more. No reporter had ever dared to ask Marina about it in person.

"What do you mean?" Marina shifted. "She's one of my dearest friends. Of course, I am excited to work with her."

"What about the rumors?" There was no sensitivity in the man's voice now. Even Milo's eyes shot up from his phone on the other side of the room. If he went further, or Marina gave any sign, Milo would stop the interview instantly.

"What rumors are you talking about?" Marina sat up straight so that her head was above the reporters. "The ones about Lara and me kissing at a party 2 years ago because of a blurry photo? The ones about us secretly dating for years and being in love? Or the ones about us getting married in Vegas?" Her voice was harsh, like she felt accused of something that she didn't do, blaming the reporter for his audacity to even consider asking about a thing like that.

The man was speechless for a moment and in another situation I would have laughed about it.

My chest hurt. The way that Marina spoke about those rumors turned my stomach upside down. There was disgust in her voice and it didn't seem like it was pointed towards the white-haired man across from her. I put the phone into the back pocket of my pants, freeing my hands to pull at two strands of my hair, sending pain through my scalp: anything to help me get through this moment.

Silence enveloped the room. Milo had put his phone away and was ready to get up from the couch. Marina caught my eyes and there was pain in them. My heart stopped for a second. Guilt and apology glistened in her brown eyes.

She turned back to the man across from her. "Well, since you can't clarify your question, let me at least clarify *this*: I love my fans. But I know that they like to assume things about me and hold onto theories and ideas. I know that most of the fandom is queer and they wish I was too but I am not. I love my husband and have never dated a woman." She looked straight into the camera now, speaking to the fans. "I'm sorry to disappoint you; I wish I could be the role model you want me to be. But, please, stop speculating about my private life. It is none of your business." Then, she turned back to the reporter. "Thank you for your questions but I believe that is enough for now." She got up from the couch and walked out of the building.

I knew deep down that this was the way she felt but I still felt my heart aching for a different answer.

If she wasn't queer, then what the hell was yesterday?

There was nothing I could have expected of her but I still felt used and betrayed. She had wanted to try something out, nothing more. And, she hadn't liked it enough to give a different answer at this interview. Of course not. Still, the pain in her eyes when they'd found mine told me something else. There was regret there. Not for what had happened the day before but for what she had to say. Maybe she was just telling herself things that she wanted to believe and she thought that, if she spoke them into a microphone, it would make them more true. Maybe she couldn't stop thinking about me the way I couldn't stop thinking about her.

I didn't see Marina again before the show. She'd disappeared, done her part of the sound check in silence and hid somewhere until her stage time. I couldn't get myself to go into the pit, didn't want to be around people, couldn't face Chloe or Liza who were both jumping up and down in the front row. I couldn't. But I also couldn't hide under a blanket in my bed because I had to work. It was already a miracle that Marina hadn't fired me after what happened. Maybe she was scared I would tell people if she did. I wanted to believe that she valued my work, though. So, I stayed in the shadows of the stage, capturing Marina and the band from behind.

Being able to focus on work was a welcome distraction. My mind was blank while I filmed and photographed. At least, it was until someone threw a pride flag on stage during *Fourteen*. First, I caught Chloe's eyes in the crowd; their glow was brighter than ever at the sight of the rainbow colors. Then, I lifted the phone to capture Marina's reaction. I thought that she'd leave it on the ground of the stage and not even acknowledge it. Instead, the camera captured her picking it up while she sang the chorus.

"Fourteen summers, fourteen falls."

Marina pulled the flag over her shoulder. The crowd cheered; Chloe was probably crying.

"Through laughter, tears, and whispered calls."

I mouthed the lyrics with her; seeing the rainbow colors put a smile on my face.

"In the echo of youthful schemes, we formed a bond from paper dreams."

When Brad started his guitar solo, Marina put her microphone in its stand and spread the flag between her hands. The crowd cheered at the top of their lungs. I picked up the professional camera to capture the moment.

When I put it down to go back to filming, Marina turned around and looked at me. The flag was still spread between her hands, her back turned towards the crowd. I froze. The glow in her eyes was back; a shiny gold mixed with the glistening of tears.

The concert was over as soon as it had started. I snuck out for a quick hug with Chloe and Liza but excused myself before they could start asking questions.

Backstage, Dari was chugging a bottle of beer while Brad was cheering him on.

Marina sat on a wooden bench, her legs crossed. She wasn't wearing her stage clothes anymore but had on wide cut jeans that had huge holes on the front, revealing her tanned legs, and a black top with cuts across the front. This was the first time that I had ever seen her in jeans, let alone wide cut ones. I had to refrain from gasping. The way her upper thighs shaped within the holes, I wanted to touch them, put my hand on her leg. The top revealed parts of her skin; I wanted to kiss each hole in her shirt.

Her hair was still wet from sweat but she didn't look exhausted at all. Her face was glowing while she watched her band mates.

"Kari, you look really hot today!" Dari laughed, before he put a bottle to his mouth.

Suddenly, I felt the need to close the top button of my shirt. His compliment made me straighten my back.

"Thank you," I laughed awkwardly. "What is happening here, actually?"

Dari was chanting for Brad to down his beer. There was an energy to this room that was unexpected after a show.

"We are going to a club tonight," Marina explained from her seat. These were the first words she had spoken to me that day.

Dari walked over to me and handed me a beer. "And I believe you should join because you're already wearing the perfect outfit."

I took the beer and nodded, even though there wasn't anything I was less prepared for than going to a club with Marina tonight. The last time she was drunk, she'd told me things that had given me hope. Now, she'd been avoiding me. What would the alcohol bring out of her this time?

I put the bottle to my mouth and twisted it between my hands; this was met with loud cheers from the boys. The liquid flew into my mouth in one big wave. I had to try my best not to puke. When the flow of beer stopped, I put the bottle down and coughed.

The sweet sound of Marina's laugh emanated from the couch. I looked at her. For a second, everyone else in the room disappeared. It was like we were communicating with our eyes, our own little language. Marina patted the space on the bench next to her. I grabbed another beer and sat down next to her before I could think about it.

The bench was long so there was space between us. Our legs didn't touch like they had the last time. I wasn't as nervous as I used to be around her, either. But, I didn't feel quite comfortable. It was more of a confused state. I felt like I had to stay as far away as possible, not just for my sake, but for her's as well. If she came too close, I didn't know if I could stop myself from kissing her again.

"Marina! Now it's your turn to do a hurricane," Dari exclaimed, holding out a bottle to her. I had to laugh again. I had never seen this man so energized before. And, the thought of Marina downing a whole bottle of beer was ridiculous.

"Well, I guess I don't have a choice." I could still hear the smile in Marina's voice.

What had changed? Was I forgiven?

She got up, put the bottle to her lips, and bent her head back. Her hair slightly touched her shoulders. She looked gorgeous, enchanting. I wanted to kiss the soft skin of her throat, whispering into her ear that she's the most beautiful woman I've ever seen. She downed the beer, letting out a slight scream of relief when the glass bottle left her lips.

When Marina sat back down, she left space between her body and the end of the bench, leaving only millimeters between our legs. My breathing quickened a bit.

Is she doing this on purpose?

What does she want?

Before, I would not have questioned her position but, after the kiss, every action of hers had some sort of meaning.

3 beers later, Marina had shifted even closer, her knee touching mine. I was tipsy and leaned into her touch. If she chose to shift closer, she wanted this. I wasn't about to kiss her again but if she did, I knew I couldn't stop her.

"Okay, let's go to the club." Marina clapped, then stood up. "If we don't leave right now, I might end up back in bed." She laughed and held out her right hand to me.

I stared at her hand for a second. Her nails were short and black and a silver ring decorated each finger. They weren't manicured perfectly, black nail polish chipped away here and there, revealing the color of her natural nails.

Before I could over think it, I grabbed her hand and her fingers comfortably slid around mine. She pulled me up from the bench and I tripped, falling right into her arms. The alcohol was definitely making me dizzy now. My head rested on Marina's shoulder for a second and I breathed in her smell as deeply as possible. She'd probably heard it. Her hand was going up and down my back slowly, maybe subconsciously.

Marina laughed, the sound ringing in my ears. "Oops, that was unexpected." She grabbed my shoulders and pushed me away from her. "You okay?"

I was startled for a moment, time frozen as I stared into the gold of her eyes. The air felt warm and her mouth was so close that, if I bent forward just a little, I would kiss it again. The wrinkles around her eyes looked prettier than ever. She bent her head toward her shoulder a bit, a crease of concern developing on her forehead.

I moved away slightly.

"Yes, yes. Totally fine," I muttered.

"Cool, then let's go," Marina replied. I didn't realize that she was still holding my hand until she pulled me toward the exit.

Luckily, there were no fans waiting outside when we left the building.

How long have we been in there?

I stumbled after Marina when she pulled me into the driveway. The night air was cold but refreshing as we began walking with my boys. My vision was less blurry when I breathed in the clean night air.

When we walked through a quiet street, I took Marina's hand and pulled her back.

"What is happening?" I asked as the guys walked around another corner. "Why are you touching me again? After that interview today, I thought you'd never want to touch me again." I tried hard to keep my voice low.

"You heard that interview?" Marina stopped walking. "I'm sorry, you weren't supposed to."

I crossed my arms above my chest. "Well, I did."

"Kari, I'm sorry." She looked to the ground. "My management tells me the rumors are bad press so I have to deny them all the time... And... I don't know... Maybe I was saying things I wanted to believe. I'm scared, okay? What happened yesterday terrifies me because I liked it."

She liked it?

"What am I supposed to do with that?"

She stepped from one foot to the other. "I don't know. I don't even know what to think myself. I'm sorry."

"Okay." I was hurt but I understood. Her situation wasn't easy at all. "Let's keep going." I let go of her hand and walked up the street.

Loud club music rushed my way and I took in the narrow street we turned onto. 2 security guards were positioned beside a cellar door on the side of the street. The interior was entirely obscured, except for blue lights shining through the little window in the door.

I tingled inside. I hadn't quite believed that I was about to go dancing with Marina until we stepped onto the street. The beer in my system took the edge off my doubts and I tried telling myself to lean into it, to enjoy her presence. If she grabbed my hand, that was her decision. I was allowed to enjoy it, wasn't I?

The security guards didn't bother to check any IDs as 3 of us were over 30. Behind the door was a steep staircase that Marina pulled me down. I had to focus on every step, careful not to trip again.

A dancehall beat drummed through my ears as we entered. The downstairs area was packed, the dance floor full of women dressed in short skirts pushing their bodies onto random men.

Around the floor was a bar and a group of red couches. A door opened out onto the smoking area outside. Most of the couches were full of people kissing or talking, playing drinking games and touching each other's bodies.

Dari brushed past us and walked toward the only empty couch in the room, motioning for us to follow. I let myself fall onto the couch; it was soft and sleek. I was still holding Marina's hand as I sat. I looked at her, expecting her to sit down next to me.

Instead of finding her spot on the couch, she bent forward, grabbing the armrest with her right hand. Her face was suddenly closer than I was prepared for. Her closeness made me feel dizzy.

"I'm gonna head to the bar and grab drinks. What do you want?" she said into my ear, her breath tickling my skin.

"I'll have whatever you're having." My voice was shaky.

When Marina pushed herself up and walked toward the bar, my middle was still pumping.

How was this really happening right now?

After the kiss, it was obvious that Marina was flirting with me now. I tried not to think about what had happened after the kiss and focused on letting myself fall for once.

Marina came back a few minutes later with 2 espresso martinis in hand and handed me a glass. I took a sip, the dark liquid felt soothing on my tongue. She sat down next to me, not even trying to keep space between our legs.

"What about us?" Dari looked at Marina from her other side, a jokingly sad tone in his voice.

"Oh, I think you guys are old enough to get your own drinks," she teased.

Dari and Brad got up and walked toward the bar without another word. As soon as they were out of sight, Marina leaned into me a little more. I could feel her shoulder resting on mine, our knees touching. Everything inside me longed to kiss her again, to unite our bodies, to get even closer. Marina let her hand wander onto my leg, slightly brushing my side on its way.

My breathing quickened at her touch and I felt dizzy. Heat rushed from my leg to my pussy. I forced myself not to touch her, not to be active. This had to be her decision. She moved her hand upward a little and everything inside me was on fire. My breathing was shallow, every breath full of anticipation, the tension in the air unbearable.

"Girls!" Dari's voice rang through my ears, pushing me back to reality.

Marina's hand disappeared from its spot in a millisecond. I felt like a fish left on dry sand.

"Let's go dancing!" Brad appeared in my vision, waving for us to get up and head over to the dance floor.

I didn't want to dance; I wanted to be alone with Marina. She got up from her seat anyway, holding out her hand for me to grab. If Marina went dancing, I had to follow. Once standing, I grabbed my glass and gulped down the cocktail in two big sips before Marina could pull me onto the dance floor. There was no way I would let Marina go without another kiss that night so drinking more felt like the best option to get my confidence up, even though it seemed like Marina was doing most of the work herself.

As soon as we stepped foot on the dance floor, Marina let go of my hand, took 2 steps backward and started dancing. She shook her hips and held her hands over her head. The way she danced here was different from the way she did on stage. It was even better. She was freer, letting herself go, floating to the music. The way she moved was angelic. I was mesmerized by every shake of her hips and the way that the wide jeans shaped her legs was one of the most beautiful sights I had ever seen. I had stared at so many photos of Marina, had watched so many videos on a loop, but seeing her in person was even more breathtaking. I wanted to put my hands on her hips and guide her through the dance but I didn't because Brad and Dari were right behind me.

Marina stepped closer again. "Kari, let go a bit. You look so stiff!" She grabbed my hands and moved them back and forth.

I had never been the kind of person that was able to let loose in clubs. At concerts, I was the first to scream and jump. But in clubs, I always felt watched. I could do a little ass shake here and there, move my hips slightly to the music, but nothing more.

Now, in this dark and dusty cellar club as Marina was grabbing my hands, I felt like I could let go. Marina pulled me toward her, then pushed me away. She let go of one hand and let me spin. Then, I walked backwards a bit, threw my hands above my head, bent my knees and pushed out my butt to the beat. Even Dari joined us, jumping up and down. We looked silly but I didn't mind. For a moment, I even forgot about touching Marina. This was about freedom and finally being a part of this group of wonderful people. Who thought 30 year olds could be this much fun? It seemed like they had been in the world and the public eye for too long to give a fuck about what others thought. That reminded me why I loved them so much.

At some point, Marina grabbed my hips and pulled me towards her. She leaned in close before she mumbled, "I'm gonna head to the bathroom." Her hand rested on the back of my head for a second and I was reminded of the magnetic force of her body. Everything inside me tingled. She grabbed my head with her hands and pushed me away just slightly, her golden eyes roaming my face. She smirked, revealing her dimple, before she let go and turned around to walk towards the bathrooms.

I watched her leave, unable to move, my breath stuck in my throat.

Does she want me to follow her?

The alcohol in my system clouded my mind, making all doubts disappear.

She wants me to follow her.

So I did. I followed the middle-aged woman I had spent countless hours dreaming about to the bathroom of a rundown nightclub.

I bumped into multiple dancing people on my way over. The narrow corridor to the bathroom was lined with pink and blue neon lights. The wall behind the lights was made of red brick stones which were plastered with stickers. It seemed like they were trying to make the club seem high-end with the lights, hiding the fact that it was just a dirty cellar.

Surprisingly, there was no line in front of the door so I walked straight through the black door with the little pink *women* sign.

An electric shock wave rushed through my body as I grabbed the silver handle.

Am I really doing this?

I was brave enough to do this. At this point, I had nothing to lose.

Right?

Right.

When I opened the door, Marina was already washing her hands, leaning over the sink. The rest of the room was empty, the 3 stalls open.

God she looks so good in those jeans.

Marina looked up from her hands and beamed at the sight of me, her eyes glowing. I let the door fall closed behind me and the music turned into a dull background sound. It was just us now.

I got as far as entering the bathroom but that was all I could do.

Marina turned around and leaned against the sink with her hips, her arms crossed above her chest. "You followed me?"

"I guess so," I said and crossed my arms above my chest while I leaned against the doorframe.

"Well, what are we gonna do about this?" Her voice was lower than usual. No one could tell me that she wasn't flirting.

I didn't move. "I don't know." She was the one who had to make a move now. "You tell me."

She pushed herself from the sink and took a step toward me. "Well…" She took another step. "I can't stop thinking about what happened yesterday." There was a dark glimmer in her eyes, darker than gold, lion-like.

"And?" My arms were still crossed. I enjoyed my position, acting like I didn't want to eat her right there. It was obvious she wanted to eat me, too.

"And…" She was less than a meter away from me now. "I know this sounds insane." Another step. "I know this is a bad idea." Her face was centimeters away from mine now. She put her right hand on the doorframe above my head and leaned forward. I felt her breath on my skin. "I would like for it to happen again."

The sensation of her breathing on my skin came in quick, hushed waves as she bit her bottom lip. Her cheeks blushed in a rosy pink. I forced my face to stay stern but my insides were having a party.

Marina was cute when she was nervous. Everything inside me was burning now and I felt powerful for doing this with her. I had control.

"Oh, would you?" I asked, letting my eyes wander down to her lips and back up.

Marina nodded, her breathing so fast that she was unable to speak. She was taller than me but seemed small right there.

I moved my lips up to her ear. "Then do it," I whispered, my top lip lightly touching her skin. Marina shuddered when I moved my head back, stopping right in front of her lips.

She didn't move for a second. The tension turned the air blurry between us. It took every ounce of power in me not to move my head forward, not to move my hands up and grab her hips, not to touch her. She looked down to my lips, then to my eyes. The fire in her gaze was burning.

"Do it," I repeated, barely audible.

This was enough. Marina let out a hushed breath before she cupped my cheek with her left hand, moving my lips up to her mouth. All the tension that had built up to this moment released like a firework as our tongues met, fighting for power. Her teeth tugged at my bottom lip and I moaned into her mouth.

Tongues. Lips. Teeth.

Hushed breaths. Gasping for air and doing it again.

She pushed me against the door, her hips pinning me against the wood.

Tongues. Lips. Teeth.

My hands found her hips, pulling her closer.

Tongues. Lips. Teeth.

I gasped for air, then pulled tighter. Her right leg wedged between my thighs.

Tongues. Lips. Teeth.

I moaned, my hand wandered into her hair, scratching her scalp. She moaned too, the softest sound.

Tongues. Lips. Teeth.

My right hand grabbed her butt. Her knee pushed up, making me gasp.

Tongues. Lips. Teeth.

Her left hand under my shirt, exploring my skin. Goosebumps.

Tongues. Lips. Teeth.

The door against my back; the door hitting me from the back. The sound of club music.

Marina pushed back, walking backwards, hitting the sink. I moved. Someone entered the bathroom. I walked into a stall and brought my hand to my mouth. Lipstick smeared across the back of my hand. My vision was blurry. Deep breaths. I sat down on the toilet. Slow breaths. Shivers. Tingling inside my body. My right leg hopped up and down.

The toilet flushed in the stall next to me. The creaking sound of the door echoed through the room, followed by the sound of water running. Every second in that stall felt like an eternity. As soon as the sound of music rang through my ears, I stood up. A cloud of dizziness flowed through me.

Breathe.

I needed Marina's lips on mine again.

I should've pulled her into the stall with me.

My hand found the door lock. I opened the door, my arm still shivering. When I stepped out of the stall, Marina was gone.

Chapter 11
Lunch - Billie Eilish

My hands clung to the sink in front of me as I stared at myself in the mirror, my knuckles turning white. The person looking back at me seemed distressed, almost messy. My bottom lip was dark and swollen where Marina's teeth had caught my skin and the perfect ponytail that I had made this morning was falling apart, strands of hair dangling around my face. The hair-tie grazed the bare skin of my shoulder where my button down was pulled down my arm. My cheeks were tomato red. *Who am I?*

I was torn. I hated the mess I became around Marina. But I also loved everything that she made me feel. Losing control felt so wrong and so good at the same time. Her presence was addictive, her closeness like a rush of nicotine. And still, she'd managed to leave me high and dry twice now.

What does she want?

It seemed like she had no idea what she wanted. She used me to explore a desire that she'd been hiding but was that it?

What about her husband?

Does she still love him?

Did she just want any woman or did she like me? Was I the one making her question her sexuality?

I shook my head and tied my hair back as best as I could. There was no room for those thoughts right now. I couldn't look into Marina's brain; time would tell what she wanted. I splashed drops of cold water onto my face, hoping that it would cool down my cheeks. The rest of the band didn't need to know about our makeout session in the bathroom. I closed the top four buttons of my shirt which Marina had opened just minutes ago.

"Just because she left doesn't mean she doesn't want you," I mouthed to the woman in the mirror. *She'll either approach you again or she won't.*

I pushed my upper body off the sink and wandered out of the bathroom. The glowy dance floor was almost empty now; most of the people were either outside smoking or cuddling on one of the couches. I scanned the room for the band members and spotted them on a pair of sofas in the far back of the room. I walked over and Marina waved at me. She patted the empty space on the couch next to her. My body hit the cushion before I could over think it, my leg touching hers. She hadn't fully moved her hand away from the cushion before I sat down; it was now resting on my lower back, slightly touching the seam of my pants.

"That was some long bathroom break," Dari laughed from the couch across from ours.

Marina's hand wandered between my pants and my butt, her fingers brushing my skin. "Kari wasn't feeling great, maybe a bit too much to drink," she told Dari before I could even open my mouth to respond.

I was about to object when Marina leaned in, whispering into my ear, "Let's leave."

"Yeah, uhm. I feel kinda sick," I said, letting my right hand circle my stomach area. "I would like to go back to the bus, if that's okay with you?."

Dari rubbed his temples, "Oh, yes, of course. We can all head home now."

"Oh, it's fine I can go with Kari." Marina slid her hand back out from behind me and pushed herself off the couch. "I'm getting tired. But you two stay here as long as you want."

Dari and Brad didn't respond immediately, an unnerving silence developing between us. Marina held out her hand to me and I grabbed it. She pulled me off the couch and didn't let go, even when I stood up.

"I promise, it's fine," Marina said as she pulled me away from the couches and towards the exit, leaving Dari and Brad behind.

As soon as we stepped outside into the cold night air, I burst out laughing. "I can't believe we just lied to your band mates to leave without them," I said, bending forward. I knew that this wasn't sexy but everything was so surreal.

Marina pulled me around a corner and pushed me towards the wall of a building. "I wanted you alone," she whispered, her lips tracing my ear this time.

The thought of us being completely by ourselves sent sizzles of anticipation through my body.

How am I living my wildest dreams right now?

Marina pulled me away from the wall and down the street. We were running now. From the outside, it must have looked like one of those cheesy rom-coms. I wanted to reach the bus as fast as possible.

We didn't stop running until we got there. When Marina typed in the code for the door to open, I wanted to push her against the side of the bus. Instead, I moved my lips to her ear.

"What about Milo? Or the driver?" I whispered.

"Milo's wife lives here so he's staying with her. The crew members are out somewhere else and the driver is sleeping," Marina winked at me while the door opened with a zooming sound.

I gave her a short kiss beneath her ear before we stepped inside. Marina was right; the bus was empty, except for the driver snoring away on his front seat. I tried not to think about the way his back must hurt from sleeping on a seat every day. Before I could over think his job, Marina pulled me to the back of the bus. She pushed away the curtain that separated her part of the bus from the rest of the crew.

Behind the curtain, there was a queen-sized bed. Half of Marina's bed was filled with black jeans and leather jackets. I could even spot a black laced bra on the pile of clothes. The fact that Marina was messy reminded me that she was just another human being; she might have been famous but she still had her faults.

Marina let go of my hand and, pulling the curtain closed, pushed the pile of clothes to the end of the bed and onto the ground with a muffled "sorry." My heart glowed in my chest, discovering more parts of Marina's personality felt like a privilege that I never thought I'd experience. She had no idea how often I had wondered about the way that she sorted her clothes or what she wore in her free time or how her bed looked.

As soon as the bed was free, Marina pushed me down onto the mattress. I was startled for a second; my breath caught in my throat at the thought of what was about to happen. Marina's bed was comfy against my back, a lot comfier than my single mattress in the bunk.

Before I could move or react, Marina crawled onto the bed and on top of me. The sight of her face above mine, her hair dangling down and a sheepish smile revealing her dimples, made everything inside me tickle.

"Why do you have a big bed, by the way?" I whispered with a chuckle as Marina pressed herself down on me.

She pressed a kiss beneath my chin. "My husband used to sleep over years ago." Then, she placed a kiss on my lips, before lifting her face back up. "We gotta be quiet," Marina whispered, her eyes scanning my face. She didn't move. The flame that had overtaken her before slowly left her eyes, replaced by nervousness. As far as I knew, Marina had never been with a woman before. As she bent back down to kiss me, I grabbed her shoulders and turned her around.

I licked the space beneath her ear. "No, *you* gotta be quiet."

I was used to being in control and there was nothing I wanted more than to explore every inch of Marina's body.

When I moved up from her ear to kiss her lips, Marina's eyes were open wide.. She bit her lip at the sight of my face and the fire in her eyes made me burn from the inside. I kissed her hard, our lips finally reuniting after that moment in the bathroom. This time, the kiss was filled with anticipation, want and need.

I sat down on her legs and unbuttoned my shirt. Marina sat up and threw her leather jacket off the bed.

Then, my hands cupped her breasts beneath her shirt. A slight moan escaped Marina's mouth before she bit her lip to quiet herself. My fingers wandered down her upper body and to the hem of her shirt. When I pulled it up, Marina lifted her hands so that I could pull it over her head. She was wearing a black lace bralette, her breasts cupped perfectly. I tugged at her bra. She took it off in a second.

Her boobs were the perfect size; not too small and not too big. Her nipples hardened beneath my gaze. I pushed her down onto the mattress. When my lips explored the outsides of her nipples, I discovered a little birthmark on her right breast. If I looked closely enough, I could see that it was shaped like a heart. I pressed a kiss to it before I circled the soft skin around her nipple with my tongue. I took it between my thumb and index finger, twisting, while my teeth tugged at her right. Marina's body tensed, pushing her hips up in my direction. I kissed her before she could make a sound. When I squeezed her nipple, she moaned into my mouth.

"Do you like this?" I whispered into her ear, my breathing fast against her skin.

Marina nodded.

"Just say stop if you don't like something," I hummed and bit the soft part of her ear before my lips wandered down.

Everything inside me wanted to leave marks on her skin, to turn the soft beige into a dark purple. I stopped myself from biting too hard, my lips just tracing her skin, my tongue circling. It was a privilege to taste the salty flavor of her body. If I concentrated enough, I could even taste bits of lavender on her throat. It must have been the spot where she sprayed perfume every morning. The smell mingled with the taste. My tongue lingered there for a moment. I could feel her heavy heartbeat vibrating against my tongue. Her breathing hushed in my ear. My own heartbeat matched hers.

Is this a delusion?

She felt like a rush of drugs.

Her hips pushed upward, reminding me to keep moving. I was here to show her something, to introduce her to my world. We didn't know when her band mates would come back so there was no time to hesitate.

I kissed down her throat and her collarbone to her shoulder. Then, I placed little kisses down her chest, gently tracing each wrinkle with my lips. The space where her skin was folded from age was softer than any skin I had ever touched. I placed a kiss on her heart-shaped birthmark then kissed down her lower belly. My lips stopped right above the seam of her jeans.

I let out a quiet grunting sound, declaring my annoyance about the piece of fabric stopping me in my tracks.

Marina answered with a soft laugh.

I pulled myself back up to kiss the smile on her lips. "Is it okay if I take off your pants?" I whispered, praying that she wouldn't back out. Ever since I had begun to think about sex with her, I had dreamed about exploring what was beneath those usual black pants.

"Yes," Marina hushed and my right hand wandered between her legs, pressing upward.

She was wet underneath her pants.

"Are you sure?" My voice was serious while the palm of my hand pressed up harder.

Marina bit her lip and nodded. If she'd spoken, she would have screamed the 'yes' out.

"Okay, let me show you what those rumors about your queerness are all about," I murmured into her ear.

Marina bent her hips farther upward, pressing against my palm. A part of me still thought that I was dreaming when I pulled down Marina's jeans, revealing a tiny piece of black underwear. I did what I had wanted to do from the moment I had first seen her round butt cheeks: I squeezed them. Marina let out a quiet gasp. Her skin gave under my fingers. I longed to turn her body around to trace the ocean waves that I had memorized but I kissed her lips instead, pinning her to the mattress. Everything about her was made to be worshiped.

My left hand wandered up her belly and back to her right breast while my hand made its way to the middle of her cheeks. I let my fingernail slightly scratch her skin. Marina squeaked which was one of the gentlest sounds I had ever heard. I kissed her with more force, biting her lip. She bit back when the palm of my hand pressed upward. The wetness of her middle made heat rush through my body. My hand pulled upward, releasing the pressure to give my fingers space to roam and explore. Her slit was so delicate.

When I started rubbing slightly, Marina's breathing intensified. There was nothing that I wanted more than to drive her crazy. I had wanted it from the day that I learned what being a lesbian meant.

"You like that?" I whispered into her ear.

I want to do this to you every day for the rest of my life.

Marina's head nodded against mine.

"More?" I breathed heat against her ear.

Marina bent her hips toward my hands as an answer.

I pushed them back down with my hand on her stomach. "Ssh, let me do the work."

Marina answered with another squeal, then bit her lip.

I strained my neck upward so that I could watch her while my fingers explored her folds, tracing and rubbing. Marina closed her eyes and pushed her head into the pillow. Her dark hair was piled around her head, decorating her beautiful face like a crown. When my

212

fingernail traced her clit, her face tightened. She pinched her eyes together, deepening the lines beneath her eyes. I wanted to follow those lines and see more appear. There was something about the deepness in her face while I made her body tense up that felt endless, infinite. Every little corner of her body, every little wrinkle on her skin, every mark, every bruise, deserved its own hour of worship.

You're the most beautiful person I have ever seen.

Marina opened her eyes, reminding me of my mission. My fingers had stopped when my eyes got lost in her face. Her hungry golden gaze searched my face in desperation. I smirked as her forehead wrinkled in confusion. Everything about the way her eyes sparkled and her lips trembled told me to keep going; they begged me to keep going without a single word. I let her suffer for another second before I pinched her clit between my thumb and forefinger. Marina's head shot up, her forehead meeting mine, while her eyes shut again. I kissed the gasp from her lips as my fingers began circling.

Her breathing was fast and huffy against my skin, every breath close to a moan.

"Do you want me to go inside?" I whispered into her ear. Marina nodded against me. I pressed another kiss against her lips then pushed her back into the pillow. "Be quiet."

I propped myself back on my arm so that I could watch her full upper body. She bit her already swollen lip when I let a single finger slide inside. Her head bent backwards into the pillow and her eyes fell closed. Even with her eyes shut, her face glowed with pleasure. My middle finger soon joined my index finger and Marina opened her mouth to scream; only a hushed whimper escaped her lips.

Her hips pushed upward and I moved my hand back and forth in a rhythmic motion. My hand and her body found their beat, falling into a rhythm.

It's like a melody, soft and sweet.

My thumb started circling her clit. Marina shivered under the pressure. My eyes were fixed on her face, the way that her cheeks darkened, turning into the color of red delicious apples. She was poisonous.

Our bodies moved to the beat.

My fingers thrust into her soft inside with every beat of her moving hips.

Exploring depths in ecstasy.

Her skin tightened around my fingers, begging for more. Her thrusts became irregular, her muscles tensing. She opened her mouth, ready to scream.

I pressed my free hand against her mouth. "Look at me," I whispered. I needed her eyes on mine, needed the fire to burn between us. I needed to see the fireworks sparkling in the deep brown of her eyes.

Marina's eyes shot open; she stared at me with desperate need. I pushed harder, then bent my fingers, lifting her lower body. Marina tensed and shivered, the warm walls around my fingers moving in. She didn't take her eyes off mine while her hips bent up one last time. She bit the inside of my hand; I suppressed a whimper of pain, pressing a tiny bit harder. Her body moved uncontrollably, her hands wrapped around my back. She clenched my skin, scratched, while every single molecule of her body urged her to the top. Sparks flowed through the air between us while fireworks exploded in her golden eyes. A river of release flowed through Marina's body as she touched the sky.

Lost in the rhythm of you and me.

Chapter 12
Don't Wake Me Up - Mercer Henderson

A pinching pain in my left hand woke me the next morning. The sun was already up, beams of light hurting my head. I rubbed my temples, then I forced my eyes open to look at my hand. There was a dark spot on the inside, deep purple turning into blue and green. It took me a second to make out the shape, the oval imprint of perfectly-formed teeth biting my skin in ecstasy. I grinned, wider than ever, reminded of the previous night.

When I closed my eyes again, I still felt the fireworks between our eyes, the way that her fingernails clawed my back. A sparkle developed in my heart at the way Marina had looked freer than ever. The way she'd held onto me after, showering me with thanks until the very second we heard the beeping sounds of the keypad. I had given her a silent kiss and disappeared into my bunk before the boys entered the bus. My bed had felt hard and cold against my back, the heat of Marina's skin and body missing, being so close yet so far from my reach. The kiss promised more while the water in her eyes dimmed the light inside of me.

What if I could never get this again?

I grabbed my phone to find some distraction. It was midday already and I was surprised that no one had woke me up to do any work.

Is this making a bad impression?

I had caused my boss to silently beg for my fingers so there was probably not any better impression that I could have made. As long as Marina didn't see me as a threat, that is.

The little green icon of my messenger app was accompanied by a red number 27. Chloe had probably spammed my phone with messages again. The thought of sharing my experience flashed through my head more than once. The fact that I could probably never let her be part of the most beautiful moment of my life left a knot of guilt in my stomach. We had talked about these fantasies for hours and I couldn't even give her a glimpse of what they were really like. I knew that Chloe would understand, if she did find out one day, but it still felt like I was betraying the most important person in my life. All this led to avoidance and my best friend wondering if I was dead. Instead of opening the messages, my thumb found the little TikTok icon. I knew that I had to talk to Chloe in person during the concert today but I wasn't quite ready to deal with her flood of texts yet.

I was watching a fan edit of Marina, when three fingers with freshly manicured black nails pushed my gray curtain aside. The phone dropped into my lap as my head shot around to the person outside my bunk. Marina moved the curtain aside and climbed into my bunk, the space barely allowing her to hover above me. She was wearing her running clothes. Her upper body was protected by nothing but a sports bra and her dark hair dangled down her face in wet, sweaty threads.

"Hi?" I asked, startled by her sudden entrance.

Marina bent forward and placed a kiss on my lips.

"Hey, sleepyhead. What have you been watching on your phone?" She let herself fall onto my body, her weight pressing me into the mattress in a comforting way.

"Uhm, nothing." I pushed the phone beneath my legs.

Marina shook her head, her nose brushing against mine.

"I don't think that was nothing." She took the phone from beneath my leg.

I tried to grab it from her but her free arm pinned mine onto my pillow. The way her hand clenched around my wrist made me think about all the other things it could do. Before I could protest, Marina had already pressed play on the TikTok.

"So you've been fan girling about me?" She laughed and scanned my face with a smirk. There was the same hungry glow in her eyes.

"Maybe," I mumbled, scanning her face in shame. I was supposed to be the cool one here, the one in control, not the creepy fan.

"Cute." Marina placed a kiss on my forehead and something inside me fluttered. "I like my little fan girl."

I felt my face go hot and red.

"In that case, I should inform you that I fangirl about you every single second of the day." I wrapped my arms around her.

"Where are the others?" I asked while her nose nestled into the space between my shoulder and neck. I felt her breath on my skin. "How long do we have?"

"They are setting up the stage," Marina said against my skin, "which means they are busy for quite a while." She kissed my collarbone. "But, from the way we both smell, I'd say we have to factor in time for a shower."

"Then let's take this to the shower."

A few minutes later, Marina and I had collected our clothes while giggling and stealing quick kisses.

How do people actually get anything done when they're around the person they have a crush on?

We found ourselves wandering through yet another concert location with our clothes and shower essentials piled up in our arms. This place was even bigger than the ones we had been in before, the building modern and gray like a convention center. The lights were bright and cold. I walked first, Marina right behind me. This place was new, even to her. At least the signs were lit with LED lights, guiding us through the hallway.

Whenever I glanced back, Marina was smiling at me, her cheeks glowing pink. Every time my eyes found hers, something inside of me sparked. There were fireworks, butterflies and so much more. In all those years of staring at her, I had never felt this kind of electricity. If I didn't love her before, I was falling for her now.

I pushed the door with a shower sign open for Marina. "Ladies first."

"Why, thank you." She stepped into the room.

When I turned around after locking the door, Marina was already putting her things on a little black bench in the corner next to 2 rain shower heads. I stepped over and put my hands on hers before she could start undressing herself.

I pulled her toward me, then put my hands on her hips. "Did you know that you mesmerize me?" I said, locking eyes with her.

"Uhm, no," Marina mumbled, her eyes averting from my gaze.

"Well." I cupped her face with my hands, forcing her to look up. "You have been mesmerizing me since I was 14. I have spent countless hours dreaming about the way you smell, the way your skin feels, what your eyes look like up close." My thumbs slightly stroked her cheeks. "I dreamed about the way your lips would feel against mine and what your body looks like beneath those tight pants and that black leather jacket."

Marina looked at me with wide, watery eyes.

I kept on talking. "You smell of the most beautiful lavender fields which reminds me of freedom. Your skin is one of the softest things I have ever touched; I wish I could kiss every single millimeter and explore every mark." I pushed the lost strand back behind her ear. "Your eyes turn golden whenever you're excited and glow with the hunger of a lion when you see me."

Marina chuckled and pressed a quick kiss to my lips.

I pushed her away. "Wait. I'm not done yet!" I laughed. "Your lips are magic." I let my thumb glide over her bottom lip. "I've kissed a lot of women but none of them ever kissed me the way you do. You kiss like you're devouring me, like it is a privilege to meet my lips. And your body?" My eyes wandered down her sports bra and over her abs. "Just wow. I mean, did you know that the stretch marks on your thighs look like ocean waves?"

Marina cried silently, salt water meeting my thumb. She stared at me, her expression somewhere between lost and amazed.

Did I say too much? Did I scare her off?

"Thank you," she said, barely audible. Then, she kissed me again and it tasted of her salty tears.

Before I could answer, Marina pressed me onto the bench, settling herself on my lap. I was startled but didn't let myself over think it. Her lips touched mine in a rush and the back of my head met the cold stone wall. Her hands wandered under my T-shirt; I felt the metal of her silver rings against my skin.

Our tongues intertwined, intensifying the kiss. The space between my legs felt hot and a deep sense of need bloomed inside me. I thought about the way that her inside had felt against my fingers the day before and I wanted nothing more than to feel it again. I wanted to hear her scream this time.

Marina left my lips to catch her breath, then tugged at my oversized shirt. I froze with a sense of insecurity. Did she want me to undress?

Does she want to touch me?

I could make my outer appearance look perfect but I could never erase the imperfections that I was hiding beneath my clothes. It already felt wrong to be around her without any makeup on, my hair still in the messy bun I had slept with. I hadn't quite considered the fact that showering with her meant undressing in front of her. I stopped Marina from pulling up my shirt.

"Eyy, it's my turn now!" she protested, her voice taking on a childish tone. When I didn't budge, she looked at me with honest, warm eyes. "Seriously, I want to see you. I want to honor your body the way you honored mine. I want to know what it feels like to touch a woman, to touch a *gorgeous* woman like you."

Her voice was so comforting and honest. I knew that she meant it. Maybe she just wanted to experiment. But, something about the way she glowed when she said the word gorgeous told me that she wanted to touch me and *only* me. I let her lift my shirt over my head, revealing the parts of me that I liked to hide.

Marina's eyes had the same lion-like glow from the day before. She placed a kiss on each of my breasts. The tension in my body loosened a little at the touch of her lips.

"Thank you," Marina said, then kissed the space between my boobs. "For letting me see you." She pushed herself up from my lap and kneeled down between my legs. Her hands grabbed the seam of my adidas shorts and slowly pulled them down.

She revealed my Calvin Klein underwear, the final layer hiding my biggest imperfection from her gaze. I tensed up but Marina pulled them down without a second thought. I held my breath. She was looking right at a surgical scar running from my belly button all the way down to my vulva.

I waited for her to react, ask about it. Marina didn't say anything; she didn't even really look at it. Instead, her eyes wandered over my hips, down my legs and back up again.

"You're beautiful," she said. She kissed my belly button. Her lips wandered downward with little kisses. Every kiss eased the tension in me. I took a long, freeing breath before Marina's lips found their way down.

She pushed my legs apart and placed a kiss on the insides of each of them. I didn't know how to behave or react. Somehow, my head quietened for the first time in a long time. Marina placed a short kiss above my clit.

"May I?" Her voice was raspy, hungry.

"Enthusiastic *yes*," I said and let my head fall back to lean against the wall.

I felt Marina smiling as she placed the next kiss on my clit. It was just a short peck but it lit a firework inside me. My hands clung to the bench beneath me. The next second, her tongue slid downward and back up. I gasped at the soft touch. A warm, comfortable feeling developed from the space between my legs.

Her tongue went up and down a couple of times, sending waves of pleasure with it. Her lips found my clit again, sucking in a melodic motion. It was almost like we were on stage, Marina singing while I took photos of her, admiring her talent. Only, this time, I was experiencing the magic of her mouth first hand. With every suck, I fell deeper into a state of calm and tension. It was close to the way photographing made me feel: no thoughts but always on edge. Photography made me feel safe, like I could step out of my own head for a moment. I was always ready to capture the next masterpiece, climbing higher and higher with every shot of Marina's tongue and lips.

She let her tongue dip inside of me and my hands grabbed her hair, burying my fingers in her dark waves. Marina singing, me shooting. I pressed her head forward, pushing her face deeper between my legs. Marina shooting, me flying. My muscles tensed as the movements of her tongue became quicker. Marina singing, me soaring. A deep wave of pleasure rushed through my body with every push of her tongue. The next twist sent sparkles through my vision. I gasped, then trembled. Fiery sparkles let me burn. She pushed me off the stage and over the edge. For a moment, I thought that I was flying.

Marina didn't stop placing wet kisses on every centimeter of skin that she found between my legs until my breathing went back to normal and my limbs stopped shaking.

"Wow," I breathed out and looked down at her.

She lifted her head to look at me. "Wow," she licked her lips. "You taste so good."

Something inside my heart sparked. "Come up here."

Marina followed my command and, a second later, she was sitting on my lap, giving me a calm kiss.

"I can't quite remember the last time I tasted myself on another woman's lips," I mumbled as I stroked her hair.

"Well, I can't remember a time that I've ever tasted a woman." Marina put her hands to her lips.

I lifted her face up to look at me. "Was this the first time you've done this?"

Marina's eyes were wide. "Yeah," her eyes darted down and back up. *Was that insecurity?* "Was it okay?"

I laughed. "More than okay."

"Really?" Her dimples showed.

"Amazing, actually," I said and gave her another kiss.

She let out a nervous chuckle, then turned around so that her back was facing me. "To be honest, I can't believe I just did this. I just wanted to, you know? Like I had this deep need to taste you, to feel you with my tongue. Is that weird? I've never felt this before."

"Not weird at all. Completely normal, actually." I stroked her hair. She had been my role model and my crush for so many years and here I was teaching her about queer sex. *How is this real life?* "Now it's my turn." I wrapped my hands around her upper body from the back, my fingertips slipping beneath her sports bra to lift it up.

Marina lifted her arms without a second thought and my hands cupped her breasts. I massaged them while I let my eyes wander to the black swallows on her back. I

227

gently pushed her dark hair away, placing a kiss on each of the four swallows, ending up at the tip of her shoulder. Each of the kisses felt like I was coming closer to her and the inked skin was soft under my lips. When I had first laid eyes on her tattoo, I had never thought that I'd ever touch it, let alone feel it beneath my lips. Here I was, kissing them, flying away with the swallows on Marina's skin.

She'd been my home for so many years and still, her presence was pure freedom. Maybe Marina was so pleased because she was discovering something new. But I was falling deeper and deeper.

My lips sucked at her neck, then at her throat. I let my hands glide to her front, sliding in between the fabric of her workout pants and her underwear. My hand wandered right between her legs. I bent it and pushed her back against me; she answered with a moan. One of the most beautiful sounds I had ever heard. Her voice was already angelic when she sang on stage but any sound that I made her produce sounded so much better. Maybe she would sing a song just for me one day.

Her butt pressed against my middle, while my fingers pressed against hers. Now I was the one moaning against her skin.

"We gotta get under the shower." I pressed her even harder against me and bit the thin skin of her throat. "You have songs to sing." My hands gilded back out of her pants and stopped at her hips to pull her up.

Marina answered with a huff of protest before she pushed herself off my legs. My eyes fixated on the waves on her thighs when she pulled her pants down her legs and off her feet.

I traced her stretch marks with the forefinger of my right hand. I could feel their outlines beneath my fingertip, as the waves were carved in a little. They were deep, like ocean water. I wanted to delve into the depths of her body.

"What are you doing back there?" Marina laughed. "I thought we gotta get into the shower."

I pressed a kiss on one of the marks. "Just tracing my favorite part of your body," I mumbled, letting my lips wander over the marks on her legs, then up to her butt cheeks.

Marina didn't answer, just stayed still until I was finished honoring the back of her body. I pushed myself to a standing position. My legs were stiff from the tense position that I had been in. I pushed off my shoes and took off the last pieces of clothing I was still wearing: my socks. Then my right hand found Marina's while my left grabbed the little plastic bag I stored my shampoo in.

As soon as we reached the shower stall, I pressed the water button and pushed Marina against the wall.

She squealed as cold water hit her skin. "Eyy!" She sprinkled drops of water in my direction. "That's cold!"

I laughed. "I guess I have to warm you up then." I pressed a kiss against her lips, then bent my knees to lower my head. The shower was still running, cooling my hot face. My body pinned hers against the wall, while my hand delved into the ocean between her legs.

When I greeted Chloe behind the barricade that night before the concert, she immediately pointed out my dark eye bags. "You look like you've had a wild night." She pinched the side of my belly, a sheepish grin on her lips.

Everything was completely unreal. I felt like I only experienced reality when I was alone with Marina. My stomach tensed, forming a cramp where everything had just felt loose and free.

What am I supposed to say?

I couldn't lie to my best friend. Chloe had every right to know what had happened but it would have been disrespectful to Marina to tell anyone about our private times together. Maybe I would've let something slip if Liza hadn't been jumping up and down next to Chloe.

But, I knew that Liza, even though I loved her to bits, couldn't keep anything to herself.

I laughed and shook my head. "Well, the boys wanted to go out last night so we hit a club." My voice was surprisingly steady, even though my insides turned upside down.

This is wrong.

"Wow. Partying with *Paper Rings and Promises*? I would literally murder for that," Liza squealed, then leaned over the barricade in front of her. She lowered her voice. "How is Marina when she's tipsy? How does she dance when she's not on stage? Did she wear the black jeans or something else?"

I lifted my shoulders, like it hadn't been a big thing. "She's just the same as she is on stage."

Liza wasn't satisfied with my answer at all but let the topic go. She smiled but there was disappointment in her eyes as she turned to talk to someone that was standing next to her.

"So, you call them the boys now, do you?" I heard Chloe's soft voice beside me. When I turned to look at my best friend, her blue eyes were sad and watery. Part of me wished that I could give my position to her, share my experience with her. She deserved it more than I did.

I grabbed her hands over the metal barrier that separated us. "Yes, I feel like I am finally becoming part of the family. I wish I could show you; I wish I could have my best friend with me."

Chloe looked down at our hands. "Don't get me wrong, I am so happy for you. Beyond happy, ecstatic even."She looked back up and smiled at me. "I just wish I could experience this with you!"

"I wish so, too, Chloe," I hugged her, the cold metal pressing into my lower belly. This barricade used to be my favorite place in the world, my home. Now, I hated how it separated us. "I promise, I will tell you all about this tour once it's over. And I promise you'll feel like you've experienced all of it yourself." I pulled her closer so I could whisper without anyone hearing my words. "There are things I can't tell you about. And it is really overwhelming and I have no clue how to handle what is happening here. I just hope I can share it with you one day. I love you, paper promise. Okay?"

Chloe nodded. "Okay." She pushed me away and we hooked our fingers together, connecting our paper rings for a short moment, before I stepped away from the barricade.

"Bye girls, I love you! Scream louder for me," I yelled as I stepped away, waving.

The further that I walked away from my best friend, the more guilt developed in my stomach.

Why am I the one experiencing this instead of her?

Sometimes I didn't feel like I earned it. Chloe deserved it just as much.

When I returned to the backstage area, the boys were already positioned at the exit, ready to walk on stage. I grabbed my camera and the band phone from a table in the corner and stood behind them, ready to follow. I was looking forward to the concert, ready to immerse myself in work to clear the fog from my mind.

Marina arrived as Dari was walking on stage. She let her hand brush my lower back when she walked past and stood behind her guitar player. I grinned to myself, knowing that Marina was thinking about undressing me right now.

As Brad ran on stage, I followed closely behind Marina into the shadows of the black stairs. Before I could set up the camera app to film Marina running on stage, I felt her hands around my chin. She placed a kiss on my lips, giving my bottom lip a short suck. The glow inside me lit up like an LED light bulb.

The kiss was short as she turned away and ran upstairs before I could even kiss her back. My fingers traced my own lips for a moment. She had left me startled.

This is more than just sex.

This is more than just experimenting.

The fact that Marina decided to risk everything and kiss me right before she walked on stage felt meaningful.

There were seven thousand people waiting to cheer her on and stare at her in front of that stage; she *still* decided to kiss me here in the shadows.

As the cheering of the crowd rang in my ears and Marina sang the first words of *In the Afterglow,* I remembered why I was there. I pulled up the phone and opened the camera app before I could dwell in my thoughts a second longer. Photographing the woman I was having sex with would at least distract me. I almost tripped as I ran upstairs and found my position in the shadows of the stage.

During the concerts, I focused on Chloe behind the barricade more than Marina on stage. Chloe waved at me multiple times. I zoomed in and snapped a few photos of her, capturing my best friend smiling from ear to ear and bawling her eyes out to an emotional song.

When Marina sang the first words of *fourteen,* Chloe's eyes found mine.

"*At fourteen, we met under summer skies.*"

Marina's warm voice filled the venue.

"*Innocence in our hearts, with stars in our eyes,*" I mouthed, my eyes not letting go of Chloe's.

"*Shared secrets whispered on the schoolyard swings,*" the crowd sang.

"*Becoming friends, tied by invisible strings.*" Chloe's mouth stood still.

"*Paper rings exchanged, promises made.*" My bottom lip quivered as I mouthed the next part.

"*Inseparable souls, our foundation laid.*"

I shook my head, shaking the sadness away. Instead of staying still in my corner, I started swaying back and forth.

"*Through laughter and tears, we found our way.*"

Instead of mouthing the lyrics, I started singing them, opening my mouth wider.

"*At fourteen, we began to sway.*"

The corners of Chloe's mouth bent upward.

"*Fourteen summers, fourteen falls,*" she sang back and dried the tears on her cheeks with the back of her hand.

"*Through it all, we answered the calls.*"

We were singing together.

"*In the echo of our teenage dreams.*"

Suddenly, I was back behind that barricade, jumping, singing and dancing with my best friend.

"*We built a bond, stronger than it seems.*"

Chapter 13
Good Luck, Babe - Chappell Roan

By the time that I got off stage and met Marina in the bathroom, I had to fight to keep my eyelids from drooping closed.

"Gosh, I am so ready to go to sleep," I moaned while Marina left a kiss on my cheek. "This day has felt like a lifetime."

"I hate to disappoint you." She nibbled at my throat. "But." A kiss. "The day is not over yet." A bite.

I moaned at her teeth against the thin skin of my throat. "Oh, what does that mean?" I asked. No matter how tired I was, I would always say yes to some night-time action with the beautiful woman in front of me.

Marina kissed me on the lips, pressing my head against the white wall of the backstage bathrooms. I had been thinking about kissing her every second of that concert. Marina was a drug and I couldn't stop taking her.

She put space between our lips. "Oh, how I wish it was what you're thinking about right now." Her hand cupped my cheek and my head leaned into the touch. "Sadly, we have a signing event happening tonight." Marina closed her eyes in annoyance and her exhausted exhale brushed my skin.

"What do you mean, a '*signing*'?"

How did I not know about this?

Marina let go of my face and turned around so that she could lean against the wall next to me. "Well, exactly what you would expect." Her hand searched for mine, our fingers entangling. "There was some sort of giveaway with a car company and whoever won got a meet and greet slash signing event with the band," she huffed. "So, basically an hour of high-pitched screaming and awkward photos."

I pushed myself off the wall. "Do you not like meeting fans?" I positioned myself in front of Marina, my hips pinning hers. Then I lowered my voice, my face inches from hers. "I mean, you're meeting a fan right now." I might've been acting flirtatious but my insides were churning. Being a fan was an enormous part of my identity, after all.

When you're a young fan, all you think about is the way that your favorite artist might perceive you. Do they know who you are? Did they make eye contact with you during the concert? How can you get their attention?

What can you post for them to like? If you've met them, did they talk to you a little longer? Did you tell the most interesting, most heart-wrenching story? Will they remember you?

In the *Paper Rings and Promises* fandom, it had always been a competition. Everyone fought for attention from the band. If you managed to meet Marina, you had won the first race. If she remembered your name in some way, you were God. No one was ever really happy for the other. Every fan wanted to be better than the others, as if we couldn't exist at the same time. I used to be captured by the fight, even though I was too young to go to every concert or even afford a meet and greet. Chloe and I found ourselves as outsiders until we got tired of it all and ended up as the nostalgic silent fans that caught a concert here and there.

Even though I had removed myself from the attention-seeking part of the fandom years ago, it still used to be a big part of my life. I was actually scared of Marina's answer to the question. Did she really not like meeting fans? Did she hate it? Did she find fans cringe? Does she find fans exhausting?

Does she find me exhausting?

Marina leaned in, catapulting me back to the present. "Well, if all our fans were like you, I'd love meeting them at any time." Her lips touched mine as she talked, making my insides warm up.

How could we ever function around each other if every interaction turned to heat?

Her words didn't feel reassuring. Of course, she liked me right now but I was still part of that group. I wasn't any better than the other fans. "And, in general?" If someone spends hours dreaming about something that the other person dreads, it didn't feel right.

"Do you really think I would be a singer if I didn't like meeting fans?" Her lips moved away a bit, her eyes scanning my face.

I didn't reply.

"I just don't really enjoy spending hours with overly excited teens when I'm hungover and running on five hours of sleep," Marina laughed, rubbing her temples. "I'd also much rather spend that time with you." She laughed softly. "I mean, how am I even supposed to concentrate on the person in front of me if you're photographing me from behind?"

Heat rushed to my cheeks. I was distracting Marina?

"Well, I'm also not looking forward to sharing you with other girls that want to kiss you as much as I do."

"Luckily, you're the only girl who gets to do that." Marina pressed another kiss on my lips, her words sending heat waves through my body.

How could she ever choose me?

"Well, I'm happy about that. " I brushed a lost strand of hair behind her ear.

Marina's lower half pressed into mine. Her arms found their way behind my back. "Good, that means I can keep you as my little secret."

My skin prickled with electricity as our tongues touched with the next kiss.

A make-out session and a few makeup touch ups later, Marina found her spot on a gray, plastic chair behind another big gray table. The other band members were sitting on similar chairs with about a meter of distance between each person. The entrance, organized with two barricades and a security guard, was on Brad's side, making Marina the last stop for each fan. There was also a stack of autograph cards next to Brad. It looked bigger than it was supposed to be, making me feel a wave of exhaustion before the event had even started.

I was leaning against a wall on Marina's side of the table: the perfect spot to snap a hugging photo for the lucky fans. Usually, I would have been excited for the fans that get to have their big moment with the woman of their dreams but all I wanted was to fall asleep in Marina's arms.

My hands clung to the camera dangling from my neck while I stared at Marina. She was wearing a fresh version of her stage outfit, the one that she had put on in the bathroom after I had undressed her. Her hands were folded on the table but her eyes were closed. It seemed like she was bracing herself for the moment to come. Her hair was gelled back in her typical fashion and she looked beautiful. I could make out the way her skin folded underneath her eyes, the little wrinkles that captivated me. She was tired but, even with her eyes closed, she was glowing with a deep energy. I liked to think that she loved what she did, although she wasn't looking forward to this event.

The first person entered the room with a shrill scream.

"Oh my god!" a blonde girl exclaimed as she appeared in front of the security guard who guided her toward Brad. She was about my age and had her hair tied up in space buns. Her eyes were adorned with blue crystals while a short white dress decorated her body. She most definitely hadn't left the concert looking this flawless.

"Hi, what's your name?" Brad asked as he grabbed an autograph card to sign.

"Leila," she mumbled while her gaze fixated on Marina. Even when Brad handed her the card and she was hugged by Dari, her eyes didn't leave Marina.

She had opened her eyes now and waved at the girl; it looked plastic as it settled across her cheeks. I propped up the camera, ready to zoom in and take the one photo Leila would use as her lock screen for the next 3 years.

There was no glow in Marina's eyes when she wrapped her arms around the girl that seemed so fragile that she might crumble under her touch. The hug did not look genuine and I felt the urge to protect Marina from doing things that she didn't want to do.

Does she dislike bodily contact with strangers?
Is it because the girl is obviously into her?
Does she hug her because she thinks she has to?

I always wanted to believe that Marina only hugged fans because she wanted to. She could always say no; shaking a fan's hand was probably enough to send them into a coma already.

The girl's hands were shaking when she took the signed card from Marina. She mumbled a nearly inaudible "thank you" and turned around to leave the room.

Before the next person could make their way to Marina, she turned her head in my direction. The glow returned to her eyes as soon as they found mine. The way she looked at me, almost like she wished that I had been the one hugging her seconds before, made a light bulb inside me illuminate. Her gaze charged me, fueling me with the electricity that my body needed to work.

When the next girl, maybe 15 years old, wrapped her arms around Brad, I stepped closer to Marina. I aimed the camera towards the people two chairs away. As I snapped a photo of their hug, I consciously leaned against Marina's chair, my lower body meeting her upper body.

My camera was still aimed toward the girl and Brad but my eyes darted down to Marina.

Her hand brushed the part of my leg hidden behind her chair. Goosebumps erupted beneath my clothes. My skin burned. I felt like the secret of our touch intensified its effect.

How was I even breathing while standing this close to her and not letting anyone see?

Marina let her hand fall down and I moved back to my position against the wall when the girl made her way to Marina. I wished that I could take my spot on Marina's left instead of being banished to the corner.

The girl was glowing with excitement when she wrapped her arms around Marina. She had shoulder length red hair that was braided down her shoulders. The way that her eyes sparkled reminded me of the way Chloe glowed whenever we talked about Marina.

"Hey, uhm, I'm really nervous," the girl mumbled, stepping from one foot to the other.

Marina seemed more comfortable now. "Oh, sweetheart, no need to be nervous." She grabbed the girl's hand and held it over the table. It almost seemed like she was filling the role of a mother to the little girl. "I'm a person, just like you."

While I wanted to be the one to hold Marina's hand, I felt a deep sense of sympathy for the girl. I smiled behind my camera while I captured their moment.

Marina's dark-nailed fingers were stroking the small pale hand; the girl had black nails just like her. With every stroke of Marina's finger, the girl's breathing seemed to slow. She was hyperventilating about meeting Marina while the same person was calming her down.

I know how you feel.

"What's your name?" Marina asked as the girl stopped shifting her weight from one foot to the other. Something made me feel like Marina would've kept stroking her hand, even if it took her hours to breathe normally again. The way that she cared made my heart flutter. It seemed like she always took care of others, like she wanted to make everyone feel happy, like she wanted to spread warmth on her way. I wanted to be her warmth, her calm and her security. I knew that I could be that for her.

"Cassie, my name is Cassie." Her voice was really high-pitched and every word a flutter of a breath.

Marina nodded slowly, "Hi Cassie." I zoomed in on Marina's dimples. "How old are you?"

"14." Her eyes darted down to their hands and stopped there for a moment. There was something that she was thinking about. I knew that there were words in her mind, a story that she wanted to tell. She'd probably spent countless hours perfecting it but she didn't quite know how to say it now. It was that moment when you finally meet your idol and suddenly every story seemed wrong or meaningless, like everything you have experienced so far was nothing compared to that moment. That was a good thing, wasn't it? A present so mesmerizing that you forget your past.

I knew what the girl thought about when her eyes darted between their hands and Marina's face. She thought about the way that she could make Marina remember her. How she could be different from all the other fans Marina met that night.

Cassie coughed, moving her free hand up to her mouth. "I outed myself in front of my parents today." Suddenly her voice was calm, sharply clear.

Marina just nodded, silence developing between them. She knew that she couldn't quite discuss queer topics with fans, always walking on a tightrope; the fans read things into it that weren't true. She must've heard fans talking about their sexuality and confessing their crush millions of times by now.

Cassie took in a long, slow breath. "You, your music and the fandom gave me the courage to do it." Her free hand was playing with one of her ginger braids now. "My parents didn't react well. The fandom showed me that it does and that it is actually the most normal thing in the world." Her cheeks flushed. "And maybe, *maybe* you were my gay awakening as well."

Marina's eyes shot up, searching for mine. Her face didn't move when she looked at me but there was this dark, golden glow in her eyes again. My body vibrated under that glow.

Why is she looking at me now?

There was a moment of silent understanding between us.

When Marina looked back at the girl, I zoomed the camera out to capture the whole scene. Marina had let go of Cassie's hand. She'd probably let go the moment the word 'gay' was mentioned and something inside me ached for that girl. And maybe it ached for me as well.

Marina smiled at Cassie nonetheless. "Thank you so much for sharing this with me." Her voice sounded generic, almost robotic, as she nodded at the girl. "It was amazing to meet you and I hope I'll see you again someday." She got up from her chair. "Thank you so much for your support." Then Marina leaned over the table to hug Cassie. She squeezed her tight, tighter than she had hugged the other girl. When Marina's face stopped next to Cassie's, her lips moved, like she was whispering something to Cassie, telling her a secret that no one else was allowed to know. I thought about our little secret and crossed my legs while I let myself lean further into the wall. Marina had been my gay awakening at 14 and maybe I was hers just now.

Chapter 14
The Smallest Man Who Ever Lived - Taylor Swift

"You know, I could get used to this." Marina pressed a kiss to my forehead, pulling me against her chest. We were in the back of the bus, lying on Marina's bed; it was about midday of the 5th show. The guys were out setting up their instruments in the next venue. Marina told them I was going to take some solo pictures of her and pulled me straight back into the bus.

"Me too." *I want this every day for the rest of my life.* "I wish the tour could last forever." My arm was wrapped around Marina's upper body, my head resting on her boobs. This had become my favorite position whenever we got to rest together.

Marina made a humming sound.

"You know that I live here in Ulm , right?" I lifted myself up so I could look at her.

"Yes?" There was a crease of concern on her forehead.

I turned my head to the side, scanning Marina's face. "We could, you know…" I started mindlessly tracing her stomach. "Spend the night at my place? We'd finally have a whole night together." My right hand cupped her left boob above her black shirt. A fluffy feeling of hope bloomed inside of me. The thought of touching Marina in my bed sent heat into my cheeks. Taking her home with me meant more than a short tour fling. And that was what I wanted to believe we were.

Marina closed her eyes for a second. "Oh Kari, I don't know if that's a good idea."

The little light bulbs burst into shards of glass, stinging me from the inside. "Why is that?" My voice was shaky; I hated the way that I had lost control. I feared her answer, deep down. Somehow, I knew what she was going to say but that didn't mean that I wanted to hear it.

"I believe this…" She touched the tip of my nose with her finger, then touched her own. "Has to stay on tour. There is just so much I could lose."

So, this will be over in two days?

I would never get to touch her again?

I didn't say anything; my eyes scanned her face, my hands touching her body. I knew that she had things to lose, I knew that our little paradise wasn't eternal. I knew that this was going to end. I just didn't want to believe it. I wanted to spend every single second we still had on tour with her.

Marina looked at me again. There were tears in her eyes, dimming their golden glow. "I..." she exhaled. "I just feel like it's better to keep this thing between us on tour. Like in the bus and in the venues, you know?"

I huffed. "No, I don't know, actually." I didn't want her to brush me away that easily. To limit me to these small spaces. We both knew that we were more than just a 'thing', even though she didn't want to accept it. Her words were hurtful, damaging; they made me angry. "Don't describe this as a 'thing'; we both know it's more than that." I pushed myself away from Marina's body and moved to the corner of the bed.

Everything inside me stung. She spoke the words that I already knew. This was limited; our time together wasn't endless. I just didn't know if I could survive that. And still, ending this in two days didn't mean that we couldn't have a full night together.

"I'm sorry, Kari." Marina brushed her hand through her hair, trying to busy her hands. "It might feel like it's more than a tour thing but it just can't be more than that. Going home with you would be the step that makes it real and I'm not willing to take that step."

I wanted to kiss sanity into her but I looked away. "It's already real for me." The anger in my voice turned into pain, my words stuffed between whimpers.

"Kari, I wish I could give you more and I wish our time was infinite. But it's not so we need to keep

251

boundaries." She pressed a kiss to my forehead. I so deeply wanted to dwell in it but I turned my gaze away. "You understand that, right?"

I brushed off her hand and moved further away. What did she want me to do? Embrace her? Kiss her again? I told her that our connection was real and she pushed me away. There was nothing else that I could do but distance myself. The pain stirred by her words was unexpected; I knew that she couldn't give me more than secret sex… I knew it the whole time. But hearing it out loud crushed me. I didn't want her to tear me to pieces completely; I rose from the bed, even though all that I wanted was to hide in her arms.

"Kari, do you *understand*?" Marina stared at me. "Kari, please." Her voice was desperate. She crawled over the bed in my direction but I turned away.

I nodded. Of course, I understood. That didn't mean that I wanted to accept it. I wasn't the kind of person to overstep boundaries. At least I wanted to believe that I wasn't. I knew that she had so much more to lose than I did; she had a whole life, a family and a career on the line. But I so deeply wanted to fight. Every second with her felt like it was meant to be. I had known it for 8 years and now that I was here, experiencing it, it was more right than ever. Her presence was like sparks flying. Her kisses were like flowers blooming. Every time her fingertips brushed my skin, a part of me healed. Her warmth, her care, her affection, was healing every wound that had come up in the past 8 years. She had kept me afloat back then, kept me swimming and fighting. Now, she was carrying me to the shore in her hands. And still, she let me drown.

"It's time for your sound check," I mumbled and walked away.

As soon as I stepped off the bus, I cried. The cold night air hit my face but I couldn't breathe. I needed to get away. I needed to breathe. Marina wanted to keep me at a distance so I let her; I broke into a sprint, running past the old houses of my own little town.

I could have gone home. My mom was going to leave for a trip in the evening which meant that she would be there for me during the day. Loki would jump on my lap, snuggling in to comfort me. But I couldn't face home. I found myself sprinting through the woods on the outskirts of the city; it was the area where I used to live before we moved away from my father. The image of the woods I would play in made my stomach turn; the pain of the past temporarily masked the pain of the present.

My body slumped onto a piece of wood in front of a lake. Pain shot through my lungs; they felt close to collapsing. My breathing was fast, my eyes fixated on the still water in front of me; the blurriness of my vision took me away from the present.

Instead, I saw a tiny hand with pink nail polish holding a bigger one, almost disappearing in its grip. The big hand led to a tanned muscular arm, dressed in a short-sleeved blue button-down shirt. The arm belonged to a middle-aged man with dark brown hair that was looking down at the owner of the tiny hand. A young girl with shoulder length brown hair beaming as she looked up at him. Her hair was woven into two braids and pink ribbons adorned their ends.

"Daddy, can we fly?" |The little girl's voice chimed in my ears. She held her hands up to her father, jumping up and down.

The man grabbed her by the armpits and turned around in a circle and she giggled in a high-pitched tone.

"I'm flying!" The girl screamed while her father turned faster and faster.

He moved so fast; their features became foggy. Through my eyes, it looked like the little girl's smile turned into a cry, her giggling into screams.

A duck landed on the water and a wave splashed over the image from my past, erasing it.

I shook my head and pushed myself off the wood. A splinter of wood cut my hand and I flinched. The sudden pain sent a sense of clarity through my body.

Stop whining.

I had no right to be upset. I wasn't allowed to have expectations. A feeling of guilt developed in my stomach.

I was the person who made her cheat after all, I was here risking her family with my presence. Marina was doing what was best for her family and her life. I was here to do a job.

My feet carried me back through the streets of my hometown in a jogging motion. Something inside me was excited to go back to photographing. This was my dream career and the thing between Marina and me was not going to jeopardize my chance of doing what I loved most. As long as I could keep my head hidden behind a camera, I didn't have to think about Marina. The lens functioned as a shield; it created the wall between us Marina so desperately wanted to keep intact.

"Kari!" Dari's deep voice stopped me. There was anger in his tone.

I looked around in confusion; I was still far from the venue. Was he looking for me? Was I late? Had I messed up my job now too? My hands instinctively went up to my ponytail, pulling two strands to tighten it.

"Yes?" My voice was weak; there was no way he could overlook that I had been crying.

"I was looking for you." He spoke softer than expected, so I took a step toward him. The corners of his mouth were curved while his eyes fixated on a drop of sweat that ran down the side of my face.

"Am I late?" I asked, my voice now drenched in the fear of messing up.

Is he going to fire me now?
Can he?

"No, don't worry." He took a step toward me. He bit his bottom lip while his eyes found my chest. "We just finished the instrumental sound check. Marina is still on-stage doing vocals."

I took a step back. "Then why were you looking for me?" This situation got weirder by the second. The low glimmer in his eyes made me want to break into a jog again.

Dari took another step forward and his long, dark hair fell into his face, "I just wanted to talk to you about something." His eyes scanned my arms and wandered down my lower body. Another step. "Something serious."

My eyes darted around for a moment. We were alone, far from any main street and about 2 blocks away from the tour bus. 3 steps behind me was a wall.

This is Dari.
The drummer of your favorite band.
Why are you even thinking about this?

"What is it?"

"I know that there is something going on between you and Marina." His voice was lower than usual as he took another step.

Instead of taking a step back, I took one toward him. "What do you mean?"

Dari let out a chuckle that sent a painful shiver down my back. "Kari." He walked toward me. I walked backwards. "We both know that there is something going on there."

My back met the wall.

I shook my head, the smile turning into fear. "There is nothing going on there."

Dari's right hand found the wall behind me. I felt his alcohol breath on my cheek and wanted to puke. He leaned forward, his long, greasy hair meeting my cheek. "I'm just worried about her."

I pressed my body into the wall; it was hard and cold against my back. A piece of loose brick pierced through my shirt. "Dari, can you please step back? You're really close," I mumbled. My eyes were focused on the floor; I couldn't look at him.

"But I gotta make sure that nothing happens to my best friend." He soaked in a deep breath. "I gotta make sure you stay away from her." He put his right hand on my cheek. His skin was so rough; it felt like it was cutting mine. "If this comes out, it'll affect my career as well, you know?"

"You don't have to worry." I turned my face away but his hand grabbed my chin, keeping me in place. "Dari, please. It's over. We ended it today."

He moved his lips to my face. The smell of beer and vodka dizzied my whole brain. I felt my breakfast coming up the back of my throat. "Well, maybe I want a taste of your little secret."

He pressed his dry lips against my cheek. I froze. I wanted to scream and kick and cry. I wanted to run away as far as I could. But I didn't move. When he moved his lips, my whole world was crumbling to pieces. This man was part of the band that raised me. The big teddy bear that always looked weird in photos with fans. I aspired to be part of their little band family, wanted to be his sister, maybe even his daughter. The big little teddy bear I always wanted to hug was now pressing me against a cold brick wall, paralyzing me in fear.

"Dari!" The sound of Docs on a stone floor rang through the alley. "Stop!"

Dari's lips froze on my skin then distanced themselves. He took a step back. His expression was somewhere between shock and fear, all lust vanished.

Marina appeared in my vision. She pushed Dari to the side, fury glowing in her eyes. "Leave." Dari was still frozen. "Now," she hissed. Her face turned toward him; her head nodded toward the end of the alley.

Marina waited until Dari disappeared around the corner before she turned back to look at me. The fury in her eyes was replaced with worry.

"Kari? Are you okay?"

My eyes stung at her words. She looked at me with so much care and compassion; it almost felt wrong after what had just happened.

When I didn't respond, Marina took a step toward me, "I'm so sorry this happened to you."

I didn't react; I was still frozen in the position Dari had left me in. Marina's features blurred in front of me and my breath got stuck in my throat. I was paralyzed. I couldn't move. I couldn't even see Marina in front of me. It felt like my body wasn't mine anymore, like I was watching from the outside.

"Kari? Are you okay?" Marina's voice echoed through my brain, bouncing off the walls of my skull.

Was I still breathing?

My eyes searched for Marina, trying to focus but finding nothing but shadows and clouds. I started breathing again but it was too fast. I panicked.

Marina was closer now; I could feel her presence. "Can I touch you?" she asked.

I wanted to scream yes, tell her she should squeeze me as tight as possible, bring me back into my body. I told my head to nod with every clear thought that I could still form.

Marina's soft hands slid around my back and pulled me away from the wall. She hugged me so tight that I thought that I'd disappear in her arms; I could delve into her and never return. Every inch of my body was hyper aware of her touch.

"Focus on me," Marina said in a calm voice.

I concentrated on the pressure her body applied to mine. I counted the times her hand moved up and down my back until I broke down.

Marina held me while I cried and the scent of lavender slowly erased the poisonous smell that Dari had left on my skin. Floods of tears ran down my cheeks and wetted Marina's white t-shirt, leaving traces of mascara behind.

This must be her stage outfit.

I wanted to push her away and apologize. Instead, Marina held me even tighter and I melted into her. My breathing slowly matched the pace of her hand stroking my back. It didn't stop moving until my cheeks dried and my breathing normalized.

"I ruined your stage fit," I mumbled into her shoulder as soon as my voice came back to me.

"Doesn't matter." Her voice was soothing, like warm tea.

"But you need to wear that tonight." My voice was steady now. "Aren't we late already?"

Now, Marina moved her body away from me. She held onto my shoulders and scanned my face. "I have enough outfits to wear but there's only one Kari."

I knew that I should push Marina away and walk away from this job, from this band, and never look back. I *knew* that I should. But all I wanted was to crawl deeper into her arms and never let go.

"Let's sit down, okay?" Marina pointed at the sidewalk. "There's no rush, sweetheart. We're not going back before I'm sure you're okay." She sat me down and kneeled in front of me, her hands cupping mine in my lap. "Are you okay physically?" Marina scanned my body from my feet up. "Did he hurt you?"

I shook my head. "I think I'm alright."

"Sure?"

I nodded.

"And how are you feeling?" Her eyes found mine, sending warmth through me.

I lifted my shoulders; they felt stiff. "I don't know."

Cold? Dead? Disappointed?

"Weird?"

Marina nodded. "That's okay. You don't have to know. There's nothing you have to be or feel right now." She touched my cheek for a second; I wanted her to cup it and kiss me. "Is there anything I can do for you right now?

Distract me. Kiss me.

"I don't think so. I'll be fine, I think."

"You sure?"

I looked to the side. "Well, you could kiss me..." The words flew over my lips before I could stop myself. This went against everything that had happened just hours before. We shouldn't. But her kiss was the only thing that could make me feel better.

"I'm sorry, Kari." She took her hands away from mine, looking away from me. "That can't happen anymore. You experienced the danger it brings. Dari's a jerk. He used to be family but the alcohol and drugs have changed him. He's been acting out lately, an anger inside him I can't fully grasp. That's no excuse, at all," she grunted, meeting my gaze again. "His actions definitely just risked his participation in the band. I want to believe he won't tell anyone but if he knows, *anyone* could. If he found out, others will too."

There was nothing for me to lose at this point. "Then why do I feel like kissing you is the only thing that can make me feel like myself right now?"

Marina's expression filled with pain. "I wish I could give you what you deserve." She looked at my lips as she spoke, like she was thinking about it too.

"Everything you've already given me is more than I could've imagined," I mumbled. "You've made my wildest dreams come true these past days."

Marina shook her head, her forehead crinkling. "Stop saying things like that, Kari. I didn't give you anything. I used you. I used the way you worship me to make myself feel better. You uplifted me, Kari. You gave me a chance to experiment, do the things that have been lingering on my mind for years. You were there, ready. And I took advantage of that." Marina put her hand on my chin, lifting my head to look at her. "I'm so sorry I did this to you. You are an incredible person. You are *mesmerizing*. You deserve someone who can love you with all they have, someone with the capacity to worship you the way you did me." She slowly pulled my face toward hers. "I want to kiss your lips as much as you want to kiss mine but I will never do it again. Nothing can ever happen between us again."

I stared at her for a moment. She hadn't said anything that I didn't already know. She'd used me from the start; I was some kind of toy to her, that was all. This whole band had never been as amazing as I had made it out to be; they had gotten me through my youth but maybe I had to let them go now that I was an adult.

"Kari, please say something." Marina's voice tried to lure me back in like a drug.

"You're right," I said, looking off into the distance. "There's nothing more I can say to that."

"I understand if you don't want to continue the internship." She sounded weak, almost like she was scared of my response. "Dari won't be an issue again; I promise I'll take care of it." She scanned my face. There was pain in her eyes; she felt guilty. "I promise there will be consequences for his actions." "You know I love your work and I don't want to lose you. Your posts have been the best our profiles have ever seen, and your photos are magical!"

Her compliments barely reached me.

Is this the end of my dream?

"Do you want me to leave?" I knew that she'd said something different but I needed to hear her answer, nonetheless.

"Oh my god, no. Kari, of course I don't want you to leave." Marina shook her head aggressively. "Yes, you might be a temptation and we have to keep our distance. But, as I said, you're doing an incredible job. Promise me you'll never stop working in the field. Promise me you'll go after those great dreams of yours. You deserve it."

I wanted to smile but I couldn't. Instead, I just nodded, "I don't want to stop working for you. It's the first time I have ever felt passionate about my work."

"But please promise me you'll go home once we leave this alley. Take tonight off and talk to someone. You're not working tonight." Her words were heavy with concern.

Anger rose inside of me. Why was she making decisions for me now? Did she think I couldn't measure my abilities for myself? I had been looking forward to work all day; I didn't want to go home and be left alone with all those thoughts without a camera to distract me.

"Promise me, please." Marina was almost begging now. I didn't quite understand why she wanted me to stay away tonight so badly.

Of course, facing Dari again was a horrible thought and I didn't know if he would threaten me. But the thought of zooming in on Marina's features on stage instantly made me feel better.

"I promise," I said, my eyes completely zoned out.

"Great." Marina let go of my face; I instantly felt the absence of her skin on mine. "Are you ready to go?

No.

"Yes." I did *want* to leave. If I had spent another second inhaling Marina's smell, I didn't know if I would ever be able to walk away.

Marina pushed herself up from the ground and held out her hand. I wanted to pull her back down toward me, wrap my arms around her and undress her right here in this alley. Instead, I let her pull me up to a standing position.

"Are you sure you're ready to go?" Marina asked. "Is there anything you still need to get from the bus?"

"Yes and no." I had a million things on the bus but my phone was resting in the back pocket of my pants and that was all that I needed right now. The thought of going back to the bus and seeing Dari again sent shivers down my spine.

Marina nodded and pulled me toward the end of the alley. She didn't let go as we walked. "Do I need to walk you home?"

I shook my head, even when the thought of walking alone scared me to the bone. "I'll be fine; it's not far. Go back to the bus and get ready for the show; it's gonna be great. Don't worry about me." At the end of the alley, I put some distance between us. "I'll see you tomorrow evening."

Marina stopped walking and nodded. She didn't seem like she was ready to walk away. She grabbed my shoulder and stopped me as I was about to turn away. "Please text your friends. Talk to someone, okay?"

I nodded, brushed off her hand and walked in the opposite direction of the tour bus.

Chapter 15
Begin - Lauren Sanderson

Kari 5:36 pm
I need you.

Chloe 5:36 pm
Where are you?

Kari 5:36 pm
Home.

15 minutes later, the doorbell rang. I pushed Loki aside and walked towards the door. My hand rested on the handle for a moment longer than it needed to. Opening that door to my best friend meant telling her what had happened. Speaking about it meant it was real. A sense of guilt rose in the deepest pit of my stomach. Chloe and I had been fantasizing about Marina together since we were teens. Now, I had actually seen Marina

from another side, I had started falling for her without telling Chloe.

I opened the door. As soon as Chloe's ocean blue eyes met mine, I choked. I started crying. Before I could break down in the doorway, she caught me. She *always* caught me.

Chloe dragged me toward my bed, placed me on my mattress, and walked out of the room. Seconds later, she returned with a glass of water. When she handed it to me, I drank a sip and coughed.

Chloe didn't hug me but found her space next to me on the mattress to sit down. All she did was sit next to me until my eyes dried and I breathed normally again.

When I turned to look at my best friend, she was lying on her side. "I knew it!"

"What?" I knew what she was talking about.

"I knew that there was a lot more going on between you and Marina. A hell of a lot more."

I lifted my hands to my face to hide a blush. "Maybe," I said.

Chloe pinched my side. "Maybe *what*?"

"Maybe we kissed," I spoke.

Chloe's eyes opened wide. "You *kissed*?"

Heat flew into my cheeks. "We didn't *just* kiss."

"Kari, what does that mean?" Chloe's eyes would explode any second now. I was sure of that.

"We, um…"

"You fucked?" Now her mouth was open so wide that it could've held a tennis ball. "You fucked the hottest MILF on the planet?"

"Chloe! She's so much more than just a hot MILF," suddenly, I felt bad for always reducing Marina to her body. She was so much more than that. Still, I chuckled, "But yeah, I guess so," I said and raised my shoulders as if I hadn't just dropped the biggest news-bomb ever.

Chloe sat up on my bed. "You *guess* so?" Her hands clung to the sheets beneath her.

"Well, yes, I *did* have sex with the most gorgeous woman on the planet." My cheeks were warm at the thought. "Please don't be mad that I didn't tell you."

"Of course, I would've liked to receive a call right after it happened, just to scream and freak out with you. But I could never be mad at you. You just broke down crying, for God's sake."

"Thank you."

Loki jumped onto the bed and pressed his head against my hand.

"The only thing I'm slightly mad about is the fact that you didn't let me be there for you before this. It seems like it didn't just start going downhill today. I hate that you had to go through that alone."

The concern in Chloe's expression made my cheeks cool. She was here for a reason and there was so much more to the story that I still had to explain. I wished that I could just talk about the sex for hours but Marina had made me promise to tell someone about the things that happened today. I wasn't ready to see the light leave Chloe's eyes when she heard what our big teddy bear had done. This band had raised us. Realizing that one of its members was a monster took a piece of me that I would never get back; I didn't want Chloe to experience the same thing.

"Based on your face and the fact that you were here alone, I can tell that Marina wasn't into it for forever. But, knowing you, you would have never left the job because of that." She cuddled Loki for a second before she looked back at me. "So, what actually happened, Kari?"

I couldn't look at her; my eyes focused on a dark spot on the wall behind her. It looked like some nail polish had splattered there years ago. I scanned every corner of it as I talked.

"I ran away when Marina told me she couldn't come home with me tonight. I knew we couldn't see each other outside of this tour; it would be too dangerous for her. But, that doesn't mean I wanted to hear it. So, I ran."

There was a second spot next to the big one. It was tiny but looked like a little heart. It almost looked like Marina's birthmark. The one that I would never see again.

"When I was on the way back, Dari cornered me." I soaked in a deep breath. Even just saying his name made me feel sick.

Chloe's expression was frozen. I couldn't tell if she was sad or mad. Just frozen. She had stopped petting Loki too.

"We were in an alley away from the main street. He said he knew what had happened between Marina and me and that I had to stay away from her. I promised him I would but he pushed me..." My voice broke. I couldn't keep going but Chloe's expression said that I didn't have to.

She was somewhere between fear and pain. The last time that I had seen her eyes this pained was the time when she came back from Innsbruck. I could see her heart breaking in the blue of her eyes.

"Fuck," was the only word that left her lips.

Neither of us spoke for a moment. Chloe probably didn't want to hear more yet either; I gave her some time to digest.

"I can't believe he did that," Chloe said, a few moments later.

"I still refuse to believe that this has happened." I bit my lip, thinking back. "Marina stopped him before he could harm me." I knew that her brain was going to painful places; I couldn't think about the 'what-if'.

"But he wanted to," Chloe said, still staring into the distance.

"Yes," I answered. "I can still feel his alcohol breath on my skin."

Chloe's expression shifted from shock to anger. "Did Marina tell you if he's ever done anything like this before?"

I shook my head.

"How is he even allowed to be in the position he's in? He's an idol for so many people for fuck's sake." Her right hand was balled into a fist. "Are they going to kick him out?"

"I don't know." I stroked Loki's head, his fur created a calming sensation beneath my fingertips.

Chloe hit the pillow beneath her hand. "That's not fair," she grunted. "He needs to go to prison or something."

I nodded. I didn't know if I wanted Dari to face full legal consequences; kicking him out of the band would probably be punishment enough.

"I know," I said calmly. "I'm sure Marina will find a way to make him pay for what he did." I *wasn't* sure.

Chloe looked back at me. "Are you okay, though?"

"No but I will be." I pulled my ponytail tighter. "Can we do something that has nothing to do with this band, please?" There was no way I would've survived work that night so I'd decided to take Marina's offer and stay home for at least one concert; there was another one the next day, anyway.

"Of course, we can." Chloe slid over to the side of the bed. "What about a *Pitch Perfect* marathon?"

Before I could formulate an answer, Chloe had already thrown my iPad onto the bed. I opened up the first movie and clicked play.

We were on the third movie, had downed a bottle of wine and eaten a pizza, when the doorbell rang.

"Expecting anyone?" Chloe mumbled. Her head was resting on a pillow, her eyes halfway closed.

I shook my head. "You and Marina are the only people that know I'm home." As soon as I said the words out loud, I knew exactly who was awaiting me behind my front door.

Chloe seemed to have realized the same thing because a sheepish grin developed on her lips. "Well, I think *I* know who it is."

She said it like it was a good thing but could it really be good to see Marina after everything that had happened?

Maybe it was the wine running through Chloe's system that made her smile. "If she decided to come here after the show, I doubt it's to tell you that you need to stay away," Chloe sat up on the bed. "She could've said that via text." She grabbed her phone and jumped off the bed, wandering towards the door. "This is either a love confession or a booty call. I guess I can sleep in your mom's room, right?"

I stared at Chloe in shock while the doorbell rang a second time. Every sane cell in my body told me not to open the door. But every blood cell rushing through my veins wanted me to believe Chloe's words. I had just started to accept that I would never get to touch Marina again, that we would go back to being 'fan' and 'singer'. And still, my heart was beating heavily with hope.

"I'll open the door if you don't do it right now! We both *knew* she wouldn't let you go like that." Chloe walked out of the room and into the hallway.

I shook my head and walked after her. Chloe had already opened the door before I could reach her. Her expression was unreadable when she saw the person on the other side. My heart fell to the pit of my stomach. Wouldn't she be *excited* if she was looking at Marina? This would be her first time meeting her idol, after all.

"She's in her room. Down the hallway," Chloe instructed them and nodded toward me. "Don't break her."

I took a few steps backward, then turned around quickly, stepping back into my room. I found a seat on my mattress and awaited the other person. Based on Chloe's last words, I knew it was Marina. That didn't mean I wanted to believe it, though. The fact that Chloe managed to stay calm and give her the cold shoulder made me proud.

I could hear the familiar sound of Docs against a wooden floor in front of my door. She stopped. I didn't think that my heart had ever beaten that fast before.

"Can I come in?" Marina's voice was soft and weak. She sounded like she had been crying. And she was nervous, *very* nervous.

I wanted to scream yes but nothing came out of my mouth. I'd lost my voice. My heart was beating in my throat, readying itself to jump right out. I knew that Marina wouldn't enter without my permission but maybe the wall between us was exactly what we needed. As long as I was standing in my own room and she wasn't, there was more power on my side.

"Kari, please," Her voice was close to breaking but I didn't budge.

A sudden wave of control rushed over me. "I don't know if I should say yes." I was suddenly sure that she shouldn't cross that threshold unless she was here to tell me she wanted me. If she wasn't going to say that she wanted to see me after the tour, she would never be more than my boss again.

"I'm so sorry for everything that happened today," Marina said. There was a thumping sound on the other side as she let herself fall against the wall next to the door.

"I know you are." I walked over to my side of the wall and sat down. The door was still ajar next to me. I was either going insane or I could make out the smell of lavender coming from the other side.

"Nothing will ever excuse the things that happened or the pain I caused you." Marina's voice was a lot stronger now, like she had practiced these words. "But, when I got on stage today, I couldn't stop looking for your eyes."

I was quiet now. I had nothing to say. Still, everything inside me was electrified. I pressed my ear against the wall, not wanting to miss a single word.

"When I sang "*in the afterglow*", I could only picture your body. And when I sang "*paper hearts*", my chest stung with the need to see you." Her words almost sounded like poetry. "When I left the stage to get ready for the encore, tears ran down my cheeks. I thought I couldn't breathe because you weren't there." I could hear her heave. "The crowd had to cheer for 10 minutes before I came back onstage." She moved on the other side and, a moment later, her hand appeared in the doorframe. "Kari,

I'm a zombie without you. I don't feel alive without you," she sniffed. "Will you take my hand? I won't let go, I promise."

There were so many doubts still knocking on the walls of my head.

How would it work?

Were we still hiding?

Were we telling the world about it?

Was she risking her family?

Did I even want that?

Do I want her to risk it all just for me?

Of course, I didn't want her to lose it all because of me. I didn't even know if taking her hand meant exactly that. But a person only had a limited amount of restraint. Every cell of my body nudged me toward her. I wanted to give in and let her hold me.

"Please, Kari. I want you." Her voice was so soft, so raw.

My hand grabbed hers before I could form another thought. A wave of electricity rushed through my body; little bees hummed in my stomach. A single touch had made me feel like I was exploding and it was everything that I wanted to feel for the rest of my life. She couldn't breathe without me and I wasn't sure I could ever breathe without her. She had been my air since I was 14.

"You mesmerize me, Kari. You made me feel alive for the first time in a long time. You're turning paper into gold. Shiny and real. You are everything. Every song I have ever sung was about you and every song I'll ever sing will be about you. I want you every day. Not just on tour but every day that is to come. I don't know how that will work; I don't know how that will look. I know it won't be easy but I know it's what I want." She squeezed my hand and it was like it wrapped right around my heart. "Can I please come in now?"

My heart glowed golden inside my chest so bright that it made my whole body feel warm and glowy. I tugged at her hand to signal for her to come in. I didn't trust my voice anymore and I couldn't stand up without falling back to my knees.

Marina pushed the door aside slowly. Her hand didn't let go of mine. Her beautiful golden eyes appeared in my doorway and every second of the day was forgotten.

The gold in her eyes was brighter than ever, "I want you, Kari."

"I want you too, Marina," I whispered; my voice was barely audible.

She pushed the door open even further and crawled into the room on her knees; her hand still held mine. Once she was inside, she pushed the door closed and sat on her legs, glowing at me. "Please tell me I can kiss you now."

I nodded so hard that I thought my head might fall off.

Not even a second later, Marina's free hand was on the back of my head, pulling me toward her. When our lips touched, it was more. Our kiss was deeper than before. There were words said between our lips we couldn't say out loud.

I needed her closer. I needed her skin on mine. I needed to crawl into her skin. I wanted to hide under her body, never having to face reality again.

When Marina's lips became wilder, needier, I pushed her away, "can we, uhm... just cuddle?" I looked to the ground. *Will this be enough for her?*

Marina put her fingertips beneath my chin and lifted my head to look up at her, "of course. There's nothing I'd like more than that, sweetheart." She pushed herself off the ground and held her hand out to me.

I took it and Marina guided me toward my own bed. She stopped and turned back around. "Do you have a t-shirt for me? I didn't bring anything" she asked.

"Of course," I grinned, and walked over to my closet. I found an old oversized *Paper Rings and Promises* t-shirt. This was exactly what I wanted to see on her.

When I handed it to her, Marina chuckled, "it's been forever since I've worn one of these."

I grabbed a t-shirt for myself, as Marina took off her stage outfit. As I turned back around, she was sitting on the corner of my bed, dressed in my t-shirt only, no bra. She was still one of the most gorgeous human beings I had ever seen.

My feet carried me to her faster than ever. I giggled, as I threw myself into her arms and pushed her onto the mattress. Her arms wrapped around me as my body united with hers.

In some way, this moment was the start of something new, like we were beginning again; everything that had happened in the days before disappeared. We were just two women, excited for each other, excited for a future together.

Gentle.

Romantic.

Excited to be in love.

My head rested on her boobs, as Marina stroked my back in slow, loving motions.

"How are you feeling now, baby?" Marina asked.

"Better now that you're here, of course. But I'm not sure how to feel. This has all been a lot. I want to be happy, but there are still images of Dari flashing through my mind. I thought I'd known him. I know I didn't, but he's been some sort of role model since I was fourteen."

Marina's hand now caressed my neck. Every stroke calmed me, grounded me. "You're allowed to not be

280

okay. I don't want to say that I get you, because I don't know how you must feel. But, I've known Dari for so long. I've seen him crumble, but of course I would've never thought he'd do such a horrible thing."

"I know, he used to be your family," I said. "How did you find us, by the way?"

"Brad told me he was worried about Dari, that he'd been saying weird things. He's never said anything like this ever before. He told me the direction Dari walked in, so I went out to search for him and found you two," Marina's voice was weak, like she was about to cry. "I don't want to think about what would've happened if I didn't."

"I don't either. I'm trying everything I can not to let my head wander there."

Marina stroked my cheek, "whenever it does, I'll be here." She pressed a kiss on my hairline.

She'll be here.

A promise.

We lay in silence for a while; Marina didn't stop caressing my back.

"How do you feel about your family now?" I asked into the silence, and lifted my head to look up at Marina.

"I don't know, to be honest. I know that the divorce is long overdue. Even without meeting you, it would've happened sooner or later. Now, I'm grateful that I don't have to do this alone."

"What about Joni?"

Marina took a moment to answer, like she wasn't sure what to say. "I'm worried about her. I really am. But she's such a smart girl. I know that she'll understand. And I think she has sensed it already. She knows that her dad and I aren't happy anymore."

"She sounds like such a wonderful girl. I can't wait to meet her."

"I think she'll like you," Marina said and kissed my cheek.

I let my head rest back on her chest. We didn't say another thing.

As Marina's breathing slowed, I looked up at the woman of my dreams, sleeping in my bed.

"I love you," I whispered, so quietly that it could've been my thoughts. "I've loved you since I was 14."

The next morning I was woken by a kiss on my forehead. "Good morning, sleepyhead! You look so cute when you sleep, it makes me want to eat you," Marina giggled.

"Hmm, you eating me doesn't sound that bad to me," I took Marina's face in my hands and pulled her toward me.

"Well, I guess I can do that then," Marian rolled her body onto mine and kissed me.

Her kiss was soft at first. The needy sensation between my legs made me pull her closer, and my tongues slipped into her mouth. I was ready now. I wanted her. Dari left my mind completely for a moment.

Every movement of our lips was pushing me to explode. Every action of the past day had placed a little bomb inside my stomach. Now they were all exploding in bright fireworks.

"May I take my shirt off of you?" I asked, as we parted for air.

"Please," Marina said. Her voice almost had a begging undertone. It was obvious that she was starving. There was no sense of hesitation on her face. All the doubts that had glistened in her eyes in the past were gone. She was ready for me, more than ever before.

I sat up, and pushed the blanket away. Marina was breathing fast, her eyes always searching for mine. She lifted her arms. I was moving too slow for her taste. Neither of us had to say a word. I enjoyed making her wait. She had given the power over to me.

I pressed another kiss on her lips as she grappled for more. I cupped her boobs over the shirt. Her nipples

283

hardened at my touch, even through the thin fabric. She soaked in a sharp breath.

Please, never let this stop.

My hands found her waist, then the hem of my shirt. I pulled it over her head and threw it to the ground. The sight of her beautiful boobs was revealed. My eyes spotted the little heart-shaped birthmark on her right one and I placed a kiss on it.

Please, let me kiss this heart every single day from now on.

Everything inside me sizzled with anticipation for her. She was majestic, the most beautiful person in the world. And she wanted me. She wanted me so badly, her breath caught in her throat when my lips touched her nipple. I didn't even have to suck or bite; the mere contact of my lips and her skin made her choke.

She moved closer and pressed her upper body against my lips so I bit and sucked. She moaned and her sounds were the most beautiful tune I had ever heard. We were finally alone and she released a moan for every single sigh she had held back before. When my other hand met her left nipple and twisted, she gasped. For the first time, she wasn't holding back, and every part of her being seemed ready.

Marina grabbed my face and pushed it a few centimeters away from her body so that she could look at me. "I want to feel you." She tugged at my oversized t-shirt and pressed a kiss to my hairline.

I pulled my shirt over my head, this time without resistance or second thoughts.

Marina scanned my upper body and grinned. She licked her bottom lip before she pulled me down to press my upper body against hers. I gasped at the sudden contact of skin on skin. I was burning, my ribs bursting open in flames. And still, I wanted to get even closer and welcome her body into my ribs. I wanted to melt into her, melt into one being. My hands grabbed her back and my fingernails dug into her skin, trying to pull her closer. She answered my pull by rolling me over to be on top.

My back hits the mattress, Marina's upper body still pressing into mine. The sudden pressure of her body on mine sent an electric shockwave through my body. My middle throbbed. Every cell of my body pulsated with need for her. I needed more, wanted her inside of me. Her lips found my throat and placed kisses down my chin and beneath my ear. She found a spot above my collarbone. She bit and sucked, knowing damn well that it would leave a mark.

She's claiming me.

That's what I wanted to believe, at least. I wanted to believe that she was so sure that she'd let me tell people that her lips had left that dark spot on my throat. We both knew that my body had been hers long before this moment but I wanted her to want it.

She won't throw me away again, once she's claimed me as hers.

A slight pinching pain developed from the spot on my throat, sending heat waves down my body.

"More," Marina whispered into my ear before I could formulate my needs myself. She pressed a kiss on my lips and pushed herself up to a sitting position.

She looked at my green, sheer underwear, her tongue gliding along her bottom lip. The tip of her index finger grazed the seam, her black nail gliding along the soft fabric. My hips pushed toward Marina's hand as I took in a sharp breath. The simple touch sent waves of pleasure through my body. The tiny bit of fabric between my legs was soaked. I wanted her fingers on me, inside of me. She pulled the seam of my underwear and let it snap back against my skin. I answered by pushing my hips even higher.

"You are so gorgeous," Marina whispered. "The most beautiful human I've ever seen." She bent forward, her lips almost meeting mine as she talked. "I wish I would've realized that sooner."

"I want to touch you every day for the rest of my life."

When I stretched my neck to kiss her, she moved her head away. I made a weird, desperate sound. Marina placed a kiss on my chin instead and gave my pussy a push with her right hand.

"Please," I winced.

The glow from Marina's eyes lit up her whole face. She was one big golden glow when she looked at me. "Be patient; give me some time to devour you first." She kissed down my throat, biting, before she kissed my collarbone and between my boobs. My heart skipped a beat with every single kiss. Marina was now looking at me the way that I looked at her. She was kissing me the way that I kissed her. I was her awakening now, just as she'd been mine all those years before.

She kissed downward, even placing one on my belly button, before her lips touched my underwear. I propped myself up on my elbows so that I could see her; her dark hair was falling across her face which was completely focused on the lower part of my belly. Her hands grabbed my waist. I loved the way her black nails and silver rings looked against my tanned skin. Her teeth tugged at the seam of my underwear before she looked back up.

"May I?" she hummed.

"Yes." My voice was weak, needy. Her finger tugged at my panties and I felt the cold of her silver ring against my skin. My hips pushed upward again and I took in a sharp breath. "Please." I was stronger now, demanding instead of begging.

"Your wish is my command." I felt every word of hers on my skin, her lips so close that I wanted to scream.

"Now," I whispered, surprised that I could still form words.

Marina's fingers slid beneath my panties and pulled them all the way down to my knees in one rushed motion.

I watched Marina as she lifted each of my feet to pull my underwear off and throw it to the ground of my bedroom. Her eyes were still glowing and the space between her eyes folded into layers of wrinkles. The morning light illuminated her face in a way that made the few freckles on her nose and cheeks visible. She was as mesmerizing as always. The space between my legs sent pulses through my body and I thought that I'd stop breathing if she didn't touch me right now.

"There is no need to rush this time," Marina said in a warm voice. She placed a soft kiss on my clit before she moved off the bed. "That means we can both take our clothes off," she laughed and got up.

Before she could pull down her Calvin Klein cotton panties, I sat up and grabbed her waist.

My lips found her ear easily. "This is my honor." I grabbed the straps of her panties and pulled them down. Marina kicked them off her feet, her cheeks blushing with happiness.

The next second, I squeezed her cheeks even tighter, pulling her toward me. The feeling of her soft skin, the little bumps of stretch marks, the artwork beneath my fingertips, made everything inside me flutter. She was an artwork, drawn by years on stage. Everything about her was soothing to me and exciting at the same time.

Marina crawled onto the bed, stopping above me on all fours. One of her knees was between my legs; its presence made me shudder, even when it wasn't touching me yet.

Gosh, this woman.

She was making me suffer, making me wait.

The audacity.

She'd made me wait for long enough. I bent my own leg and let my knee shoot up, pressing it into the space between hers.

Marina gasped. "Kari!"

This was the first time that she'd said my name during sex and it was probably the most beautiful word that I'd ever heard. She said *my* name, in *my* house, in *my* bed. She was here, in my life. I shifted my leg so that the pressure of my knee was right on her clit.

"Fuck," she sighed. Here she was, swearing in my house, the most gorgeous woman on the planet.

So, she is a talker?

Everything inside me smiled; the corners of my mouth couldn't go up far enough.

I stretched my neck to whisper into her ear. "Never thought that I'd hear you swear inside of my room but it might be the sexiest thing ever."

Marina pushed back with her own knee now.

"Fuck!" I swore.

"So, you didn't make up scenarios about this? Dream about this while staring at those giant posters of me?" Marina whispered and nodded towards my walls, without ever releasing an ounce of pressure.

"Oh, I dreamed about even wilder things." I tried to be sneaky, flirty, but my voice was barely a whisper, lost in the tension of my body.

Marina removed her leg, crawled backwards, and stopped with her head between my legs. She kissed the inside of both of my thighs, sucked for a millisecond. I moaned.

She looked up at me. "Let's make all your delusions come true." Her voice was loud and steady, sure, and the warmth of her breath stroked my clit as she talked.

The next moment, her head sank between my legs. Her tongue licked through my slit and my body answered with a shiver. She licked another time, sending a flame rushing from deep in my stomach up to my throat. Marina was burning me from the inside with her tongue alone.

When I pushed my hips into her face, her lips settled above my clit. She kissed and I moaned. She sucked and I burned. She bit and I screamed. I was burning all the way to my fingertips and down to my toes. My skin prickled, tensed, tingled.

"This…" My heart beat so fast I thought it'd jump out of my chest. "Is…" My words were hushed breaths. "Amazing."

Marina's mouth moved even faster, her lips sucking while her tongue danced. It slid down and inside of me, then back up to circle around my clit; every movement sent another electric shockwave through me.

Marina's hands wandered beneath my bum to lift me up a bit further, deepening the way that her mouth and tongue were able to move. I needed to come, it needed to happen right now. The tingles, the waves, the electricity, made me shiver and lunge upward uncontrollably.

"Marina," I moaned. "More."

Her nails dug into my skin. She kissed my clit, sucking harder and longer than before. Every second that she sucked, she stoked the fire inside of me, pushing me higher into the sky. The moment that her lips let go of my most sacred part, I fell from the sky.

I collapsed.

I screamed, I gasped, I shivered and I *burned.*

My body moved in uncontrollable motions, jiggling with pleasure until I hit the ground and found myself gasping for air.

Marina crawled up my body. She kissed me and I tasted myself on her lips. She let her body rest on mine, comforting me with warmth and pleasure while I regained conscience. The bees slowly calmed and hummed comfortably through the warmth and pressure of Marina's body on mine.

Her face was buried in my neck and my hands found the back of her head, combing through her hair. It didn't take long until my breathing returned to normal and I wanted to touch her, give back to her. But there was nothing that I wanted more than to feel her breathing on my neck and her arm wrapped around me. This was so much closer, so much more intimate, than we had been any of the times before.

I was so used to being the one that pleased others, that touched others, made others come. And when I did, they usually left. If I got them high enough, soaring above me, they flew away. Even if they wanted more and I let them in, they left because I got "too much", just like Tate had done. I feared that Marina would do the same. She knew me now; she'd seen every part of me. I'd let her into my life.

What if she realized that I wasn't enough if I made her come now?

Marina made humming sounds while I massaged her back for a moment.

"I could get used to this," I said and placed a kiss on Marina's hairline.

Can we stay in this position forever?

"I don't think I'll get used to this," Marina mumbled. "In a good way."

"I want to touch you right now." I was surprised by the calm in my voice. "But I'm afraid you'll leave if I let you go."

Marina propped herself on her hands under her chin so that she could look at me from below. "Sweetheart, I'm right here. I'm not leaving." Her voice was so soft, so soothing. I wanted to record it, bottle it up and listen to it whenever I was anxious. "Why would you think that?"

"It's because I'm so used to *giving*. I'm always the one to touch and never the one to receive. Usually because I don't *let* people touch me. I don't like to show people my insecurities. Those things always stayed temporary in some way. Once I pleased the girls, they left."

Marina took my left hand from my side and placed a kiss on the back of my hand.

"You were different because I felt like I'd known you for years, even when we'd just met in person. You accompanied me through all of that in some way so I didn't hesitate as much to reveal myself to you. But we were still temporary." I bit my lip. "Now you're here, in my bed. I've never wanted anything, anyone, more than you. I'm starting to realize that this can't stay temporary, you know? So, here I am, fearing to please you because nothing scares me more than the thought of you leaving this room." The words rushed out of me like an outside power had taken me over, even though they came from deep inside of me.

When I finished speaking, silence developed between us; the only audible sound was the heavy beating of our hearts. Marina held my left hand, stroking its back. With every second that passed, my heart beat faster; it'd jump out of my chest if Marina didn't speak sometime soon.

Marina pushed herself into a sitting position. Her legs were now wrapped around mine.

Was this too much?

She let go of my hand and my heart sank to the pit of my stomach.

Her index finger, decorated with her signature black nail polish, traced the scar on my lower belly. It went all the way from my belly button down to my pussy. My biggest imperfection. I wanted to pull her hand away but I let her trace it anyway.

"Tell me about this scar," she said. Her voice was as soft as always, no trace of disgust or judgment. She looked up at me, her deep eyes searching for mine. They glowed with nothing but golden interest.

"It's, uh." I let out a deep breath; I had never really told anyone about it, never *needed* to. "It's surgical. A few years ago, I had a cyst on my ovaries. It was so big that it pressed on all my organs… I was close to dying, *really* close."

"I'm sorry that happened to you," Marina said and caressed my scar with her lips. Her lips were the first to ever touch it, the first to ever worship it as something beautiful.

For the first time, I wanted to talk about it. I wanted to share the story of my scar. Even though I so often refused to think about it, to even look at it. "My stomach grew over the years; it got bigger and bigger with time. Shortly before the surgery, I looked like I was pregnant. I always thought it was just air inside my stomach, that something was wrong with my digestive system. Making appointments at the doctor scares me so it took me forever to get it checked out. And even then, the first doctor told me it was just air as well. When I finally found a doctor that did an ultrasound, he sent me to the hospital right away. It took them two weeks to find out what was happening. The cyst was 8 kilograms when they took it out. It had consumed one of my ovaries. That was the closest I ever got to losing my life." I sucked in a sharp breath, "My ex-girlfriend left me at that time, claiming I was too much for her, and my dad never reached out to me. You'd think almost dying would've changed something for me but everything was just the same when I left the hospital." My eyes watered. "Sometimes, I feel ashamed because I know they could've found it a lot earlier if I had gone to a gynaecologist at some point sooner in my life. I just never really needed to so I didn't. Now, I regret all of that. The scar would've been a fraction of this. I wish I would be more comfortable talking about it. It can happen to any young woman and not enough of them know about it."

"Thank you for sharing." Marina kissed the top of my scar. "You are so strong." She kissed downward. "And this scar is beautiful." She kissed the end of it, right above my clit. "Because it is part of your masterpiece of a body."

Everything inside me fluttered at her words. She was worshiping me, honoring me the way that I honored her. She wanted to know everything about me, just like I wanted to know everything about her. It was almost like she was fan girling about me right there. She didn't call my scar ugly or blame me for not doing enough to prevent it; she liked it because she liked *me*.

"I am not planning to leave you anytime soon. I am not planning to leave you, *period*." She crawled upward and pressed a kiss between my boobs. "Not if you touch me and not if you don't." She pressed a kiss to my left boob. "I came here tonight because I want you more than anything." She pressed a kiss to the other. "Because you're the only person in the world that has ever made me feel like myself." She pressed a kiss to my lips.

"You're the person I wrote all those songs about when I still wondered if you even existed."

Butterflies fluttered beneath my skin. This was real. This was *realer* than real. Marina wanted me, more than anything.

She wants me.

I grabbed her hips and turned her around so that I was sitting on top of her. "That was all I needed to hear." I sucked at her throat, careful not to leave a mark. Just because she wanted me didn't mean that she was ready to share us with the world.

Marina answered with a moan, her fingers digging into my back, and I let my hand slide between her legs.

"Ready?" I hushed.

She nodded; her chin met the top of my head. I let my index and middle fingers glide along the inside of her thighs. Marina sighed.

Those sounds.

Her voice was almost more magical now than it was when she sang. I propped myself up to a steadier position so that I could look at her while my fingers slid along her folds.

Marina closed her eyes and let her head fall back on the pillow. Her dark hair spread around my pillow; she looked like an angel. My fingers moved faster, gliding in and out of her folds, but never quite meeting her clit. Her breathing became hushed.

"Kari." Her voice was barely a whisper as her hips bent upward towards my hand.

I circled around her clit and her lower body began moving against my hand. When I moved my fingers faster, up and down and to the sides, her breathing matching their pace. Marina's hands shot to her sides, clinging to my bed sheets. When I let one finger glide into her, meeting her soft walls, her face tensed and her mouth shot open, every breath a loud moan.

I wanted to photograph this moment so badly. I wanted to capture the way her dark nails and silver rings looked against my white sheets. I wanted to snap a close up of her mouth agape and her eyes pinched together. I wanted to photograph the contrast of her tanned skin against my pale skin. I wanted to photograph every single inch of her body in this state, on my bed, in my room, with my fingers inside of her.

I pushed harder, bending my fingers.

"Kari!" She almost screamed. Hearing my name had never felt this good. Her hips pushed up against my hand and we fell into our own little rhythm. With every push, her body tensed more. I could even make out the tension in her abs. She was an artwork in my sheets and I was drawing her with my movements. My breathing almost matched hers. The more she tensed, the more my stomach fluttered. There was nothing that I wanted more, nothing that could make me happier, than lifting Marina all the way to the sky.

Her breathing was so hushed that I thought it'd stop and her knuckles were so white that I thought they'd break. Her motions broke the rhythm, her pushes slower, but hard. On the next push, she stopped, pressing as hard against my hand as she could. Her body tensed and lifted off the mattress. For a second, she was floating above my bed, her only anchor my hand inside of her. Then, a shudder went through her body and she fell.

I fell with her.

Do you know this feeling when your biggest dreams are right in front of you?

That moment when they learn to walk and then fly?

When you can't quite grasp the concept of those things being real?

Everything else, your whole life, suddenly seems to shift.

Reality shifts.

Suddenly, the only real thing is that dream.

I was experiencing dreams that I hadn't even dreamed yet.

Dreams I didn't know that I had.

Our bodies collapsed onto each other.

Chapter 16
Be Your Man - G Flip

"It sounded like you were having fun last night." Chloe winked at me while she filled her plastic bottle with tap water.

I buried my face in my hands, feeling the heat creep into my cheeks. She stared at me with her blue eyes, waiting for an answer. I wasn't ready to talk about this; I didn't know if I'd ever be able to put last night into words.

The splashing sound of water hitting the sink forced Chloe to look away. Her bottle was overflowing and I chuckled.

"It seems like my love life is distracting you more than me," I laughed and walked over to the kitchen counter to prepare a coffee for Marina. I hated coffee but there was nothing I wanted more than to prepare coffee for the 35 year old woman that was still sleeping in my bed.

"Well, how can it not be distracting if my best friend is sleeping with the hottest milf on earth?" Chloe asked as she sat down on the little wooden chair in the kitchen.

"Oh, so I'm a milf?" Marina asked behind me.

I turned around so fast that I knocked over the cup. Luckily, it wasn't filled yet. Marina lunged forward and caught it before it could hit the ground.

My breath stuck in my throat. Marina was standing right in front of me, only a few inches separating our bodies. She was wearing one of my old, oversized *Paper Rings and Promises* t-shirts.

"I took a shirt from your closet; I hope that's okay."

I was still staring at her upper body in my old shirt. She wasn't wearing a bra and the outline of her nipples was visible beneath the thin cotton. "It's more than okay," I said, my eyes focused on the band's logo of a paper heart on the shirt. "Technically it used to be yours once," I mumbled.

It was like only we existed in this world. Chloe wasn't sitting in the corner, watching our conversation. We weren't even in this kitchen; we were floating somewhere in the clouds. I looked back up to her face and our eyes were immediately glued together.

The coffee machine was beeping behind me. Marina's eyes darted over, then to the cup in my hands.

"That's for you," I handed her the cup.

Marina smiled. "I was wondering why you were holding a coffee cup, considering I've never seen you drink any." She walked over to the machine, placing the cup beneath it.

Nobody said a thing until the machine beeped again. Marina grabbed her full cup and let herself fall into the chair across from Chloe. When I looked back at Chloe, I couldn't help but laugh; her eyes were open so wide that they looked like they were about to fall from her face.

"Seen a ghost?" Marina asked and crossed one leg over the other, leaning back in her chair.

Chloe shook her head. "I- I'm sorry for calling you a milf," she muttered.

We only had two chairs in the kitchen so I stood beside them and leaned against the counter, watching the scene unfold in front of me.

"No need to apologize." Marina took a sip of her coffee. "I take it as a compliment." When she put her cup back down, she looked up at me and patted her lap.

What?

Marina wanted me to sit on her lap. In my own kitchen. While she sipped the coffee I made her.

Chloe's eyes darted back open as she looked back and forth between Marina and me. She stared at me as if I had presented her with a dinosaur. I walked over to Marina and carefully sat down on her lap before I could over think it.

She wrapped her arms around my lower stomach and everything immediately started to tingle. The little bees were back in action, producing enough honey to glue me to the other woman. Everything inside me glowed at the warmth of Marina's body beneath mine. This felt right. This felt *real*. I belonged right there, close to her, making coffee for her, waking up in the same house as her, sharing the same kitchen with her. Marina and I belonged *together*.

I looked over at Chloe; She probably thought the same thing. There was so much happiness in the blue of her eyes; she was happy for me, genuinely happy.

She seemed as happy as I was when I had seen her face light up at the first *Willow* concert I accompanied her to. There was a different kind of happiness, a different kind of peace and safety in my best friend's body, when her favorite singer walked on stage. All the fear and anxiety that I was so used to seeing in her eyes disappeared with the first beat of the intro. I had never seen her that way before and nothing made me happier than finally seeing my best friend finding a community she could call home.

I guessed it was my turn now, at least that was what the glow on her face told me.

Is Marina the person I'd soon call home?

She could be. She already felt like home. But the fear of the future nagged at me, like a bear licking away the honey that glued me to her. I didn't want her to give up what she *used* to call home just to become mine. I didn't know if I could live with myself if Marina gave up her family just to be with me. And still, there was nothing that I wanted more than to be with her.

"I'm gonna leave you 2 lovebirds alone now," Chloe decided, breaking the silence. "Have fun on your day off." My best friend got up from her chair, grabbed her water bottle, nodded at us and walked out of the room.

Marina wrapped her arms around me even tighter as we sat in silence. I knew that I should walk out of the kitchen and see my friend to the door to say goodbye.

I can't just let her leave like that, right?

I wanted nothing more than to melt into Marina's body but Chloe was important too.

"I'll be right back," I mumbled.

Marina's soft lips kissed my shoulder before she pushed me off her lap. Her hands wrapped around both sides of my hips to hold me steady. I didn't want her to let go; I wanted her to pull me back into her safety instead.

I walked away from her anyway. Chloe had her tote bag swung over her shoulder and was just about to open the front door when I stepped into the hallway.

"You can't just leave without letting me say goodbye properly," I said and walked down the hallway.

Chloe paused at the door and turned around to look at me.

I closed the distance and embraced my favorite person. "Are you gonna be okay?"

Chloe shook her head, her curls tickling my face. "Are *you* gonna be okay?"

I swallowed hard; all those fears and doubts still lingered in the back of my head, dropping down to nag at my heart. Marina decided she wanted me now. She promised that she'd stay. I believed her but all those outer circumstances seemed to make that impossible, even if she wanted to.

"I hope so," I mumbled. "Right now, it seems like I will be."

Chloe nodded again. "Promise me you'll look after yourself," she said.

"I will." I didn't know if I could. I used to be so good at protecting myself, at keeping my walls up, but Marina seemed to break them down just by looking at me.

Chloe took a step back. The little crooked heart on her silver ring glowed in the morning sunlight when her hand fell to her side. I didn't want her to leave, even though I wanted nothing more than to be alone with Marina.

"Have an amazing day off together. I'll see you tomorrow," she said, loud enough for Marina to hear it in the kitchen. Then, she lowered her voice to a whisper: "Don't let her break you just because she's breathtaking."

"Text me when you're at your hotel." I didn't react to her last sentence, didn't even nod. She knew that I couldn't promise anything; we both knew that Marina would break me if she wanted to.

Chloe stepped through the doorway and into the sunlight of Ulm. When she heaved her suitcase down the stairs of my front garden, I screamed a soft "I love you!" after her. She turned around, waved and left my garden. I closed the door behind her.

Marina was still sipping on her coffee when I entered the kitchen. The corners of her mouth immediately went up when she saw me coming in. "Everything okay?" she asked.

"More than okay," I opened the cupboard above the stove to take out a pan. "Scrambled or fried eggs?"

"We have catering at the venue, even on days off, you know?" Marina said. I heard her pushing back her chair to get up when I took a carton of eggs out of the fridge.

"But I want to make you breakfast."

But I want to be like a normal couple, making each other breakfast.

I took two eggs out of the carton.

"Well, if that's the case, I'll take them fried." I could hear the grin in her voice without even turning around to look at her.

I turned on the stove and put butter in the pan. The tapping sound of Marina's bare feet against the tiles of my kitchen floor told me that she was approaching. I took two plates out of the cupboard and put a piece of the now cold toast on each of them.

Marina's hands wrapped around me from behind. I immediately felt warm and glowy from the inside. "Ooh," was all I could say.

Marina's hand grabbed an egg while the other held me by the waist. "I can't just let my girl cook for me all by herself."

My girl?

"You look way too hot doing that." She cracked the egg on the side of the pan with one hand while the other moved around the front of my stomach.

Heat crept into my cheeks and flames burned me from the space where her hand touched my body. She placed the shell of the egg back into the box and her other hand cupped my breast.

"So, uhm, I'm your girl?" I asked and grabbed the other egg. When I cracked it against the pan, a piece of shell fell in.

"I mean, if you agree to be," Marina whispered, her lips almost touching my ear. I didn't realize that she was fishing the piece of shell out of the pan until she dropped it into the box.

I answered by giving her a kiss on the cheek. There was nothing that I wanted more than for her to call me hers. I let myself sink into Marina's touch. Everything burned; I wanted to grab her waist, turn her around and undress her right there in the kitchen. I couldn't distinguish if there was fire burning me or butterflies making me tingly as I buried my nose in her hair for a moment.

How did she smell like lavender right after waking up?

"Our eggs are ready," Marina whispered into my ear and let go of my body. She took a spatula from the wall and separated each egg from the pan to drop them on our toast, taking them over to the table.

If she wanted me, I'd be hers.

This time I was sitting on Chloe's chair, even though I wanted to sit on her lap again. We ate in silence for a moment. My thoughts were running circles inside my head.

How long is this magic going to last?

I didn't know if we had to go back to the bus in a few hours or in a day. There could be press things that we had to do. The bus might be leaving early, in which case we'd spend the day off in the next city. I didn't even know how she'd left her band mates or what she'd told them when she came to my place the night before.

"When do we have to return to the bus?" I broke the silence, right before I took another bite of my toast. I didn't even feel hungry; the thought of going back to the place I used to love made me feel sick. Marina's presence helped me forget what had happened the day before, at least partially. That didn't change the fact that I never wanted to see Dari again, though; I never wanted to see him pull his long, greasy hair up or see him chug a beer ever again. The mere thought of the man disgusted me; I couldn't quite distinguish if the tightness in my throat was caused by anger, fear or hatred.

"Not before late tonight." Marina placed her toast back on her plate. She grabbed my free hand in the middle of the table. "It's going to be just the two of us for the whole day."

Did she see the fear in my eyes?

"Are you sure?" My eyes widened. "Aren't there any press things you need to do?"

Marina shook her head. "No."

"And the bus isn't leaving this morning? I mean, the drive to Berlin is really long…"

"No," Marina answered again.

"What about the crew? Don't you want to spend the last day off with *them*? Tomorrow is the last show." I still couldn't quite believe that I'd get a whole day with Marina without having to hide anything.

"You're part of the crew as well. And I'd much rather spend my last day off here with you." The dimples beneath her eyes showed. "I'll take a chance if I see it." She fixated her eyes on a crumb on the table. "I'll just have to make a call in a bit to organize a replacement for Dari."

"And what about your family? They're waiting for you in Berlin. You could see them sooner if the bus left earlier." I didn't want to bring up her family, I would've rather forgotten about them until we had to face reality, but my need for security wanted to hear what she was thinking. "And you didn't have to kick Dari out for me."

"Don't say that." Marina took my face into her hands. "First of all, DaRI doesn't deserve to be on a stage ever again and you would never have to accept being put into a position like that. *Ever*. Do you understand?"

I nodded.

"I wouldn't want to be on stage with him either and I hate that this industry even sees it as an option." Marina shook her head. "Second, I choose you. That doesn't mean I'm forgetting about my daughter or the confrontation with Greg that's awaiting me. I know it's not gonna be easy and it's gonna be a process but we don't have to face that just yet. As long as I'm officially

311

on tour, even on a day off in Berlin, Greg wouldn't show up, not even if I asked him to."

"I hate him for that." I knew that I wasn't allowed to judge her relationship but I couldn't quite keep it back. Of course, he didn't really deserve the troubles that he'd have to face if Marina decided to go public with me but Marina was worthy of someone better than him.

Marina took another bite of her toast and swallowed audibly. "You know, sometimes I think that, too."

"Had you ever thought about leaving him before you met me?" I knew that she had but I knew why she hadn't actually left; Joni was her everything. I could tell by the way that her face lit up with love whenever she heard her name or spoke about her.

"Do you think I would be here if I hadn't? Even before I met you, I thought about leaving him more than once." She stared down at the table as her hand fumbled with her coffee cup. "I loved him once but I don't love him anymore. He hates the one thing that ignites me, that makes me feel alive. The stage is where I'm myself. I feel like he hates the version of me that is really *me*. I wasn't ready to leave him, though; I guess I needed another reason to. I want *you* and I'll take the step but that doesn't mean I'm not scared. He'll start a legal war, I'm sure. He'll want to keep Joni away from me. I love her so much and I don't want to be the reason she suffers." She took a deep breath, like she was preparing for a future that wouldn't let her breathe. "The whole thing will be public and the thought of that makes me feel sick."

I put my hand above hers on the cup, calming her fumbling. She looked up from the table and into my eyes.

"I'm sorry." I didn't really know what else to say at first. "Joni will be hurt, nothing will ever be the same for her." I knew so well how Joni would feel and I hated that I could be a reason for that. "She'll suffer but there's nothing worse you could do than stay with Greg to keep Joni happy. My mum tried that and it resulted in even more pain and chaos. Don't be the same. Don't let Joni be the one to pick you up from the floor because you get lost in a relationship that isn't right for you anymore. Take the step as long as it's yours to take, as long as you're still in control. Joni will understand one day." The words flew out of my mouth before I could stop them.

"Thank you." But her eyes were watery.

I hated seeing her cry. I hated that her husband treated her the way that he did. I hated that she was in this position now. I hated that I couldn't take the pain away from her.

"You are the most wonderful woman I've ever seen," I said. "You deserve to be with someone who supports everything you do because what you do is incredible. You've saved me more than once. I wouldn't be at this point in my life if it wasn't for your voice. I know that I'm not the only one. Anyone who doesn't see that, anyone who doesn't see the importance and beauty of your work, doesn't deserve to be in your life."

Marina let go of her cup and let her hand fall into mine. "With everything else that's happening, sometimes I forget that."

"You deserve to be reminded every single day. I'm your physical reminder that your work saves lives."

Her bottom lip quivered and she bit down on it. My heart broke for her pain; I had seen her cry on stage a few times but never this close, never this personally.

I pushed my chair back and walked around the table toward her. "Babe, don't cry." I let myself fall to my knees in front of her chair and placed my hands on her thighs. "You deserve everything and so much more. You are mesmerizing. All I want in life is to see your smile, to *make* you smile, because you've managed to make me smile in times when I thought I never would again."

Marina sniffed, sending a dagger through my heart. "I'm just so grateful that you've stepped into my life; I feel like now you're saving me. You're my awakening, Kari."

The daggers turned into flowers blooming in my heart. It glowed and tingled, full of life. Everything that used to be gray turned to color, rainbows inside of me. I pulled myself back onto my feet. I took Marina's face into my hands and pulled her head towards mine. The closer that I got, the more star-like freckles my eyes could count. Before my lips touched hers, I whispered, "You're everything to me, Marina."

I kissed her and she kissed me back. This was more than any other kiss; it was the first kiss that was deep with compassion. I'd almost call it *love*. The way that her lips parted to welcome mine, slow and soft, was everything. Before I had kissed Marina that day in my kitchen, I had never been in love. Kissing her so deeply was better than any concert that I'd ever seen. No, it was every concert I'd ever seen all wrapped into one. It was every time that I'd listened to *Paper Rings and Promises* songs and felt seen. I was thrown back to the day that I'd discovered Marina's voice on the radio.

My stomach fluttered the same way that it had done when I'd seen Marina on stage for the first time.

My heart bloomed the way that it had when I finally hugged Chloe.

I experienced the perfection that I'd been searching for. At the same time, I felt free of any expectations.

When we parted, Marina wasn't crying anymore; she was glowing. "You're everything to me, too, Kari." Her lips brushed mine briefly. "And so much more."

315

Evening came sooner than I was ready for. Marina and I were lying on my bed, my head resting on her naked breasts, and my TV was playing the third episode of *The L Word;* but the volume was so low that we could barely pay attention. I had put it on to introduce Marina to the show which, now that she was really entering the queer world, was mandatory. After the first episode, we stopped watching, undressing each other again, having sex and then snuggling in the limbo between waking and sleeping.

"Have you ever considered coming out to your fans?" I mumbled against Marina's skin. I could see her heart-shaped birthmark through the corner of my eye.

"Not really," Marina's voice was too cold for our situation. "I never really had a reason to."

I pushed myself up so that I could look at her. "So, you've never thought that you were queer before?"

"No." Marina's voice was almost offended.

Mine was insecure. "Really?" My eyes scanned her face. "I mean… I thought with all the rumors going on, the thought must've crossed your mind."

She put her palm on my head, like she was holding a baby. My face dropped back onto her breasts. "I convinced myself they were just rumors. That way, I had no reason to give them any thought."

I didn't quite want to believe her words. "Is that really what you thought or was it the easiest option?" I took her palm off my head and lifted myself back up to look at her. "You're feeling something now that you're with me, right? I mean, you obviously liked what I was doing to you.," I breathed against her skin and goose bumps erupted around her nipple. "That felt pretty queer to me."

Marina didn't look at me, choosing to stare at my ceiling instead. "I just don't like people making assumptions about me, okay? I hate it when people think they know me, even if they have no clue who I really am."

I thought I knew you.

I ignored the slight sting in my heart. "Are you sure that's the reason you're reacting this way?" I knew that I was overstepping, making her uncomfortable. But I wasn't quite sure if there was such a thing as overstepping between us anymore; we'd crossed all borders already.

"Maybe I was scared." Marina still wouldn't look at me, her eyes fixated on the ceiling.

I pressed a kiss on her chin, hoping to make her feel better, more comfortable. "Scared of what?"

She looked down at me, her eyes watery. "Admitting it to myself, having to go into conflict with my management and my husband. Being what everyone already knew I was. Giving in to secret thoughts I'd had for years."

"I know you're a public figure. I know that there are thousands of people who have their eyes on you." I pressed a kiss to her birthmark. "But you also have a strong queer fan base who love you more than anything and who'd support you with everything they have. You could have even helped, or still *could* help, so many more people. If you would have come out years ago, it would've changed my life. There are so many people that see you as their gay awakening and looking up to an openly queer idol would give them so much strength; they would feel empowered to be their true selves."

Marina swallowed. "I don't know if I want to be a queer idol, though. It would be an honor, yes. I love my queer fans. But I'm scared. Having so many queer fans means hearing so many painful stories about *being* queer. Young girls have told me they've been kicked out of their family's house because they bought a gay flag to wave at one of our concerts. I've heard of people getting hate comments and being bullied online. People fled their hometowns after coming out. I know that it's easier when you're an adult and you can choose the place you live. And I know that things change for the better every day. But I don't know if I'm ready to be part of it. I don't know if I'm ready to fight, to be an advocate. Being openly queer as a public person is always political and some kind of protest. I don't want to do that. All I want is to make music."

I understood what Marina was saying but my mind could barely grasp the meaning of her words. I had never really seen it from that side, had never really considered what it meant to her career. Coming out, especially for female artists with a large, queer audience, usually meant a career boost, even if there was backlash from other sides of the industry. I was sure that queer fans were the strongest, building a sense of community that straight people couldn't understand. I had thought that if Marina came out, it'd just make everything better. But if she didn't want to be that kind of person, if she didn't want to be the person I so desperately wanted her to be, there was nothing I could do.

"I believe that you could do it and that you'd love it. But that's not my choice to make." I rested my head back on her boobs. I didn't want to think about what it'd mean if she chose not to out herself publicly; I didn't know if I could be with her in secret forever. I so desperately wanted to be by her side but I also wanted her to proudly present me to the world. I once promised myself to never date any woman who *wasn't* out, to never be a 'dirty' secret. But Marina meant so much to me; I was scared that I would stay, even if I was her secret forever.

"I'm sorry I couldn't give you the answers you wanted to hear, sweetheart," Marina said and placed a kiss on my hairline.

I was supposed to live in the present, right?

My present was so beautiful that there was no reason to think about the future, *right?*

Marina was here with me *now*.

She was everything to me and I was everything to her.

Chapter 17
Light On – Maggie Rogers

When I let myself fall into my bunk in the bus that night, it felt like I was lying down on a rock. I longed to be back in my own bed, Marina's arms wrapped around me. We hadn't kissed goodnight, hadn't even had a chance to *say* goodnight. I wanted Marina to be able to reveal us at her own pace, not meeting everyone with my hand in hers.

She left to sort out some things with her band mates and Milo, probably making some calls to organize a new drummer to meet them in Berlin. Marina had told me that Dari was already gone and was on a train back to Berlin.

Instead of hiding in Marina's arms, I was alone. It was still way too early to sleep; I checked my phone and shot a message over to Chloe. She had a notorious problem of not letting me know when she'd arrived somewhere safe.

Kari, 8:25 pm
Did you get to Berlin okay?

She replied instantly.

Chloe, 8:25 pm
Yes, safe and chilling at the hotel.

For a second, I wished that I wasn't lying on this uncomfortable bunk bed... that I was sitting in a hotel with my best friend, bubbling with excitement for the concert the next day.

I turned around and the bed made a creaking sound.

Chloe, 8:26 pm
How was your day with Marina? ;)

I thought about the time that I'd spent with my idol. I was thrilled at the image of Marina naked in my bed.

Kari, 8:27 pm
Everything and so much more.

I bit my bottom lip.

Kari, 8:27 pm
She called me her girl.

322

Chloe, 8:27 pm
Only her girl?

Kari, 8.27 pm
Well, she called me many more things but that was the
most exciting one.

I grinned at my phone; the way that Marina had said
my name was still ringing in my ears like my favorite
song.

Chloe, 8:28 pm
Soo, she didn't call you her girlfriend?

I would've never expected her to call me her
girlfriend with everything that it meant.; I would've never
expected her to call me *anything*. I wished she did, of
course. I wished that we could already walk out into the
world as girlfriend and girlfriend. I took a deep breath
and stared at the slatted frame above me; I didn't want to
answer Chloe.

Chloe, 8:30 pm
Or did you at least talk about what's going to happen
after the tour?

Kari, 8:31 pm
She said she wanted to see me after.

Chloe, 8:31 pm
And how do you feel about that?

I didn't know how I felt. I didn't know how I was *supposed* to feel. She wouldn't have done it, wouldn't have risked all of that, if she didn't believe in us.

Kari, 8:32 pm
I don't really know but I do believe her words.
She did say that she wants a divorce but she's scared.
I don't want to force her to do anything. I understand her.

Chloe, 8:33 pm
Just don't let her hurt you, okay?

Kari, 8:34 pm
I'll try my best.

The bus door made its typical beeping sound. I dropped my phone to my chest and closed my eyes.

I heard Milo's voice, "This is such a mess; I hope the new drummer gets everything quickly."

"I understand that but we both know Dari had to leave," Marina said; she sounded stressed.

"Of course." Milo stepped into the bus. "Don't worry about it. I'll make sure everything goes smoothly."

"Thank you." Marina wandered toward her bed and her Docs hit the ground beside mine. I tried to bring up images of her body against mine, of her skin meeting mine. The rest of the crew entered the bus and the door closed behind them. I heard shuffling bed sheets and the changing of clothes. I stayed in my position until they turned off the lights.

The engine started. I closed my eyes but couldn't fall asleep. Dari wasn't here but I couldn't help thinking about the things that he had done. The fact that I had slept in the bunk beneath him for so many nights and didn't know what a monster he was made me feel sick. I turned around on my mattress and hid my face in my pillow. I thought about screaming, the need to release my feelings scratching my tongue. Instead, I suffocated myself, pressing my face deeper into the pillow until my body forced me to breathe.

Before I could press my head back into the pillow, an index finger with a chunky silver ring and black chipped nail polish stroked the back of my right hand. Marina grabbed it in support. The mere contact of her skin created a feeling of security and longing inside of me. I wanted to pull her into the small bed with me. Her lips placed a soft kiss on the back of my hand but she didn't stop holding it with hers. She was trying to show me that she was there, thinking about me. My heart bloomed at the thought of her thinking about me, wanting to touch me just the way that I wanted to touch her. I felt that, as long as she was there, nothing could happen to me. I just hated that I couldn't feel her body on mine at that moment but even her small gesture made me feel bubbly.

I closed my eyes, imagining us laying in bed together. I thought about our future together, her taking me on dates, introducing me to Berlin. I couldn't wait to spend the rest of my life with her. Dari disappeared into the back of my mind as Marina rubbed her thumb over the back of my hand in circles. With every stroke of her thumb, my breathing slowed, and my insides calmed. I was okay.

Chapter 18
Still Into You - Paramore

When I woke the next day, the bus was already empty; only our driver was snoring away on the front seat. I crawled out of my bed, pulled my suitcase out from underneath and picked out a tight white top with a short black miniskirt. I wanted to show Marina that she'd made the right choice; I had to give everything I had. I changed and pulled my hair up into the usual tight, sleek ponytail. As my hands pulled it tighter until I winced, a small tear escaped my eye and I immediately dried it.

Don't cry, she chose you.

I took out my makeup bag and rummaged for a palette with a small mirror. Even though I had barely slept, there was a glow in my eyes.

She chose you.

I applied a bit of waterproof mascara on my upper eyelashes.

I received a text from Milo, calling me into the venue to snap a few pictures of each band member during sound check. The sun was high in the blue sky, burning my skin. To the right side of the bus, the tall, iconic buildings of Berlin touched the clouds. To my left, the industrial area around the concert venue, which was an old fabric production hall, shone in dusty gray. The city was full of possibilities and I couldn't wait for the new life that was waiting for me here.

I walked toward the back entry of the venue. The big metal doors screeched when I pushed them inward; they were heavy, straining my breathing. The backstage area was completely empty, a messy buffet that consisted of empty plates and a few lonely pieces of fruit lined the back wall. A big leather couch, which reminded me of the couch I had sat on back on my first day, stood in the middle of the room.

My fingertips sizzled at the sight of it, reminding me of the way that it felt to have Marina's skin touch mine for the first time. The way that my body had been squeezed next to hers, our legs meeting. The way that the mixture of excitement and alcohol ran through my veins, making me glow from inside. I had been so scared, so nervous. I had still been so naïve. Everything had been so new and the smallest gestures and touches had suddenly been the biggest in the world. Every single thing that she had done, every little movement of her body, had had an effect on mine. I could still feel my heart jump at the memory of smelling her lavender scent for the first time. I had gotten so much closer to her since then. Now, I just wanted more and more because I knew what it felt like to have her. Could I ever live without her again? It had just been a week but there were lifetimes between that moment and this last night of the tour. I'd probably never fully be able to grasp how I'd gotten from there to here.

Since there was no one else in the room yet, I let myself fall onto the couch. Someone would call me when they were ready; they always did. Right now, I was happy to be alone. Maybe it was right to take it step by step; make it from one room to the next with a fresh breath. A week ago, I would have ran towards Marina, would have ran towards any work task I could. Now, I wanted this to be over, to leave with Marina and walk towards a new future.

"Kari?" I didn't even turn when I smelled her. Nevertheless, a wave of goose bumps ran down my back at the sound of Doc Martens hitting the floor.

Marina wandered around the old couch and let herself fall down next to me. The couch was way too big for just us two but she didn't bother putting space between us, our thighs meeting. The warmth of her body against mine melted some of the ice-cold fear inside me. Marina didn't say a word, didn't even ask how I was doing. There were a million things to do but nothing to be said.

Marina took my hand and wrapped her fingers around it. The soothing feeling of silver rings scratching at my skin reassured me, reminded me of what she'd said the night before. Everything was going to be okay, wasn't it? There was a reason that Marina had turned up at my apartment the day before and it wasn't a bad one. She wanted *me*. She wanted to *stay* with me.

All I wanted was to kiss Marina, to hide in her arms and never come back out. I started crying. I didn't quite know if it was fear of her backing out or happy tears because I'd finally gotten what I wanted. I didn't turn to hug Marina, didn't even let her see my tears. I had to bite my lip to silence a sob. She still didn't speak but put her arms around me and pulled my face towards her chest. Marina pushed me against her body even tighter with every sob. She stayed silent but I could hear her heart beating where my ear rested on her chest. The beat was fast but calm. Like the slow drum counting down before the start of a song, giving security to the rest of the band. My hushed breathing slowly matched the pace of the drum. She didn't need to speak for me to know she wouldn't let go; she'd hold me as long as I needed her.

I flinched when the sound of real drums emanated behind us. Marina grabbed my shoulders to position me a few centimeters away from her body.

"It's not him; he's never going to hurt you again," she said, her voice steadier than my hand holding me up on the couch. I knew that if I tried to speak, my voice would barely be a whisper.

Marina's thumb gently rubbed my shoulder. "I promise."

My eyes widened and I stared at her. I tried to focus on her features, the little freckles on the space between her eyebrows, but all I could do was recall the images imprinted in my brain. My eyes couldn't focus. Everything was blurry. The painful events of the previous days crashed down on me with every beat of the drum.

"I'll be here by your side to protect you. Dari's gone." I knew that she wanted to make me feel safe but it sounded more like she was trying to persuade herself.

I nodded. I knew that her words were the truth, even when the images still roamed through my mind.

Milo appeared in the doorway behind Marina. His eyes caught mine in a hushed gaze. My body tensed. He was a good guy but that didn't mean Marina would keep holding me in front of him.

Marina looked at me in confusion.

"Milo," I mouthed before Marina could turn.

Marina let go of my shoulders and I thought that she'd leave. Instead, her right hand grabbed my left and her left hand ended up on my thigh, high up, almost obvious. She turned her upper body to look at her manager.

"I'm just dropping by to let you know that we're ready." Milo smiled at her, then at me. "But take your time, please." His eyes lingered on each of Marina's hands for a second.

Does he know?

How much does he know?

Is he mad?

Is he happy?

My heartbeat quickened again but this time with excitement. Whatever his lingering gaze meant, he didn't look surprised, nor mad or angry in any form. Milo turned around and left the room.

Marina's eyes returned to mine with a warm glow, as if nothing had happened. Her left hand wandered higher on my thigh. I couldn't hide the question mark on my face.

"I had to tell him *something* when I left last night," Marina said and barely lifted her shoulders. My mouth stood open in confusion.

She told him about us?

And she's happy?

What happened to the Marina before last night?

I felt played by the lightness on her face. All her features were completely relaxed, like she hadn't been driving me insane the past few days because she didn't want anyone to find out about us. She looked at me as if telling Milo that she had fucked me was the easiest thing in the world.

"Milo is my manager, Kari," Marina's left hand kept wandering. "He's almost like a therapist to me. Of course, it wasn't easy to tell him; I can't quite believe I did," she laughed softly. "But he always has to know where I am, even when I come rushing to your door to beg for you to come back to me." She cocked her head to the side just slightly. "I told him that I had to see you because you mean a lot to me." She looked down at her hand on my thigh. "I guess he figured out the rest."

Her words slowly turned my vision sharp again and soft freckles danced on her nose when she scrunched it up.

"Do you know how freaking beautiful you are?" Marina said, her head turning my way.

I shook my head.

Marina stroked my left cheek. Goosebumps developed as her silver rings lightly touched my skin.

"I love the way you blush when I look at you, the way those little freckles," she began, touching a few of my freckles on my nose up to the space between my eyebrows. "The way they turn into stars dancing in the night sky, when you see me and your face lights up." Her right index finger wandered down my nose and toward my lips; she touched the upper one, sending a shiver down my back. "Your lips are pink, like my favorite roses, and kissing them is like smelling each flower on a never-ending field." Her finger slid down to my lower lip, giving it a slight push down.

I imagined the way that her dark nail polish, the nail polish that I had admired for 8 years, looked against my lips.

"I wish I could kiss them every second of every day," Marina whispered before she leaned forward. Her hand moved my face toward hers gently. Her finger didn't let go of my lower lip until her lips kissed mine.

The kiss was soft and gentle, safe. Her lips moved against mine in a reassuring way, promising. "You deserve the world and so much more," Marina said against my lips as we parted for air.

"You do, too."

She put her hands back on my thighs. "Let me know when you're ready to go inside. If you don't feel like you can do it, that's okay as well. All of this is in your own time."

I nodded. I had to go in at some point, didn't I? There were only a few hours left before the last concert so it was kind of crunch time.

"It's fine. We can go in," I said but looked away from Marina.

My hands wandered to my sleek ponytail to pull the strands tighter but Marina stopped me. She put her hands on mine, forcing them to relax. "You're perfect the way you are," she said, her voice so warm that I wanted to sink into its sound. "Please don't."

I let her guide my hands back down and place them into my lap.

Marina rested her forehead against mine. Everything inside me was electrified, starting from the space our foreheads met; almost like we were each other's source of energy.

"Okay," I whispered, even though I couldn't promise that I wouldn't pull at my hair once she turned her back and we walked into the room. I breathed in her breath.

Can't we stay like this for the rest of forever?

"I wish we could stay like this forever," Marina whispered, her lips almost touching mine as she spoke.

I let my tongue glide along her bottom lip as an answer. I still couldn't believe that Marina and I wanted the same thing. How was that even possible?

I inhaled her breath another time; it was a mixture of coffee and granola. I could almost taste her breakfast on my tongue as I placed a short kiss on her lips, biting down on her bottom lip.

"Let's do this," I whispered and forced myself away from her.

"Sure?" Her dark eyes scanned my face.

I could melt into her gaze right there, let it consume me. The way that she held me safe, made sure that I was okay, even though I had a job to do for her. It felt as if I was more important than her job, than her band, than her life.

I nodded. I had to go through this at some point and, if I sat with her on this couch any longer, I would never leave.

When we walked into the concert hall, the new drummer waved at me. He looked completely different to Dari and his eyes focused on mine instead of my body. The way that he smiled comforted me; it seemed real.

Marina's hand briefly stroked mine as she stepped beside me before she swung herself up onto the stage.

How can someone make jumping on a meter high stage so sexy?

The memory of my younger self fixating on Marina's ass as she swung herself up after stage-diving made me grin. It was insane how she could shift my emotional state so effortlessly; I glowed because Marina had done something simple.

That's how love is supposed to be, isn't it?

Marina winked at me before she stepped toward the microphone. For the rest of the sound check, I focused on her and snapped a few beautiful photos. It felt good to be behind the camera again, to zoom in on Marina's features and capture them as she sang into the microphone. She was the most precious thing that I had ever seen, my favorite thing to photograph. When I could focus my camera on her, it was like the rest of the world dropped away. I don't mean in the way that everything dissolved when I was with her or the way that my heartbeat quickened and the space between my legs throbbed with heat. The world simply stopped existing because nothing else mattered; there was nothing but the camera and her. All worries disappeared when I took photos of her. It was pure peace.

After the sound check, I followed Marina into the bathroom to watch her get ready. And maybe because that door was also the only one we were able to lock. As soon as we entered the bathroom, which was small but modern, I pushed Marina against the wall and locked it behind her. My hand stayed at the height of the lock and turned to cup her ass.

"You know, I've wanted to do this ever since you swung yourself up on that stage?" I whispered into her ear before I pushed her wavy dark hair to the side to reveal her bare throat. I kissed her throat, then sucked, then bit. I didn't care about leaving marks anymore. I wanted to eat her, to inhale her, to consume her.

"Do you mean when I swung myself on that stage today or when you were fan girling about me?" Marina huffed between ragged breaths. Her voice became muffled in my hair.

"Both." I bit down on the soft skin of her throat, making her moan.

The sound was almost more beautiful than any lyrics that she had sung into a microphone. Maybe that was because I made her do it. When I bit harder, she moaned harder. She knew that her throat was turning red and purple beneath my lips but, instead of pushing me away, she pulled me even tighter. She pressed my body into hers, her hands clinging to my back.

"Fuck, Kari," she whimpered.

I let go of her throat and moved my mouth up to her ear. "Yeah?" I whispered.

"You're..." She tried to lift her head higher so that my mouth was level with her throat again.

Damn.

I breathed on her throat, licking the spot that I had been caressing but I didn't bite it again.

"I'm what?" I whispered.

"Everything," she finished her sentence and my teeth stroked her skin again.

The contact of my lips against her throat was instantly answered with a loud moan.

I'm everything to her.
She is everything to me.

Our time behind locked doors ended as fast as it had started. Marina stood in front of the little mirror that was lined with light bulbs, applying mascara. Her hair was gelled back, giving it that wet look that always made me melt. Her lips were slightly red, both from kissing me and from the tinted chapstick that she'd applied. She was wearing the same black jeans that she always did, highlighting her beautiful curves.

"You're gorgeous." I hugged Marina from the back.

"Thank you."

"But you might want to apply some concealer on this." I placed a little kiss on the spot on her throat which was now a shade of purple and red. It had the shape of a heart; I loved it. "Or everyone will see what's been going on in this bathroom."

Marina shook her head, her hair tickling my forehead. "What if I want them to see?" Her eyes found mine in the mirror; they were glowing golden.

"I guess I can make more then," I laughed and bit beneath her chin.

"Later," she said and took my head between her hands, placing a kiss on my hairline. "Later, you can do anything you want to me, baby."

My body was aflame.

Chapter 19
sun to me - MGK

I spotted Chloe's bright red hair behind the barricade before the concert started. Liza was grinning from ear to ear next to her. I greeted both of them with a hug. I chose to stay close to my friends during the show because Marina had told me to do what I felt comfortable with. I always took my best photos from down there, anyway. I ran towards my best friend right after Marina had said goodbye to me for the show.

Chloe gave me a tight hug, like we hadn't just seen each other the day before. She smelled like watermelon vape and a sense of comfort spread through my body. Of course, I was scared of this concert; the end of tour was never easy.

8 years ago, every song on the set list had been a step closer to the end. I'd followed my favorite band for weeks at a time and the rest of my world had ceased to exist. For a moment, when my favorite people had left the stage, it felt like my life was over.

How does your life go on if your biggest dream ends?

How do you keep living?

Marina's eyes were fixated on me as she stepped on stage. She let her head fall back to the loud cheers of the crowd and the dark spot on her throat shone in the blue glow of the stage spotlights.

I gave Chloe a look over my shoulder; she winked at me and pointed to her throat with her free hand. I nodded. Chloe's eyes widened and there was something like pride in her expression. I giggled when I turned back around.

The first few songs were filled with glances. It was almost like Marina was addressing the songs solely to me; her eyes played with me. I stayed close to Chloe for most of the concert and only took a few steps left and right for better angles.

I put the focus on enjoying and doing my best work instead of dwelling in sadness because it was ending.

If it's real, this isn't the end, right?

Maybe I was growing up, too. I was learning that the end of this tour wouldn't mean the end of my life. I had cried for the end of a tour so many times but always found myself back screaming in the front row at the next. This wasn't the end of my life; it was the start of my better future.

It felt like I was 14 again, holding Chloe's hand during our favorite songs, but older this time. Wiser, maybe. I was holding a camera and doing the things that I loved most. Even if things with Marina ended after tonight, even if there was only a kiss goodbye after this concert, my life would go on. Maybe that was the reason for it all; dreaming, growing and learning. Just to keep going.

When Marina stepped back on stage for the encore, the band didn't follow. She walked over to Brad's side and grabbed his acoustic guitar from the stand. Hushed voices arose from behind me, asking what was going on and why the band didn't follow. Something was different.

What was she doing?

Marina found her place in front of her microphone stand and fixed her gaze on me. She started playing a melody on the guitar without saying a word. I lifted the camera up to film but she motioned for me to put it down. My whole body was frozen under her gaze. I stopped breathing and my heart drummed loud in my ears. Marina almost looked nervous when she lifted her mouth to the microphone.

I've been traveling this long, winding road,
Singing my heart out, feeling the load.
But there's a light, shining bright, in the crowd;
A beacon of hope. You're making me proud.

You caught my eye with your smile so sweet,
A moment in time where our worlds meet.
And every night, when I'm up here singing,
I feel your love; oh, it's got me believing.

This song's for you, though no one knows,
A secret love that quietly grows.
Every note, every word, it's true;
I'm pouring my heart out, just for you.

I see you standing there, swaying to the beat.
Your eyes reflect the rhythm, making me complete.
It's our little secret, hidden from the rest,
But in this melody, I've given you my best.

You're the reason my voice soars high.
In the darkest times, you light up my sky.
And, though the world doesn't know your name,
In this song, you're my burning flame.

This song's for you, though no one knows;
A secret love that quietly grows.
Every note, every word, it's true;
I'm pouring my heart out, just for you.

Every whisper, every sigh,
Is a promise that we'll never die.

In the shadows, we find our way.
With every lyric, I want to say...

This song's for you, though no one knows;
A secret love that quietly grows.
Every note, every word, it's true;
I'm pouring my heart out, just for you.

So, here's to us, in this hidden light.
A love that's strong, burning bright.
In every song, you'll hear me sing;
You're my everything, my everything.

I didn't start breathing again until Marina turned and left the stage.

Holy shit.

Marina hadn't said a word to explain this song. Chloe and I were the only people in the audience who knew who this was about.

Every fan's biggest dream is for their favorite artist to write a song about them one day. Even after what had happened between Marina and I, I would probably never be able to grasp that this had actually happened.

"Oh my God!" Chloe squealed behind me.

I let go of her hand and turned around. I hadn't realized that I had been crying until I felt the wetness on my cheeks when I lifted my hands to hide my face.

"That was like the most beautiful thing I've ever seen!" Chloe giggled.

I would have said the same thing if I had seen Marina sing this song about another woman, let alone a fan. I dreaded the speculations that would arise from this scene but I also felt excitement bubbling inside of me at the theories fans would come up with.

Will they guess that it's about a woman?

Did they see her looking at me?

Will this make all the queer fans feel as good as they hoped it would?

There were so many thoughts running through my head and at the same time it was like I couldn't formulate a full sentence. I was speechless.

"How are you feeling?" Chloe asked and grabbed my hands to move them away from my face. "Just lift your shoulder if you don't know."

I lifted my shoulders and let out a shaky laugh. If I said anything, I would've started crying.

"But good?" Chloe's eyes searched my face for signs of pain.

I nodded. I didn't know how I felt but whatever it was, humming down there inside of my stomach, it was good.

We remained in this position, Chloe holding my hands over the barricade and me being unable to speak for a moment. It was peaceful in a way, a quiet

346

understanding of 2 friends about the life-altering moment that had taken place on stage.

I could've remained in this position forever but the silence was interrupted by Liza hysterically tapping on Chloe's shoulder from the side. "What the hell just happened?!"

Chloe glanced over at my friend. Liza had no idea what had been going on between Marina and I over the past week. She *mustn't* know; she's the kind of person that just couldn't keep a secret. I definitely didn't have the energy to interact with her, let alone come up with rumors that weren't true to keep my secret. I looked from Chloe to Liza and back to Chloe in a rather panicked manner.

Chloe looked back at me with a nod. "Go get your girl," she mouthed silently.

I nodded. "Bye Liza," I said and forced myself to walk away; Chloe would handle it.

When I entered the backstage area, Marina greeted me with 2 glasses of champagne in her hands and gave me one. I could see the rest of the band and crew, even the bus driver, standing in a group behind her, each of them with a glass as well.

I took mine gratefully. "You know that none of your fans will sleep tonight; they will be wondering who that mysterious new song was about."

Marina grinned behind her champagne glass, clinking it with mine. "Let them wonder. The only person that's supposed to know, *knows*." Both of us took a sip.

What about her family?

I still wondered where the shift in her emotions had come from. Why did she decide to risk her family for me?

Marina stepped from one foot to the other. "But I do wanna know what you thought of the song," she mumbled, taking another sip of her bubbly drink. She was cute when she was nervous.

"Words could never express how much it means to me," I said. "I could show you in a different way, though." I winked. "*If* we were alone."

I wanted to kiss her so badly. I wanted to kiss every part of her body, worship her for her beautiful talent. I wanted to make her scream, yell and sing my name when no one was around. Nothing could ever compare to the gift of a song written about me. Maybe I could never make her feel the way that she made me feel, mean as much to her as she did to me, but I guessed that was okay.

"Oh, how I wish I could be alone with you right now," Marina said and lifted her hand to slightly touch mine. Everything tingled at the contact. Sometimes small touches, the hidden ones, were even stronger, more electrifying, than pressing my body against hers.

Marina and I stood in silence for a moment, dwelling within the touch of our hands. The rest of the band and crew were chatting and mingling in the backstage area behind us. I focused my attention on the beautiful woman in front of me, the background turning blurry.

She looked at me and bit her lower lip. My heart fluttered at the way that the dimple in her right cheek became visible.

How can anyone be this gorgeous?

Her whole face glowed the way my insides sizzled.

"Marina!" Milo interrupted our silence. He approached from behind her and put his hands on her shoulders. "I really don't want to interrupt."

She let go of my hands but turned around to look at her manager.

"It's fine." Her forehead crumbled in annoyance when she glanced back at me, while her voice raised to a happy tune. "What is it?"

"I just want to make sure that you 2 are ready for the fans coming in tonight," Milo said. "You know, the drinks we talked about?"

Marina nodded; I had no clue what they were on about.

"Well, they're coming in like 15 minutes. I gotta find them at the entrance and take them backstage. You don't have to be there right at the moment I walk them in, just don't let them wait too long."

Marina nodded again, then grabbed my hand. "Can you get Kari's friend, Chloe, too? She's the red-head."

"Of course," Milo said and left.

I looked at Marina with a visible question mark on my face. "What is happening?"

Marina laughed, "To be honest, I don't really know." She lifted her shoulders. "Milo plans these things and lets me know at the last minute most of the time." That wild glare was visible again. "I guess they're fans that won a chance to join the after-party with us."

"For some reason I always seemed to miss these things. Otherwise, I would've seduced you years ago."

Marina giggled. "Well, I don't have any clue about my appointments. But what I do know is that we have 15 minutes to spare before I have to be anywhere." She looked around; the rest of the team was busy chatting and drinking, none of them eager to go anywhere. "May I escort you to my humble home on wheels, m'lady?"

I laughed, my stomach humming with anticipation. 15 minutes was more than enough time to make her scream my name. Marina pulled me through the room. We exchanged our empty champagne flutes for new ones on the way.

I felt like I was 15 again. Marina pulled me into a dark street somewhere on the outskirts of Berlin and pressed me against the side of the tour bus. It felt just like I was running away from school with the first girl I ever crushed on. The way we kissed on the school grounds behind the cafeteria. The way we touched hands in class under the table, not letting anyone see what was going on between us. Being with Marina was like falling in love for the first time all over again.

Marina found the skin that was visible between my skirt and my top. A wave of electricity shot down to the space between my legs. She grabbed my waist and pushed me even harder against the bus, her right leg pushing up between my legs. Everything inside me vibrated.

She lifted her lips up to my ear. "You know, it's incredibly hard to be on that stage and see you standing down there and not being able to touch you?" The wetness of her lips grazed the sensitive skin of my right ear as she spoke. "I just wish I could eat you every second of every day."

I giggled at her words.

Yeah, definitely not 15 anymore.

Marina pressed a kiss beneath my earlobe. "You know..." She nibbled at the space beneath my ear. "I still gotta take revenge for what you did to my throat earlier." Her teeth stroked my throat and I let out a deep groan.

Damn.

"I guess you gotta be quick if you want to do that within 15 minutes," I moaned, my voice a mere hush under her lips against my throat.

351

"Oh, my pleasure." She bit down harder, sending a wave of pain and pleasure through my body. Her lips sucked on my throat, my head falling back against the cold surface of the bus, her free hand typing on the keypad to my left.

When the door opened with a beep, Marina pulled me off the side and into the bus, her lips not leaving the spot beneath my ear. I needed more. I needed her closer, my throat throbbing with her marks, her skin on my skin. As if Marina could hear my thoughts, she pulled my body against hers and guided me up the steps of the bus, her lips just briefly letting go of my throat to hold me up.

Once inside, she pushed me onto the bed and climbed on top of me. She took out her phone from her back pocket and set a timer to 10 minutes before she lowered her body onto mine.

"Okay?" she asked, awaiting my approval.

The spot on my neck was still electric from her touch.

"*So* okay," I whispered before I grabbed her face to pull her close.

Our lips connected in a hushed kiss filled with need and want. A firework exploded in my chest. Everything I had ever experienced before vanished. The woman that I had been wanting my whole life suddenly wants me back. Her tongue slid over my lips before she placed kisses on my chin and cheek. Finally, her lips found my throat again. I let my head fall back onto the pillow as she placed kisses on my neck in a circle around the already sore spot. She sucked on my skin, a millimeter above or a millimeter below, making me moan with each bite. A fire was burning inside me, silently begging her to put her lips back on the spot that was pulsating with the need for pain.

"Please!"

Marina bit down right on the spot, her knee shooting up between my legs. I gasped and my fingers clung to the satin of her top. God, how I had worshiped different versions of that black top over all those years. My hands wandered beneath it and pushed it upward. Marina placed a gentle kiss on my throat before she let go to lift her arms.

Now I'm the one taking that top of.

The satin shirt ended up on the ground a second later. I opened her black lacy bra and threw it to the ground. I tingled inside at the sight of Marina's bare breasts and I let my thumb glide over the little heart shaped birthmark. Her nipple hardened at my touch. She gasped.

Gosh, how am I the one doing this to her?

Before Marina's lips could return to my throat, I lifted my own arms as well and Marina pushed my top off my upper body.

"I'll never get tired of this sight." Marina scanned my upper body and licked her lips. Her eyes darted over to her phone where her timer was still running. "I only have 3 more minutes. I don't think that's enough time to take your skirt off."

She cocked her head to the side, seemingly considering the situation. A second later, she lowered her body onto mine again, her nipples pressing against my skin; I gasped at the sudden contact of skin.

"I don't think I even need that," she whispered and bit down on my throat again. Hard. I let out a muffled scream.

Her right hand found the space between my legs, wandering underneath my skirt and pressing against the fabric of my underwear. Everything inside my body was vibrating.

Holy shit.

She rubbed her fore and index fingers against my underwear, every rub sending a wave of pleasure through my veins.

"Harder," I moaned, meaning both her teeth and her fingers.

Marina pushed and bit harder. Her fingertip was now placed on my clit, pressing down, her knee pushing against it to intensify the pressure. With every push, every bite, every circle of her tongue, she took me higher. Every motion made me sizzle.

My arms wrapped around her upper body, clinging to her back, pressing her boobs harder onto mine. My fingernails clawed her skin as I pushed my hips up against her hand.

When her finger pushed the fabric of my underwear away and found contact with my most sensitive part, my muscles clenched. All she needed to do was circle my clit once and everything tingled, burst, electrified. My body went upwards in a wave, everything clenching together in a rush of pleasure. I screamed. I shot to the sky and even higher, out into the universe. The alarm went off and I fell.

We were fully dressed in record time. The bathroom in the bus was dark and poorly lit so Marina took on the job of fixing my hair and make-up. She sat cross-legged in front of me on her bed. She carefully removed the hair tie which was strangled in knots. Her eyes scanned my face while her fingers tried to detangle the knots as gently as possible.

"Why do you always do that?"

"Do what?" A sudden jolt of pain shot through my head as Marina pulled out a hair. My eyes closed.

"Sorry!" Marina looked concerned and put her palm on my head, calming the pulsating feeling of pain. "You know what I mean." She nodded toward her hands in my hair and resumed freeing the hair tie. "You know you're perfect no matter how your hair looks, right?" My eyes darted away from hers. Marina freed one of her hands to lift my head. "Please."

I took a deep breath of lavender air. "It's not that I feel insecure or that I think I have to look perfect constantly. It's more about control." Marina freed the tie and my hair fell around my shoulders. A wave of pain and relief shot from my head down to my toes; I wanted to pull it back up immediately.

"My appearance is the one thing I can control, at least partially. Whenever I pull my hair, it's like I'm pulling my life back together. If one hair falls, I'm losing control," I huffed. "I know it sounds stupid but I just can't help thinking everything will fall apart if I let go."

Marina looked at me, her hands ruffling through my now loose hair. The brown waves fell just slightly past my shoulders. "I'll be here to catch you if you fall." She took my face in her hands and pressed a kiss on my lips. "I'll always be here to hold you together."

My heart thumped in my chest.

Maybe it's okay to fall apart once in a while.

When we walked back into the backstage area, the ends of my hair tickled my bare shoulders and Marina's hand brushed mine with every step.

There was a group of women gathered around Milo in the middle of the room. Each of them had a glass of champagne in hand. Chloe stood about a meter behind the circle, her arms crossed, leaning against a wall and sipping on her glass. The rest of the band was scattered around the room; they probably had already said hello to the fans.

Marina stopped in her tracks before the people in the room could realize we were here. She took my hand and pulled me back into the shadows, pressing another kiss to my lips.

"You know I don't want to share you tonight?" I whispered and kissed her again.

"Just a few hours and I'll be all yours again." Her words were more of a whisper as her fingers traced the dark spot on my neck. "Anyway, we claimed each other, didn't we?" She grabbed my hand and pulled me out of the shadows.

We walked over to the bar and took 2 more glasses of champagne before Marina made herself visible to the group. The fans started screaming when they spotted her, jumping up and down. I slowly drifted away from Marina to greet my best friend.

Chloe scanned me in disbelief when I approached. "What did she do to you?" she asked. Her eyes jumped back and forth between my hair and the dark spot on my throat.

I laughed and embraced her. I let my hand brush through my hair as we parted. "Don't you like my new style?" I said.

"I *love* it!" Chloe exclaimed. "I'm just not used to it."

"I guess she makes me feel perfect enough to be imperfect." I lifted my shoulders.

Chloe grabbed my hands. "I love that for you, Kari. I really do." Her eyes now fixated on the spot on my throat and she laughed. "But what did she do to your throat?"

I giggled and pointed toward a couch in the back. We sat down and I expanded the 15 minutes in the tour bus to a 30 minute over sharing session. We heard a squeal or scream from the middle of the room here and there but we mostly used the time to debrief from best friend to best friend without distraction.

I could see the way that Marina took her time to clink glasses with every single one of the fans, granting them the time that they deserved. She hugged each of them tightly. She listened closely to all of them. My heart beamed at the sight; there was no jealousy from my side because all their eyes lingered at the purple spot on her neck in confusion. None of them would ever get what I have, would ever get as close to her as I got.

I used to hate thinking this way, even when my subconscious wouldn't stop comparing myself to other fans. It was this mindset of constant comparison that destroyed most fandoms for me. Someone had always gotten more selfies with her, had hugged her more times, had been to more concerts. There was always something 'more', almost as if you couldn't get close to her if someone else had. Just because one fan developed a bond with Marina didn't mean that she couldn't develop a friendship with another as well. To be honest, it took some time for me to realize that maybe fandoms aren't all about the artists; they were about the *fans*. It was about the beautiful people you got to meet along the way. Isn't it gorgeous how people could connect on such a pure level, no matter the distance or age difference, a simple connection over love for the same thing?

My heart bloomed seeing Marina make other fans glow with excitement. I knew how much it could change a life, and every single fan out there deserved to know that feeling.

"I love the way she handles fans," I said, my eyes still focused on Marina. "Not every artist does it with so much love." My heart beat in the rhythm of Marina's movements.

"It's special," my best friend agreed, turning her head to look at me. "It's always been special."

"*She's* special." I looked at Chloe, taking my eyes off Marina.

"We're so lucky." Chloe's blue eyes were warm. "Not everyone gets to experience something like this."

Not everyone gets to experience something like this.

I recalled the moment Marina pushed me against the wall in the backstage bathroom a few hours ago.

Saying hi to all the fans had taken way longer than I had been ready for. As soon as everyone, including Chloe, had left the room, Marina pulled me into the bathroom. All I wanted was to lay in bed with her, to press my body against hers. Instead, I had watched her for hours just to sneak into a bathroom for a kiss. Her breath smelled like champagne, sweet and bubbly, when I kissed her. She was *my* champagne, my little drug, her fizziness making me dizzy.

I pushed her a few centimeters away. "Is this the last time I'm going to feel you this close?" Marina might've said that we would keep seeing each other after the tour but I still couldn't quite believe it would ever feel or be the same.

Marina actually had the audacity to grin at me. "Oh, you really think so? Do you really think I'd waste our last night on the bus?"

Marina took my face into her hands, her thumbs circling my cheeks. "I booked a hotel room for us, babe." She kissed me softly. "It's only us. One last time before this tour is over."

"Then why are we in this bathroom?"

Marina laughed. "Because I couldn't wait." She pressed me harder into the wall, her leg nudging between my thighs.

Chapter 20
Shh... Don't Say It - Fletcher

My jaw dropped in a gasp when I entered the hotel room. It was a suite, bigger than any hotel room that I had ever seen. A golden, metallic king size bed decorated with a green velvet blanket, waited for us in the middle of the room. Two deep red bathrobes that looked rested on top. The room looked more like it was part of a palace, not a hotel. It smelled of vanilla, as a red candle burned on the nightstand. I felt the taste of it on my tongue.

An image of our bodies tangling beneath those velvet sheets flashed through my mind.

When did she book this?

She would've been with her husband tonight, in her own bed, if she hadn't met me.

This is all for me.

"Wow." I approached the bed in slow, swaying steps. The champagne in my system created a comfortable dizziness. I sat down on the corner, my hands stroking the soft velvet. "This is amazing, Marina."

Her whole expression glowed. "You deserve more than amazing." She stepped toward me, her index finger touching the tip of my chin. "This tour was the best time of my life." She placed a kiss on each corner of my mouth. "And that's just because of you." A dimple showed on her right cheek. "I wanted just the best for the end of this tour."

The mention of the word 'end' stung in my chest for a millisecond but the way that her eyes sparkled at me made me fall deeper.

How can a person be this gorgeous?

She sat down on the bed next to me, her hand finding its space on my upper thigh. Her touch still sent sizzles through my veins like the first time that her skin had connected with mine.

I needed to ask about it, one final step of reassurance. "What about Greg? And Joni?"

Marina smiled. "I called Greg and told him to leave before I even went to your place the other night. He didn't take it well but that's a problem for the future. Joni is still on a class trip."

"Okay." I looked down at the blanket beneath me, my fingers stroking over the soft velvet.

"Anywhere you are will always be the best for me and I'm willing to risk it all for you." She turned my face back toward her and my lips grazed hers briefly.

"Let's take a shower, baby girl." She put distance between our faces and winked at me. "I really wanna try these bathrobes!" A second later, she stood in front of the bed and started taking off her clothes. "And I really gotta get rid of these stage clothes; they're nasty," She laughed and unbuttoned her black jeans.

"You don't have to ask me twice!" I pulled my shirt over my head, the warm breeze of the room tingling against my nipples.

Our clothes were soon scattered across the floor and Marina pulled me toward the bathroom. The shower was big, the tiles decorated with golden lines.

I stepped in immediately, the water brushing over my skin in a comfortable way; calming me, grounding me. I was ready to enjoy the final night of the tour with this beautiful woman. I turned her body around, pressing her against the tiles.

"Kari! What are you doing?" She laughed at me.

"I just like the back of your body," I said, letting my finger trace the outline of the swallows on her shoulder. It tickled downward, the way that drop of water had wandered down her body on the day when I had first seen her beautiful body. Then, I felt softly along her shoulders, her spine, her curves, down to the wavy stretch marks on her butt cheek.

"I wish I could take a photo with my mind so I could look at the art of your body every day," I said, my voice barely audible under the sound of the running water. I moved closer to her face, speaking against her cheek. "You're the most beautiful being."

Marina didn't answer. I turned her around and kissed her and she kissed me back. There was so much love in the unity of our lips.

The fanciest shampoo bottles that I'd ever seen rested on a little tabletop next to the shower. I grabbed one, squeezing a generous drop onto the palm of my hand. I applied the shampoo to Marina's hair and massaged her scalp. Her wet, dark hair felt so soft beneath my fingertips. She closed her eyes as she let her head fall back under the shower rain. She looked so beautiful with her head bent back, her make-up slowly losing its form, washing away. This was her most gorgeous version, her raw version. My heart beamed.

We applied shampoo to each other's hair and shower gel to each other's bodies. Taking care of the other, cleaning each other, calming each other, exploring each other. She dried the water from my body and I dried the water from hers. We left our hair wet, the bedroom screaming for our presence. We left the bathrobes lying on top of the toilet, knowing that they wouldn't stay on for long.

I pulled Marina back to the bedroom, pushing her onto the bed, climbing on top of her. My hands immediately went to her boobs, exploring her body.

Marina took my hands away, grabbing my hips to push me off her. I ended up next to her, resting on my side. She turned over and rested on hers.

"Tonight is all about you, baby girl," she said, her finger now the one to trace the shape of my hip. "May I guide you tonight?" Her eyes shimmered dark brown, a comfortable warmth flowing through my body.

I didn't know what it meant but Marina could guide me anywhere.

I nodded.

Her face glowed in the red light of the candles. "I'm a bit nervous." She bit her lower lip, taking her hand from my body to push herself into a seated position. "I've never done this before." She turned around and bent over the side of her bed. "I just…" She shuffled through her bag that rested next to the bed. "I want to see you free." When she turned back around, a pair of handcuffs and a blindfold dangled from her hand. "I want to make you lose control, to make you forget about all those doubts in your head."

A fire burned between my legs.

Fuck.

She had thought about this. She wanted to do something special for me. Where did she even get those handcuffs? Yes, my heart was filled with fear. I didn't know what it meant to let go, didn't know if I could do that. But I wanted to learn. If there was one person that I trusted, it was Marina.

"May I?" She nervously played with the silver chain between the handcuffs. "You can always tell me to take them off if you're not feeling it. I just think it's worth a try."

"Yes." I held out my hands for her to cuff them.

Marina put the cuffs around my wrists. I expected them to be uncomfortable but they were soft, the insides furry. She didn't connect them with the metallic chain yet but let it dangle from my hand.

She took the blindfold that rested in her lap. "Ready?" she asked.

I nodded so she pulled it over my head. Everything went dark and, with that, my mind went blank; I was in Marina's hands now.

I felt her hands on my hips, slowly and gently turning me around so I lay on my back, my butt tickled by the soft velvet beneath me. Her hands wrapped around my wrists, pulling them upward, so I had to stretch out my arms. The sound of metal clanking against metal created a vibration between my legs. My hands were tied to the bed frame now, my arms stretched out above my head.

My brain sounded an alarm, telling me to regain control. For the first time, I chose not to listen. I chose to give up control.

Marina's finger slowly traced my neck and boobs. I focused on her touch, blacking out the fears in my mind. All that existed was the contact of her finger on my skin.

Her thumb and index finger grabbed my nipple, twisting it slightly and making me moan. The small touch exploded into the most intense feeling; all that existed was the little sensitive patch of skin that her fingers touched.

"How does this feel?" Her words were soft.

"Good," I huffed.

Amazing.

Her lips grazed my ear, the sensation of something wet meeting my earlobe. Marina took it as a sign and licked the space beneath my ear. Her tongue traced down my throat to my collarbone and down to my nipple. When the sensation of her soft lips brushed my nipple hit, I moaned louder and my torso bent upward, moving towards her lips. The metallic chain of the handcuffs made a clinking sound against the bed frame as my hands pulled forward, the manacles straining against my wrists. I couldn't move further, couldn't touch Marina, couldn't really guide her lips. A sense of freedom made my body feel like it floated above the bed.

I was so used to being in control, so used to taking care of others, being the one who guides others. I had always clung to every piece of control that I could grasp. Suddenly, there was nothing more freeing than giving that control to someone else. There was nothing that I had to think about, nothing that I had to do, no one that I had to consider.

Marina bit down on my nipple.

"Fuck!" I exclaimed.

"More?" she asked, her lips stroking my skin as she talked.

I bit my lip and nodded.

Fuck, yeah.

Marina placed a kiss between my boobs. "You are the most beautiful woman I've ever seen," she said and placed a kiss beneath each of my boobs, her hands exploring. "You deserve to be caressed, to be worshiped. I wish I could kiss every single part of your body."

Her words let me float; every single one of them made me feel like I was above the world.

"And you deserve to let go," she placed a kiss on my belly button. "You deserve to be free." She kissed downward, her lips nudging the space above my clit.

My body tensed in anticipation, awaiting her lips between my legs. Nothing happened.

The next second, her breath was close to my ear again, her hands still at my sides. "Let go, Kari," she whispered against my ear.

Her hand moved to my front, her finger sliding down to the inside of my thigh. Everything burned and sizzled at her touch. I needed her inside of me; I needed her to push me to the sky.

Her finger stroked my clit slightly. "I'll be here to catch you." Her fingers slid downward through my folds, stopping at my opening.

My head was dizzy; nothing existed except for her touch. It wasn't Marina and I anymore; it was Marina's hand and my body. All other thoughts were gone, letting me float without restrain. I might've been cuffed down but I was free at her touch.

"May I?" Her words now tickled my lips, her face now level with mine.

I bent my forehead upward as an answer, searching for her lips. She pressed a gentle kiss on mine, not letting go as she pushed one finger inside me.

I bit down on her lower lip and she pushed harder, my hips moving upward against her hand, the cuffs clinking against the bed frame.

"Harder," I moaned as our lips parted for air.

A second finger slid into me, bending inside. Marina's head nestled in the space between my shoulder and neck, her tongue caressing my neck. I gasped and moaned, almost screamed, at every push. There was nothing holding me back anymore, nothing keeping me quiet, nothing keeping me from flying, nothing that I had to control. With every push, my insides pulsated; fiery, electric. I flew higher and higher, knowing that Marina would catch me if I fell.

"Fuck," I moaned, pressing harder into Marina's hands.

She simpered against my throat before she bit down on it. Aware of my wrists straining against the cuffs, the metallic sound grew louder and louder.

All that existed was my body and every space that was being caressed and touched. The only thing that was left was the universe above, awaiting me. Stars appeared in the darkness behind the blindfold, my muscles tensing; I really was flying through the night sky.

With the next push, my muscles tensed around Marina's fingers. My hands almost slid out of the handcuffs as my body bent upward uncontrollably.

Everything ignited in fireworks, the last push sending me to a place that I'd never been before. I burst.

When I fell back to earth, Marina wrapped her arms around my body, holding me tightly as I shivered with pleasure.

Marina didn't let go of me for hours that felt like minutes.

As I was drifting off to sleep, she whispered into my ear, "I can't wait to spend my life with you."

I fell asleep with a smile on my lips.

Epilogue
Meine Liebe – Wilhelmine

"Kari! She posted it!" Chloe's shrill voice chimed through my phone speakers. The phone vibrated with her scream, almost falling off the corner of my nightstand.

Why did I put her on speaker again?

I rubbed my eyes. It was 1am and my body was still recovering from the tour. Now, I was lying in my bed in Ulm, in a room that didn't feel like mine anymore; I'd left my heart and brain on tour.

Of course, Marina had promised to see me again once she'd figured out her marriage but being back in my old life wasn't easy. I wanted to be there for her as she faced her divorce and talked to Joni; I wanted to support her, even though my presence would've probably complicated things. I'd be there for her during future fights but this was *her* battle.

Therefore, I had spent the past few days sleeping, not able to function in any way. I didn't feel like talking but, when Chloe called, I *had* to pick up.

Before I could respond to Chloe's question, she screamed into the phone again. "Kari! She posted it!"

Who posted what?

My tired brain couldn't quite follow Chloe's words; I wasn't quite sure it even wanted to.

Chloe's voice got louder, if that was even possible. "Check your Instagram. *Now!*"

I turned around to grab my phone from my nightstand. The streetlight from outside my window blinded my eyes when I tried to open them to unlock it.

"Do I really have to open my eyes now?" I mumbled into my pillow.

Chloe squealed. "Trust me. You *want to* see this!"

How can someone be this excited in the middle of the night?

When I opened my eyes and unlocked my screen, an Instagram notification was waiting for me.

Paper Rings and Promises just posted a photo.

My hands started to tremble. The last time that they had posted, it was Dari announcing that he'd left the band.

What is happening?

"Kari, are you there? Did you see it?" Chloe's voice was shaky with excitement. Good excitement.

I didn't respond but clicked on the notification instead. The loading process seemed like an eternity. I couldn't wrap my head around the fact that someone had posted on this account without my approval, nor could I understand why a post made Chloe so excited.

A familiar image came into focus and my heart immediately jumped into my throat. Marina's dark brown eyes were glowing into the camera, a big smile spread across her face. I had taken that photo; she was beaming at *me*. There were many photos that I had taken of her during the tour but this was the only one that glowed that way, the only one where she was looking directly at me behind the camera. I could feel my heart drumming the way that it did on the day when her eyes had caught mine.

Marina had her gaze turned away from the crowd, her back towards them, so that she could face me. The crowd was cheering in the background and a big pride flag was spread from Marina's left hand to her right; she was wearing it like the queer idol that she was meant to be. This was my favorite photo of Marina and the last that I would've expected her to post.

I scrolled down to the caption; it was short, no hashtags. When I read it, my heart jumped out of my throat in a scream. Chloe laughed on the other side but didn't say a thing. Every dream that I had ever dreamed and those that I could've never imagined dreaming were

375

becoming a reality. Marina would look at me the way that she had in that photo every day from now on. She had told her fans what we've been wanting to hear ever since the first day that we had seen her. I was excited for all the little girls that shared their queer stories with Marina, for all the fans that had discovered their sexuality because of her, for all the people that had found their safe space, a community that accepts them, no matter what color of the rainbow, through this band.

I whimpered, tears running down my cheeks.

This was it.

Everything that I had always wanted was right in front of me.

Paperringsandpromises, 00:57am

I am proud to announce that y'all knew before I did.

I find women fucking breathtaking!

Songbook

in the afterglow

(Verse 1)
In the dim-lit room, where whispers turn to sighs,
Fingers intertwined, tracing secrets in your eyes.
Lost in your touch, we dance a delicate line,
Bodies in motion, syncing in perfect time.

(Chorus)
It's like a melody, soft and sweet,
Our bodies moving to the beat.
Exploring depths in ecstasy,
Lost in the rhythm of you and me.

(Verse 2)
Breathless gasps and tangled sheets,
Skin on skin, our hearts meet.
In the silence, our desires speak,
A symphony of passion, reaching its peak.

(Chorus)
It's like a melody, soft and sweet,
Our bodies moving to the beat.
Exploring depths in ecstasy,
Lost in the rhythm of you and me.

(Bridge)
In every touch, a story unfolds,
A masterpiece of love untold.
With every kiss, we rewrite the script.
In this intimate dance, our souls eclipse.

(Chorus)
It's like a melody, soft and sweet,
Our bodies moving to the beat.
Exploring depths in ecstasy,
Lost in the rhythm of you and me.

(Outro)
In the afterglow, we lay entwined,
Two hearts beating as one, transcending time.
In this indie pop serenade, our love's decree,
Forever bound in the harmony of you and me.

Paperhearts

(Verse 1)
Folded whispers, secrets untold,
In the quiet corners, our story unfolds.
Paper hearts, delicate and shy,
Yearning for love, reaching for the sky.

(Chorus)
In the dance of maybes, we find our start,
Lost in the yearning of paper hearts.
A love that whispers, a love that could be,
In the tender embrace of you and me.

(Verse 2)
Faded words on sheets so thin,
Echoes of a love waiting to begin.
In the silence, we find our voice,
In the realm where dreams rejoice.

(Chorus)
In the dance of maybes, we find our start,
Lost in the yearning of paper hearts.
A love that whispers, a love that could be,
In the tender embrace of you and me.

(Bridge)
Though uncertain, our hearts beat strong,
In the melody of a hopeful song.
With each fold, a promise is made,
In the fragile beauty of love displayed.

(Chorus)
In the dance of maybes, we find our start,
Lost in the yearning of paper hearts.
A love that whispers, a love that could be,
In the tender embrace of you and me.

(Outro)
So, let's hold onto this fragile chance,
In the dance of love's sweet romance.
In the whispers of a love set free,
In the silent echo of what could be.

Fourteen

(Verse 1)
At fourteen, we met under summer skies;
Innocence in our hearts with stars in our eyes.
Shared secrets whispered in the schoolyard swings,
Becoming friends, tied by invisible strings.

(Pre-Chorus)
Paper rings exchanged, promises made,
Inseparable souls, our foundation laid.
Through laughter and tears, we found our way,
At fourteen, we began to sway.

(Chorus)
Fourteen summers, fourteen falls,
Through it all, we answered the calls.
In the echo of our teenage dreams,
We built a bond, stronger than it seems.

(Verse 2)
With guitars in hand, we strummed our tales,
In melodies and lyrics, our friendship prevails.
From basement jams to midnight drives,
Together, we soared, feeling alive.

(Pre-Chorus)
Paper rings turned into melodies sung,
Our journey started, our hearts were young.
Through highs and lows, we held each other tight.
At fourteen, we found our light.

(Chorus)
Fourteen summers, fourteen falls,
Through laughter, tears and whispered calls.
In the echo of our youthful schemes,
We formed a bond from paper dreams.

(Bridge)
From paper rings to stages grand,
We faced the world, hand in hand.
In the music, our souls aligned,
At fourteen, our destinies entwined.

(Chorus)
Fourteen summers, fourteen falls,
Through laughter, tears and whispered calls.
In the echo of our youthful schemes,
We formed a bond from paper dreams.

(Outro)
So here's to us and here's to now,
From fourteen on, we take our vow.
In the music, our story sings,
Forever tied by paper rings.

Acknowledgements

My girl. It hasn't been long but being with you has taught me what romance novels are all about. This book is the first with a happy ending because with you, writing romance around spicy scenes suddenly comes easy to me.

Lena. Thank you for being the Kari to my Chloe and bringing this character to life.

My found fan family. Claudia, Janina, Willis, any fan I've met along the way. You gave me a sense of home and community in times I thought I'd never fit in. Thank you for showing me what being a fan is all about.

Wilhelmine. Thank you for creating a community that I feel safe and welcome in. I found a family through your music and I couldn't thank you enough. And thank you for making me believe in myself and my art. My books wouldn't exist without you.

Dad. Thank you for always cheering me on, for supporting what I do, for believing in me and my crazy dreams.

CiCi. Thank you for your editing advice and everything that you've done to always push me forward.

Malin. Thank you for sticking with me and bringing my characters to life on the cover.

Romy. You're the best editor that I could've wished for; thank you for doing this with me.

Faith. Thank you for giving this book the final polish that it needed.

And to all the fan girls out there. Thank you for everything that you're doing, for spreading love in a world of hate and creating a sense of belonging where people drift further and further apart. Never stop.

About the Author

Emely was born and raised in Germany but her heart is scattered around the world from a series of long travels in the United States and other countries. While she chooses to live in Düsseldorf, she's always traveling somewhere for pride events and concerts. With her writing, she wants to create the representation that her younger self would've needed. She is currently enrolled in the Creative Writing BFA program of South Gate Creative Writing School in Denmark.

Check out: *I Fall in Love Once a Year*!

Chloe attends Cologne pride every year – it's a place and time where she can express herself and explore her sexuality. It's just that this year, everything seems to be different.

The first night of pride weekend, between sweaty bodies and loud music of a lesbian bar, Chloe meets Mel and her world turns upside down. Mel is older, mysterious, and stirs something inside Chloe she didn't know existed – Is it just sexual tension or true romantic feelings?

The world of quick hook-ups and short-term crushes suddenly turns into the beautiful ups and downs of an emotional rollercoaster. Within the color and clamor of one of the biggest prides in Europe, the lesbian universe seems to be the size of a small town. As Mel's ex-girlfriend steps into the picture, the delusion of a dreamy weekend is shaken up...